THE DARK CIRCLE

The Dark Circle

A Patrick Dawlish Mystery

**John Creasey *writing as*
Gordon Ashe**

ISBN: 978-1-5040-9864-9

This edition published in 2025 by Open Road Integrated Media, Inc.
180 Maiden Lane
New York, NY 10038
www.openroadmedia.com

THE DARK CIRCLE

CHAPTER ONE

MAN AND WIFE

'I don't like it here,' said Dawlish.

'*You* don't like it. How do you think *I* feel? Don't let go of my arm!' His wife's voice rose, she was near panic.

'Let this teach you what a wonderful husband you have, precious. A strong arm in time of need, a strong nerve on a dark and eerie night. Just to show that I forgive you, you may put your arm round my waist. I must have my hands free, I want to strike a match.'

Her arm stole round his waist; it had a long way to go, but it was a determined arm. It wasn't very steady.

'What is there to forgive?' she asked.

'You brought us here, looking for a Greek god. You must drop everything, you said, and come. I *know* I have some matches somewhere.'

'He's only a boy.'

'Somewhere I've heard those words before, Felicity. I wonder just how many deluded women have uttered them, and even more deluded men listened to them!'

'*Can't* you find those matches?'

'No. Keep quiet a minute, while I concentrate. Dwell upon the folly of an intelligent and mature woman getting herself mixed up in murky mystery because of a beautiful boy.'

'Darling, I *hate* you. How dare you call me intelligent and mature!'

'Will you please *hush*?' hissed Dawlish.

Felicity hushed. All about them was darkness and silence. They stood on the landing of a strange house. There were houses on either side, houses at the back and houses in front, yet it seemed like the only house in the world, a lonely place, filled with whispering.

Dawlish held the matches in his left hand; they had been there since he'd said 'I don't like it here', but Felicity didn't know that. Felicity hadn't his acute sense of hearing—didn't hear the creaking footsteps above, didn't know that he would not strike the match because it would give their position away. They stood still at the head of the narrow stairs, and suddenly Felicity's arm twitched and she pressed closer to him. She didn't speak, but she had heard that sound and knew they weren't alone.

'I must have left them on the table,' Dawlish said. 'Take it easy. Left foot forward, one step at a time, arm stretched out so that we'll know if we're going to run into a wall. Ready? One—'

There was no wall in front of them, but there was someone else above and behind them. The creaking came from the stairs. They had come up only one flight in a three-storeyed house. The unknown was trying to creep down without being either heard or seen. The Dawlish's were not the only people here with thumping hearts and taut nerves.

'Two—'

Dawlish's right hand touched a wall or a door. He put his lips close to Felicity's ear and whispered: 'If you can hear me, take your arm away.'

She took her arm away, but still pressed tightly against him.

'Take one step forward, and stay put.'

She hesitated. The creaking continued; the unknown was now behind them, but not above. It was easy to imagine that they could hear his breathing. Dawlish drew away from Felicity, who took the step forward as he said: 'Three.' Now he stood on his own. He turned slowly, until he faced the stairs. There was a turn in the stairs which hid the front door and the dim street lighting. It was pitch dark and he could distinguish nothing— not even a vague shape; nor could he now hear anything, so the other also must be standing still. Was he at the foot of the stairs? Dawlish went forward one step, then tore off a match with infinite care; it was of cardboard and made no sound. He felt for the red tip and held it on the striking surface. As he did so there was another creak.

He said in a muted voice: 'There must *be* a wall. Four—'

He struck the match, and a bright yellow flame sprang up with an angry hiss, showing walls, doors, staircase and the man with his back to Dawlish. He was a little man, a hand on the banisters, about to step down from this landing. His head was turned, so that Dawlish had a distorted view of his face and clearly saw his long nose. Dawlish sprang forward and the match fluttered and nearly went out.

He didn't see what the little man threw at him, but he felt it, heavy and hard, in the pit of his stomach. It drove his wind out in a gasping grunt, then it dropped to the floor with a crash.

'Pat!' cried Felicity.

The little man raced down the stairs, stumbled, recovered and ran on.

Felicity groped her way back to her husband.

'Pat!'

He grunted as he straightened up—and as the little man

reached the half-landing and sped down the short flight to the front door.

A door banged.

'Wonderful! Aren't I good? Give me a medal, darling.' Dawlish was savage with himself for having mistimed the effort—and his stomach hurt. Running footsteps sounded vaguely. 'Did he turn right or did he turn left, why did he run and what has he done? I'm going to strike another match.'

Flame flared again, and showed him a scared Felicity, with her grey-green eyes rounded and close to him. He was bent nearly double and his stomach muscles were still contracted. The missile lay near his foot, a round glass paper-weight.

'Well, it could have hit me on the nose. I suppose that would have been worse.' He let the match go out, and darkness dropped on them again, but this time without tension. He rubbed his stomach gingerly. 'I'm going to find that main switch so that we can have a proper light. Will you stay here while—'

'No!'

'Look here, he's gone. You heard him, I felt him.'

'No!'

'Right. Then I'll go first.'

He groped for the top stair with his foot; after three steps, Felicity found the edge of his coat and held on to it. They went down, a step at a time, negotiated the half-landing and then the final flight, and stood in the narrow passage which served as a hall. An electric lamp brushed Dawlish's head; he knew there was a bulb inside and also knew that when he pressed the switch down nothing would happen, because he'd tried it when he had come in.

'Strike another,' pleaded Felicity. 'Or—'

'Or what?'

'Pat, I'm sorry. It was crazy to come here. I don't mind what happens to Charles. It's his business, nothing to do with us. I don't want to stay. We can find the front door without any light, and then forget all about it. No one need know we've been here. I don't suppose I shall ever hear from Charles again, and—'

'Not being psychic, you almost certainly won't.'

'Pat, what do you mean?'

'That proves you're not psychic. Charles expected trouble, and all that's happened here tells us that it's come. It reeked suspicion when Charles gave you a key so that we could get in if he were delayed. Do you really want to turn your back on it now?'

'Where do you think the main switch is?' asked Felicity.

She held his arm as they went along the passage by the stairs and found the kitchen; the main switch was in a corner cupboard. Dawlish drew down the lever, and light came on immediately— here, in an old-fashioned kitchen which smelt faintly of stale food, in the dingy hall and also on the gloomy landing, where there was a low-powered lamp. Dawlish went to the front door, pulling on his gloves, and stood on the porch for a few seconds, peering up and down. It was a short street with tall terraced houses on either side, and only two street lamps. No one was about. A church clock, not far away, struck a sonorous ten.

'It's getting late,' said Felicity.

'Ten o'clock is only late for country bumpkins like you and me; it's mid-afternoon for Londoners.'

Dawlish drew her inside and closed and locked the door, then, as an afterthought, shot the bolt. He returned to the kitchen and did the same there, with Felicity watching him meekly. He glanced at the window and saw that the catch was fastened.

'If you'd like to be useful, you could check some of the other windows,' he said.

'Why do you think someone else might come?'

'I don't. I just want to make sure that if they arrive they don't take us by surprise. We've had enough surprises for one evening.' Dawlish looked into her solemn face, judged the state of her nerves, and smiled. It was a good smile, reassuring and strong. 'You were right to want to come, you know.'

'You really think so?'

'Isn't this evidence of trouble?'

'Do you expect to find him—dead?'

'It's anyone's guess. If you were right, he was afraid of being killed. Presumably he had reason for fear. Our paper-weight expert didn't want to be seen, which makes him suspect as having no right in the house. He hurled that weight hard enough to smash my skull, so he doesn't oppose murder on principle. That doesn't make him a murderer, but it does prove that he was desperate. Shall we fasten the windows?'

They went round the ground floor. Only two windows were unfastened, both in the dining-room, which overlooked the small back garden. The ceilings were high, the decorations hideously Victorian. The furniture was all old and heavy, the carpets threadbare.

'Odd setting for Charles.'

'Pat, let's go upstairs; I'm feeling sick with uncertainty.'

This time they didn't stop at the first landing, but went to the second, because the unknown man had started from there. A third flight of stairs stretched up towards a dark attic landing. A low-powered light spread a gentle radiance over brown walls and big dark doors, all of them closed. Dawlish, still wearing gloves, opened two doors and looked into empty bedrooms.

'Do you know who lived here with him?'

'His uncle and aunt, I think. He said very little about it,' Felicity looked at the third and last door, and moistened her lips. 'I suppose—this is the room.'

Dawlish turned the handle and pushed. The room was dark. He stood with his hand on the light switch, while Felicity held her breath. He flicked it down. Light sprang out, and they saw the dead man.

CHAPTER TWO

THE BODY

Felicity spoke after what seemed a long silence.

'It—it's not Charles.'

'No.'

Dawlish went farther into the room. The man in bed was elderly. Horror crept into their minds, because everything except the man's head was neat and tidy. There had been no struggle. This man had been murdered while he slept; a hammer lay on the floor.

Felicity said in a low-pitched voice:

'I'm going to be sick.'

'Take it easy, my darling.' There was warmth in Dawlish's tone, and real compassion. He took her out on the landing, and hurried with her down the stairs to a bathroom. 'Sit down a bit. It'll pass. I won't be long.'

He heard her coughing as he went back to the room and the body. He stood in the doorway, and his gaze roamed. Yes, everything was in order. He could imagine that the old man had gone to bed, as usual—there was an open book on the bedside table and a pair of *pince-nez* on top of it. A glass of water and a bottle of dyspepsia tablets made the scene both homely and terrifying. The body was in the middle of the large bed.

Was he Charles's uncle?

Dawlish opened the drawers of the dressing-chest and glanced into the wardrobe; nothing appeared to have been disturbed. The old man's clothes lay folded neatly on a chair at the foot of the bed, coat and waistcoat placed carefully over the back of the chair. You couldn't jump to conclusions, but it was a fair guess that robbery had not been the motive for this crime.

A pale and subdued Felicity appeared in the doorway.

'Do you think the man we saw killed him?'

'If I were a policeman, I'd like to have a word with him, for a start. Talking of policemen, I haven't noticed a telephone about. Have you?'

'No.'

'This may be the uncle. But where's the aunt? And where is Charles? Didn't he promise you he would be here?'

'Yes.'

'And did you promise him we'd come, or only promise to try to persuade me?'

'I said I was sure you'd come. I wish—I hadn't.'

'I shouldn't wish that,' said Dawlish gently. 'The old chap might have lain there for the night, even for a day or two. The police will have a good start now, and we can describe the length of the little man's nose, if nothing else. I wish I knew whether he wore gloves. I shouldn't have handled that paper-weight. I wonder where the nearest telephone is.'

'Shall I go and find one?'

'Thanks. Call Bill Trivett at his home, and if you can't get him, call Scotland Yard. If you actually meet a copper you'd better tell him to come along, but don't go out of your way to find one.'

'All right.'

Felicity went out quickly. Dawlish waited until she was on the stairs, then followed. He leaned over the banisters watching her tall, graceful figure going down. She didn't fumble with the lock or the bolt of the front door and she closed the door when she went out. He hurried after her, and watched from the porch until she reached the corner, and only then was he satisfied that no one had shown any interest in her—so, presumably, no one was watching the house.

He went to the first floor and opened a door opposite the head of the stairs. This room struck a different note from any of the others. It was brighter, gayer, more modernized. There was a small desk littered with papers, a single divan bed, and near it an ashtray filled with cigarette ends. The fluorescent strip-lighting had certainly been newly installed, and seemed incongruous in this melancholy house. There were also oddments which told of Charles being a young man of taste; a fastidious, almost feminine taste. What little Dawlish knew of him suggested he was a tailor's dummy of a man with film star looks.

Felicity knew more about him than Dawlish; presumably Felicity saw something beyond the dummy, or she wouldn't have promised to help.

She had lunched with Charles that day, and telephoned Dawlish, who had been at their Surrey home. 'Darling, will you come up right away? There's something I want to talk about.' He'd argued, because he had been away from home for three weeks and was eager to work in the garden and on his small fruit farm; but when Felicity wanted something badly she knew how to get it.

All she'd been able to tell him was that Charles was scared, needed help and didn't want to go to the police. Young men in trouble who didn't want help from the police had usually a guilty conscience. Also, many of them called on Dawlish, who had a reputation for crime investigation and for working without confiding in the police.

Was the fact that Charles had poured out his heart to Felicity induced only because she was a lovely woman prepared to lend a sympathetic ear? Or because she was the wife of Patrick Dawlish? Probably a little of both had influenced Charles. It was either a bane or a boon to Dawlish, depending on his mood, that so many knew him by reputation; or thought they did. There were those who saw him as a private detective; those who thought him a secret service ace; others who believed him to be a throwback to a lawless age, loving excitement and adventure for their own sakes, willing to plunge into any wildcat scheme which offered the chance of either of them. Even Felicity had been heard to say that he ought to have been born a policeman; but it was a policeman, William Trivett of the C.I.D., who had come nearest to the truth.

'He's simply a magnet for crime. Nine people might ask his help and be turned down. The tenth will get it—and what a case it'll be. I've never known him pick a loser yet!'

Trivett knew Dawlish well, for they were old friends. Trivett was forbearing, too, and took no umbrage when Dawlish investigated those affairs which he knew were the prerogative of the police. Trivett had but to wait, and Dawlish would come; and his help, and sometimes co-operation, were worth waiting for, for he had an uncanny knack of being right.

Now, in this silent house, Dawlish pondered.

What was there here, to tell him more about Charles Horden? All he knew was that Charles 'wrote' and lectured to literary societies. Judging from the state of the desk, he was an untidy young man. He wrote mostly short stories—abstruse themes without a beginning or end which occasionally appeared in exclusive journals whose sponsors believed in art for art's sake.

Dawlish didn't know whether Charles earned enough by his writing to live on, whether he had any other occupation or had private means. The papers on the desk were obviously the result of recent labours; Dawlish read a couple of paragraphs and sniffed.

He sat at the desk. Searching a desk with gloves on wasn't easy; searching without his gloves would tell the police that he had let his curiosity gain the upper hand. Except for Trivett, they would object strenuously. They would certainly assume that he knew more than he professed, and had a stronger motive than Felicity's urging for being interested in Charles. Even Trivett might think that.

Here was a bank statement—the *MidPro* Bank in Kensington High Street. Charles had a balance of a hundred and twenty-three pounds nine shillings, which didn't make him rich. The statement covered a three-months period; Dawlish totted up the credit figure, saw that in the period Charles had banked a little over a hundred pounds, all in small amounts; that didn't make him rich, either. There were a few unpaid bills, none of them of a frightening amount or overdue. There were eleven unsold manuscripts, neatly typed and with tantalizing titles—*The Psychology of Silas Clay; The Double Life of Reginald Fulton; The Mind Divided.* There were letters from editors in this country and in the United States, and everything in the desk was orderly—Charles, presumably, was untidy only during a period of literary gestation. He'd been at work recently; probably that day—yes, certainly that day, the ink on some of the sheets hadn't as yet turned dark. He had been worried enough to beg for help, but settled enough in his mind to come back and work. Or had he worked out of sheer desperation, to try to keep his mind off danger?

Why *had* he asked the Dawlishes to come and see him that night?

Had he known, or guessed, what was going to happen?

Dawlish finished his search, and was baffled; nothing here betrayed a dark secret. He noticed that there were no photographs, either on the desk or about the room. A few futuristic water-colours hung on the walls in narrow black frames—tiny things, surrounded by large pieces of white cardboard, all of them signed with the name Fay. In fact, almost the only distinguishable feature on the picture was 'Fay'. Was it a surname, or a woman's Christian name?

The front door bell rang.

Dawlish went out immediately, switching off the light in the room, and hurried downstairs. Felicity had been gone for fifteen minutes—time enough to have passed on her message and returned. He hoped she hadn't met a patrol policeman. He opened the door, and the girl standing on the porch began hurriedly:

'Oh, Charles, I—'

She stopped and drew in her breath when she realized that this wasn't Charles. She was a tiny thing; Dawlish dwarfed her. She was hatless and her golden hair accentuated the deep blue of her eyes. She was out of breath, as if she had been running, and there was anxiety—was it as high geared as fear?—in her expression.

'Hallo!' said Dawlish. 'Looking for Charles?'

'Who—are you?'

'A friend of Charles,' said Dawlish, and drew aside for her to enter.

He wished it were Felicity; it wouldn't take him long to start worrying about Felicity and blaming himself for having let her go alone. That was why he fluffed a job for the second time that night. For the girl turned and ran, and he was too late to grab her.

He rushed after her, but it was no good. She had a few yards start and ran like a deer. And she didn't once turn to look at him. A man appeared at the corner, heard them running and stopped in astonishment. The girl sped past him, the man stepped in front of Dawlish.

'What—'

'I'll miss my train.' Dawlish handed him off, but had lost precious seconds and still more precious yards.

The girl was now in the busier road, and he could hear her running, but no longer see her. When he reached the next corner she was thirty yards away, and waving wildly—at what? A taxi was on the other side of the road, with its 'free' sign glowing with light.

'Taxi! Taxi!'

She ran into the road. The driver obligingly leaned out and opened the door, and she sprang inside. Dawlish was fifteen yards away and on the wrong side. Short of flinging himself in front of the taxi, there wasn't anything he could do. The girl didn't look at him, but sank back out of sight as the taxi passed him.

Felicity beckoned frantically from the door of the house.

'Pat, where have you been? You scared the wits out of me.' She clutched his arm. 'Why do you always do crazy things?'

'It's in my blood,' said Dawlish. 'And if ever there was a time when I wanted to grab a flighty damsel, this was it. She was my revenge for Charles, and the prettiest thing I've seen in months.'

'*Is* this the time to chase after a girl?'

'It was. I must have scared her by the glitter in my eye. Who did you speak to?'

'Bill Trivett.'

'And he said in a heavy voice, "What's Pat up to now?". Why didn't you confess that it was all your fault?'

'He wouldn't have believed me.'

'What a woman!' Dawlish led her to the house again, telling her what had happened.

Felicity was more than interested.

'Pat, what do you think this girl wanted?'

'I know what she wanted, and I was very glad to discover it. She wanted Charles. There isn't any doubt that Charles leads a double life. He lunched with you, spending money he couldn't afford at an expensive restaurant, and all the time this poor neglected little woman was waiting for him at some low-priced café. I've never seen a girl across whose face the word was writ so large.'

'What word?'

'*Betrayed!*'

'Listen, darling,' said Felicity. 'Stop fooling. I brought you along to help Charles, not to chase mysterious people all over London. How did she arrive?'

'She rang the bell. What did Trivett say?'

'That he'd better come along himself, but a squad car would be here first. Also, that you were to tell him the whole truth, and not keep anything back. He said that if this was one of those jobs where you think you're so much better than the police, he wouldn't have any mercy on you. He said—'

'I can guess. Don't go on in that depressing way.'

'Oh, well, I wouldn't have telephoned you, but Charles was so obviously frightened. He tried to hide it and make light of it, but it showed all right; I couldn't fail to see it. That kind of man—'

'*What* kind of man?'

Felicity sat on the stairs and looked straight at the open front door. It was chilly, but not really cold; it had been a warm April day.

'The kind that makes most men unsympathetic, I suppose. For he *is* clever. Some people think he's a genius. I've always liked his work. It's rather slight and tenuous, but there's great depth of feeling; he seems to be groping for something that the inner, kinder, more innocent part of oneself gropes for. He makes you feel that his characters might be you. That means he's not much good at ordinary things, doesn't it?' She flashed a glance at Dawlish, but he stood bent slightly forward, pressing a hand gently on his bruise. 'He couldn't hide his feelings if he tried.'

A car turned into the street.

'Well, well,' breathed Dawlish, 'discounting the rarefied bits, is there anything at all, anything, I mean, as brutal as a *fact*, that Charles told you that you didn't tell me?'

'No, I don't think so.'

The car pulled up outside, and Dawlish grinned.

'Let me hear you explaining the nuances of genius to the police, won't you?'

'There's no need to be beastly,' said Felicity.

The car door slammed.

Dawlish leaned forward, put a hand beneath his wife's chin and peered into those grey-green eyes. She was still pale, beneath her make-up. She was not really beautiful, but undoubtedly she was lovely.

He kissed her.

'All right, I'll do what I can to help Charles,' he said. 'I'll be his cotton-wool, and you can be his inspiration.'

The front door bell rang.

'You'd better wipe off that lipstick,' said Felicity. 'I'll open the door.'

CHAPTER THREE

MAN MISSING

Trivett was tall and well-dressed; a man more easily taken for a lawyer than a policeman. Dawlish and Felicity were in Charles's room when he came up the stairs. He thrust one hand in his pocket as he came in, stood by the doorway, and looked Dawlish up and down.

'So you're at it again.'

'It's almost routine, isn't it? I get to know a man and murder is committed. How are you?'

'Suspicious.'

'I give you my solemn word that neither Felicity nor I killed the chap. And that he was entirely unknown to us.'

'You almost make it sound convincing. I suppose that means you took up the murderer's cause. He persuaded you that he was in need of help, brought you along here and left you with the corpse, hoping you'd get hanged instead of him.'

'Isn't he in a nice mood?' suggested Dawlish. 'Come down to the level of erring humanity, Bill.'

Trivett laughed. 'You're a ruddy nuisance. This was my first night off for two weeks. You can give me the official story now and tell me the truth afterwards—Grace said she'd have some coffee ready.' Grace was his wife, and the Trivetts and the Dawlishes were very good friends. 'I've already warned Felicity, Pat—no funny business.'

'She's certainly the one you ought to warn. All right, where's your shorthand writer? I'll say my little piece, and go along quietly.'

'It may even come to that,' said Trivett.

The statement made and signed, Pat and his wife left Number 13 Wyman Street and were driven by Trivett to his flat near Westminster Cathedral. There was no lift, and they walked up several flights of stone steps. Dawlish grunted now and again, still conscious of the bruise. Grace Trivett heard them coming, and had the door open and coffee ready.

Dawlish sat down in an easy chair and beamed at the dark-haired beauty who was Grace Trivett.

'We came to talk about this Charles Horden,' Trivett said.

'My night off,' grinned Dawlish. 'Felicity's on duty, she knows all about the budding genius.'

He smoked thoughtfully while Felicity repeated what she had told him, embroidering it with more detail but adding no new facts.

'I seem to have heard the name somewhere before,' Trivett muttered.

'I know it well,' Grace put in quickly. 'He has written some wonderful stories.'

'You, too?' mourned Dawlish plaintively. 'But even cutting genius out—which I'm more than willing to do—this is a queer show. It would be easier to understand if Charles had turned up, or been murdered. Where *is* Charles? Is the old man his uncle? If so, where's the missing aunt?'

'It's possible they've gone out to a late show and supper,' Trivett suggested.

Dawlish shook his head.

'Far too banal. The affair doesn't smell that way to me.' He yawned. 'I confess I hope I hear more about it, Bill. Just in case you decide to tell me what you uncover, I'll stay in London for a few days. Okay, Fel?'

Felicity didn't speak.

Trivett said: 'If you think you've convinced me that this is all you know, you've another think coming. Where is Horden, Pat?'

'I've only seen him once. He came down to address a literary club a month ago. Felicity is secretary of the club. We usually give a cocktail party on the evening of the meeting for the members and their lions. This lion took advantage of my absence and called again—and then persuaded Felicity to lunch with him in London today.' He yawned again. 'Bedtime.'

'Where are you staying?' asked Grace.

'We—' began Felicity.

'The *Mayfair*,' said Dawlish suavely. 'It won't take us ten minutes to get there.' He stood up. 'Ready, Fel?'

When they'd gone, Grace said: 'I really think Pat was telling the truth this time. Don't you?'

Trivett laughed. 'Possibly. But now he's begun, nothing in the world will make him let go. Felicity started something she'll probably regret. I wonder where they're really staying tonight.'

Grace looked startled. 'Surely—'

'Felicity started to say that they hadn't booked anywhere, and Pat jumped in because he didn't want to stay here. I've seen the great Patrick at work before. And it wouldn't surprise me if we're not glad of his help before it's over.' Trivett chuckled. 'Never tell him so, my sweet; he'd be impossible afterwards.'

*　*　*

Dawlish took the wheel of the green Bentley, and Felicity said: 'If they haven't a room at the *Mayfair*, we'll have to spend half the night chasing round for a hotel. Why can't you be sensible sometimes?'

'It's the genius in me.' Dawlish drove towards Victoria Street and turned left; and then past Victoria Station and turned left again, away from the West End of London and the *Mayfair* Hotel.

'What *are* you doing?' Felicity demanded.

'We're going home.'

'You told Bill—'

'I don't know much about Charles Horden, but I can imagine he's persistent. I'm told that all breeds of writers have to be; it's the only way they ever get anywhere. Having once asked us for help, he'll probably ask again. If he needed help before, he needs it much more now, and he certainly won't try to find us at a Scotland Yard man's flat. That reminds me, I won't be a jiffy.'

He pulled up near a telephone kiosk, left Felicity, and made a call, talking briefly to a man with a deep voice.

Back at the car, he said: 'Rest your head on my shoulder, little one, and have a nap.'

Felicity sat straight up and aloof, for a little while, but soon leaned against him as he drove through the quiet, starry night, past the wooded land and gentle scenery of Surrey.

It was exactly two hours from the time they had left Victoria to the time when Dawlish stopped the car outside the gates of *Four Ways*, their home. No light shone at the windows, but the shape of the house was clear against the starlit sky. A gentle wind rustled across the fields. Felicity, wide awake now, sat waiting for Dawlish to fasten the gates back. The drive to the house ran upwards, with steep banks on either side.

Dawlish drove straight into the garage, the doors of which stood open.

'Had a nice nap?'

'I dozed. Do you think Charles will telephone?'

'I hope he doesn't until the morning. I could do with forty winks.'

Dawlish yawned again, his arm about her waist as they approached the front door. The hall was in darkness, and he switched on the light.

'There's a note!' Felicity leaned forward.

Dawlish looked at the hall table.

'Three notes.' He picked up three slips of paper on which brief messages were scrawled in Norah, their maid's, pencilled writing. '*Listen, sweetheart! Ten o'clock—Mr. Horden rang up. Eleven o'clock. He rang again. Ten to twelve—he rang again dear Mrs. Dawlish I've gone to bed.*'

'You're lying!'

'Gospel truth. Note the finality, the unwritten ultimatum, of the last—"I've gone to bed, and to hell with Mr. Horden if he should ring again". She couldn't have said it clearer.'

'Pat, you scare me sometimes.'

'*I* scare *you*!'

'How did you know that he'd try to get in touch with us?'

'Even I can add two and two,' said Dawlish. 'He wanted to see us, was prevented from going home, possibly fearing violence. That would make him even more anxious to see us. You see, I'm allowing that he's a victim, not a villain. Like to make some more coffee?'

Dawlish went into the drawing-room, a long, narrow room with wide windows, and a charm which was almost wholly due to Felicity. A telephone stood near the fireplace by the side of Dawlish's large armchair. He sat on the arm and lifted the receiver, while Felicity watched from the door.

'Hallo, operator . . . This is Alum 133 speaking. Have there

been any calls for me in the last two hours, do you know?'
He winked at Felicity, nodded, nodded again and then said:
'Thanks very much.' He put down the receiver. 'I hate to break
it to you, I hate to break it to myself, but our chance of a quiet
night is nil. We had a call at twelve-twenty, another at twelve
forty-five and the last at one thirty-four, which shows you how
exact these telephone operators have to be. The missing Charles
is very anxious to find us. I—here we go!'

The telephone bell rang. He lifted the receiver with the
resigned smile of one about to be proved right.

'Hallo . . . Yes, this is Alum 133, and I'm expecting a call.' He
watched Felicity coming towards him, and hissed: 'Listen in!'

Felicity flew out of the room, and reached the extension, in
the bedroom, as the operator said: 'You're through.'

'This is Patrick Dawlish,' said Dawlish.

'Mr. Dawlish,' said the distraught voice of a woman, 'is
Charles there? *Is* he there?'

Dawlish said: 'No, I haven't seen him tonight. What makes you
think he might come to see me?'

The girl said weakly: 'I—I don't know.'

'I suppose you do mean Charles Horden?'

'Of course I do.'

'And I suppose you're the girl who ran away from me earlier
this evening.'

'Yes, but I didn't know then who you were.'

'And you've been waiting for Charles, but he hasn't turned
up—when were you supposed to meet him?'

'At eight o'clock.'

'And you waited until after ten before going to the house to
see him?'

'Yes, but—'

'Why? And why do you think he might have come here?'

The girl said: 'He told me that he was getting in touch with you. I said that he was crazy; but he would try it, and—I'm so afraid that he's been hurt. He *is* in danger. He ought to leave the country; there's no point in his staying here now. If—if you see him, will you ask him to leave? He knows where to go, he knows that he needn't worry about money or anything like that. If only he weren't so independent—' she broke off, and caught her breath. '*Will* you tell him that?'

'I'll pass on the message. Where are you?'

'That doesn't matter.'

'It matters a lot. Unless you tell me who you are and where I can find you, the moment I get a chance I'll turn your Charles over to the police.'

She gasped: 'No!'

'Where are you?'

'At my home. 19, Lincoln Square, Mayfair.' She almost whispered the words. 'My name is Downing, Fay Downing. You will tell Charles—'

'I'll tell Charles what you've said, and I shall call at your house at twelve o'clock in the morning,' said Dawlish. 'And listen, Fay Downing. Odd things happened at Charles's house tonight. Don't look at a newspaper, don't go there again, don't do anything until I've seen you. Is that clear?'

'*Clear?* How—'

'And I'll see you at twelve o'clock, precisely.'

Dawlish put down the receiver and heard the 'ting' as Felicity replaced hers. He wondered what she made of this. Of course, he ought to tell the police about this telephone call; there wasn't any excuse for keeping it to himself, but—Felicity came into the room, looking tired but bright-eyed.

'My mistake,' he said. 'I didn't expect to hear from Fay.'

'Pat, if Trivett knew—'

'He doesn't know, and I'll lay a pound to a penny that Fay Downing will talk more freely to you and me than she will to Bill. That is, if you'll come tomorrow. When we've heard the girl's story, we can decide how much to pass on to Bill. She sounded jumpy, didn't she? And she's so fond of Charles that she'll stake him to leave the country, and complains bitterly that he's too stiff-necked about accepting money from girl friends. That's almost the first nice thing I've heard about Charles. Shall we have some coffee, or—'

The front door bell rang, followed by the sharp rat-tat-tat of the knocker.

CHAPTER FOUR

VISITOR

'Or shall we go straight to bed?' Dawlish finished, closing his eyes and looking away from the door. The bell rang again. 'Hallo, what's this? Visitors? Wonderful!' He looked at his watch, shook it and held it to his ear. 'Why, it's only three o'clock. If that bell hadn't rung, we might have been in bed by half past—lazing away while all the world is awake and searching for Charles.'

The bell rang again.

'Aren't you going to let him in?' asked Dawlish. 'He's your friend.'

'I'll come with you,' Felicity said. 'And, Pat, don't be flippant with him. He's terribly worried, and—'

'It will do him good to wait. It will also tell us what he's likely to do if we don't answer. He might go away, he might come round to the back door, or he might break a window.' He paused, raising his head, listening. 'No sound. He was impatient when he first arrived, knocked three times in quick succession, and now—a long silence. Why? He must know that someone's in, because the light's on.'

The silence continued.

'*Pat!*' breathed Felicity.

'Be patient a little longer,' he pleaded. He took her arm, led her towards the door, but before they reached it, slipped an arm round her shoulders and another beneath her knees, and dumped her into an easy chair in the corner. 'Rest, darling, and don't get up. I'm going to put out the light.'

'Pat—'

His long arm stretched out and the light faded; it was pitch dark for a few seconds. Then the starlight gradually filtered into the room from the pale shape of the window. The silence was intense now—only Felicity's breathing broke it. Dawlish smiled, knowing what she was thinking of him.

He heard the movement first; a footstep, outside. Dawlish moved silently towards the window, but kept close to the wall. He heard Felicity draw in her breath sharply, for a shadow appeared; the blurred grey round shape of a man's face. Next came the dark outline of head and shoulders. A hand moved and pressed against the glass pane.

'*Pat,*' whispered Felicity. 'What are you trying to do?'

'Unravel the mystery of the three o'clock caller,' Dawlish whispered back. 'Just stay where you are.'

He went out of the room. There was no light in the hall; none anywhere in the house now. He groped for the front door and opened it. Poking his head round the corner of the porch, he saw the dark shape of a man standing by the window. It was impossible to see his face or figure, to judge whether he was young or old.

The path outside was of gravel; silent movement on it was almost impossible. Dawlish judged his distance, and sprang forward. At the first sound the man started violently, then turned and ran. But he didn't know the garden, tripped on the edge of the lawn and fell into a rose bed. As he fell, he cried out.

Her endurance strained to the utmost, Felicity switched on the drawing-room lights. The bright glow, streaming through the uncurtained windows, showed a stocky, powerful-looking man with dark hair; certainly not Charles.

'Good evening,' said Dawlish. 'I'm sorry about the rose bed.' He helped the man to his feet, but kept a hand loosely on his arm. 'Coming in for a moment?'

The man did not speak, shrugged his coat into position, and allowed himself to be led to the front door. There Felicity waited.

'You didn't know Charles was an expert in disguises, did you?' asked Dawlish. 'Slightly studded by thorns at the moment, but I suppose a genius wouldn't worry about a little thing like that. He—'

'Darling,' said Felicity, 'the genius joke is dead.'

'As far as I'm concerned, it died some time ago. I was only trying to be nice.' He tightened his grip on the stranger's shoulder, but the man made no attempt to get away, and walked firmly into the drawing-room. There he looked into a mirror, scowled, and gingerly felt for his handkerchief. Dawlish plucked several thorns from his coat and another from his hair. The man dabbed rather peevishly at his face.

'Perhaps you'd better bathe those scratches,' Dawlish suggested.

The stranger had dark blue eyes and a firm chin. He was of medium height and broad with it. Dawlish towered above him, and in breadth could give him a full three inches. They made a strange and striking contrast, Dawlish having hair and eyebrows the colour of ripe corn, big features and a nose which had once been broken in an early skirmish. It was said by his friends that Dawlish had been born to the ways of violence.

The stranger spoke. 'May I?'

'I'll take you to the bathroom,' said Dawlish. 'Care for a drink afterwards, or would you prefer coffee?'

'Beer, if you have it.'

'Darling,' muttered Felicity, 'if you talk to him behind my back I'll never forgive you.'

Dawlish grinned at her as he led the way out. The stranger followed without a word. In the bathroom he sponged his face and the backs of his hands gingerly, and Dawlish gave him a pot of ointment, which he rubbed gently into the scratches. His suit had been cut by an expert tailor and the set of the lapels was perfect.

'Finished?' asked Dawlish.

'Thanks.'

They went downstairs again. Felicity had put out beer and tankards, and made tea for herself. Gravely, Dawlish offered the stranger a cigarette; then lit it. Next he gave him beer.

'Now,' Dawlish suggested gently, 'perhaps you can explain an over-close juxtaposition to my rose bush?'

The stranger smiled faintly; but he didn't look at Dawlish. He shrugged.

'Let's start at the beginning, or at least a little further back. Why didn't you answer when I rang?'

'I wanted to put you at a disadvantage.'

'You certainly did that,' murmured the stranger. 'There are more comfortable, and less painful, positions in which to be found.'

'And your reason for coming?'

'Is this. Dawlish, I understand that Charles Horden has asked for your help. He's not worth it. He isn't worth anyone's time or trouble. To put it concisely, he's a rat, a coward and a crook. He'll involve you in a nasty mess if you give him half a chance. Don't listen to him. And if he's worked through your wife, don't listen to her. I can never understand why, but he's a great success with women. Too great. He's ruined several, to my knowledge.'

'Ah! So I am to take it that you are St. George, whose only desire is to succour such damsels in distress.'

'I'm only interested in one damsel. I'll stop him from making a fool of her, if I have to break his neck. I didn't come here to tell you anything except this, Dawlish. Horden is a nasty piece of work. You'll be a fool if you believe his story and try to help him. You're just the type of genial idiot who would feel sorry for him and start making trouble. I—'

'Trouble for whom?'

'Me, among others.'

'And you don't like trouble?'

The stranger smiled again. 'I can face it with the next man if it's necessary; if it isn't, it becomes a bore. In this case if you stir up trouble you, too, will get hurt, and do yourself no good with your friends the police. Once they know the truth about Charles Horden, they'll have a pretty poor opinion of anyone who tries to help him. I'm talking for your own good.'

'Forgive me if I mention that such entire disinterest is unusual. More beer?'

'Thanks.' The stranger held out his tankard. 'Is Charles Horden here?' he asked.

'That's a leading question.'

'You may as well tell me—ah, thanks. I was ready for a drink,' said the stranger, and finished half the beer in a single gulp. 'I thought he might have broken in and been waiting for you. Or that some kind lady had given him a key. He has a genius for getting front door keys as well as a genius for kind ladies. Just at the moment he's on the run, ready to accept help from anybody, and when he goes, their choicest bits of silver go with him. That's Charles. Take my advice, Dawlish, and keep away from him.'

'But supposing he doesn't keep away from me?'

The stranger shrugged. 'You can deal with Charles Horden all right, if you've a mind to. Anyhow, you can't say I haven't warned you.'

'No, I certainly can't say that,' murmured Dawlish meekly. 'Who's the girl you're worried about?'

'Let's leave her out of this.'

'A charming voice,' murmured Dawlish, reminiscently.

The stranger started. 'You know—'

Dawlish laughed. 'Listen to me, little man. I am not quite an imbecile, and I don't plunge into sinister affairs with my eyes shut. There's a lot about Charles Horden which interested me. I'm still interested.'

'You're wrong,' said the stranger.

'You think so?'

'I'm sure of it. I'll go farther than that and say you're an ass. Anyone who knows anything about Charles and still wants to help him, must be one. You married the wrong man, Mrs. Dawlish.' The stranger finished his beer and stood up. 'I must be going. Thanks for everything. You might grow some thornless rose-bushes in future; it would be a kindly deed. Sure you won't tell me whether Charles is here?'

Dawlish shook his head.

The stranger shrugged. 'Pity,' he said, and dropped his right hand towards his pocket, as if reaching for his cigarettes. He was facing Dawlish. His movements were leisurely, his composure remarkable—until Dawlish sprang across the room and grabbed his arm. There was a short, furious struggle, and a gun fell heavily to the floor.

The dark blue eyes blazed with anger but the man made no attempt to struggle until Dawlish slackened his grip. Then he drove his clenched fist towards Dawlish's face. Dawlish moved his head sideways, and the fist whistled past. Dawlish caught him off balance, and tipped him backwards on to the sofa.

'Your mistake,' Dawlish said, picking up the gun. 'Why do you want Charles as badly as that?'

The man didn't speak.

'Your second mistake,' said Dawlish. 'I don't want to hurt you, but by jingo if I do, you'll get a lot you don't expect. *Why* do you want Charles?' Suddenly, unexpectedly, Dawlish dived his right hand into the man's inside coat pocket, drew out a wallet and a letter, and tossed them on to a chair. 'Got your glasses, sweetheart?' he asked Felicity.

'I think I can manage without them,' she said. She looked doubtfully at the wallet and a letter before picking them up, outraged at the idea of examining them, then looked at the gun and decided that its appearance had somehow altered her ideas of what was done and what was not. 'If this is addressed to him, Pat, he's a Mr. John Downing, and he lives at 19, Lincoln Square, Mayfair. That's a terribly expensive district, isn't it, darling?'

'Terribly. See what's in his wallet, will you?'

'Dawlish, if you—'

'Be quiet. You came uninvited. You also threatened me with a gun which surely allows me in return a certain slackening of gentlemanly etiquette. We'll have a chat about Charles, too, and about his uncle and aunt and everyone else, including dazzling damsels who've got themselves mixed up with Charles. Any luck, precious?'

'There's a driving licence, and *that* belongs to a Mr. Downing. And another letter addressed to him. There are some stamps and lots of money and—oh, Pat! Here's a photograph of Charles!'

Downing growled: 'You'll be sorry about this, Dawlish.'

'Well, Fel? Any other pictures?' Dawlish asked.

'There's one of Mr. Downing himself with a girl. On the back is written: "With Fay, Cannes, March nineteen fifty something".'

Downing growled: 'She's nothing to do with this. Leave her out of it. Dawlish, you'll regret the whole business. I came to get Charles away and to tell you to have nothing to do with him. He's poison. If you want to keep your hands clean, tell me whether he's here, and if he is let me take him away, and then forget about it. I'm serious.'

'You didn't ask the proper way,' Dawlish said. 'Nothing else in the wallet, darling?'

'Only the letters.'

'No!' cried Downing.

'That's one way of asking us to read them, but we'll leave it for a moment,' Dawlish said. 'Anyhow, it's not our job, but one for the police. I don't think the local people ought to handle this, do you? Better give Bill Trivett a ring.'

Downing said sharply: 'Don't go to the police!'

'Oh, but I'm a law-abiding man. Of course, if you were to tell me what it's all about I might be in a better position to decide what to do. You see, Charles has stated categorically that he's in fear of his life. He's almost certainly afraid of you. You can't go about scaring the wits out of people, carrying lethal weapons and trying to search other people's houses with impunity. It's a series of criminal offences. But if you care to tell us what Charles has done to make you dislike him so—' Dawlish broke off, with a shrug.

Downing didn't speak.

'I don't *like* disturbing Bill in the middle of the night,' said Felicity. 'I know he's a Scotland Yard man, but he does need sleep. Couldn't we shut Mr. Downing up somewhere—lock him in the box-room, for instance—and then talk to Bill tomorrow?'

'I suppose we could,' conceded Dawlish. 'On the other hand, this is the time of night when human resistance is at its lowest ebb. If we really try to make him talk now, we'll probably succeed. After all—'

He broke off.

He heard the sound before either of the others, and looked towards the window. Felicity said: *'Not another!'* Downing stared tensely into the darkness. After a few seconds, a man's footsteps sounded clearly. Whoever it was, was in a hurry.

Dawlish said: 'Cover our Mr. Downing with his own gun, sweetheart, and if he tries to get up, shoot him.'

He went out, reaching the hall as the front door bell rang. He opened the door and beamed at the caller.

'Come in,' he said softly.

Charles Horden came in.

CHAPTER FIVE

FRIGHTENED MAN

The light fell on to terrified eyes in a long, pale face; on to silky, fair hair, ruffled by the wind—hair badly in need of cutting. Charles wore flannels and an old jacket; his tie was carelessly knotted.

'Were you followed?'

'I'm followed everywhere. Dawlish, I'm desperate. I must have your help. *Shut the door!*' Until then he had spoken in a whisper, now his voice rose. 'They might shoot; they might do anything.'

Dawlish pushed him gently away from the open door and stepped into the porch. No one spoke in the drawing-room. Outside nothing stirred. Dawlish peered down the drive, making out the shapes of flowers, bushes and trees—it would be easy for a man, or men, to hide there. But no one appeared, there was no shot to break the silence.

'You're crazy!' gasped Charles.

'Everyone's telling me that tonight.' Dawlish closed the door, and for Charles's peace of mind, pushed a bolt home with his foot. 'Are you sure you were followed?'

'I think so.'

'The night is easily peopled by devils, Charles. Take it easy.'

If you could forget the fear, the over-long hair, and the tremulous mouth, Charles was a good-looking young man. He was more than that, he was the epitome of Greek perfection. Just now, his pale hands were fluttering in agitation, as his eyes stared hauntingly at the door, as if he expected to hear a bullet thud against the wood.

'Devils,' he muttered. 'You're right there. They've been after me for weeks; I can't stand it any longer, Dawlish. I'm not a brave man, I've never been brave, and now—my nerve's broken, hounded until it's snapped! I can't work, can't do anything. I'm finished—finished. *Will* you help me? Your wife said—'

'Yes, I will.'

'Dawlish, I shall *never* be able to thank you enough!' But the promise of help brought only words in response; there was no lightening of Charles's fear. 'If only I could rest for a few hours! I can't sleep, I daren't—I haven't had a good night's sleep for weeks.'

The red rims at his eyes, and their glassiness, suggested there was a lot of truth in what he said. Felicity had not exaggerated his need for help.

Dawlish said 'Who's gunning for you, Charles?'

'That's the devil of it, I don't *know*. That's what I want to find out—who's behind it all.'

'Why didn't you wait in tonight?'

'I was too scared. I was going to dine with a friend and go home afterwards—but I was followed. I couldn't get her into a mess, so I cut the dinner and dodged about, to get rid of the chap who was following me. Then I came down here. It's bad enough for me, but if she starts getting mixed up in it I—I shan't be able to stand it. One can take just so much, Dawlish, and I've taken that and more!'

'Yes, I believe you,' said Dawlish.

That didn't mean that he accepted everything that Charles said.

He took Charles's arm and led him towards the drawing-room door. Snatches of the conversation must have been heard there, but neither Felicity nor Downing had spoken audibly; and Downing hadn't moved, or Felicity would have fired, to frighten, not to wound him. She would, entirely against her inclinations, scrupulously co-operate with Dawlish in this affair. It was she who had brought him into it, and for that she would accept responsibility.

Dawlish smiled at the thought, opened the door, and ushered Charles inside. He was quick to follow, eager to see Downing's face. Did Downing know who had called?

Charles gasped: 'John!'

Felicity sat where Dawlish had left her, nursing the automatic. Downing put his hands on the arm of his chair and leapt at Charles.

'No!' screamed Charles. 'No!'

He made no attempt to protect himself, just cowered back against Dawlish, who pushed him aside and stood squarely between the two men.

Downing growled: 'Let me get at him!'

'Later,' said Dawlish. 'What's it all about?'

'I'll break his neck!'

'Well, before you start,' said Dawlish mildly, 'what about telling me all about it. Have you been gunning for him for long?'

Downing set his lips stubbornly.

Dawlish swung round on Charles. 'Is this the man you're scared of?'

Charles gulped. 'I'm sorry I behaved like that, Dawlish. It's just that my nerves are so bad, when I saw him coming at me, I thought he would kill me.'

'What you might call a premonition of things to come,' said Downing acidly.

'What's your grouse?' Dawlish demanded.

Downing didn't speak, but Charles waved his hands and said: 'He thinks I'm pursuing his sister. As a matter of fact, it's the other way round.'

'That's a lie,' said Downing.

'He won't listen to reason,' said Charles. 'Could I—could I have a drink?'

Felicity poured him out a whisky and soda. Downing looked as if he would like to knock the glass out of Charles's hand.

'How did you get here, Downing?' Dawlish demanded.

'By car. I left it at the cross roads.'

'How did you know the way?'

'I came out to see you this afternoon.'

'Why?'

'Because I knew Charles had appealed to you for help. My sister told me. At least she had the sense to tell me that. He's lied to you about her. He won't leave her alone, and he's not going to score another of his filthy triumphs with Fay, if I can help it.'

'How did *you* get here, Charles?'

'I came by train,' muttered Charles. 'I couldn't get a taxi, so I walked the three miles from Haslemere Station.'

'What made you think you were followed?'

Charles licked his lips. 'I *know* I was.'

Dawlish said: 'You're in the frame of mind that imagines a lot of things that don't exist. Downing, what's your quarrel with Charles? Simply that you think he's after your sister?'

'Yes.'

'Isn't that a little extreme?'

'Maybe I'm old-fashioned, but in my opinion she's not old enough to know what she's doing. I wouldn't have her mix with this swine and his set if there was no one else on earth. Don't make any mistake, Dawlish, I'm going to run him out of the country before it's over. It's the only way to stop him from pestering Fay.'

'What did you propose to do with him?'

Downing said slowly: 'I was going to beat him up. I had the gun, to scare him. I thought I'd get him away, if he was here. Then I was going to drive out into the country, and thrash him to within an inch of his life. If you had a streak of decency in you, you'd let me go ahead. It might even knock some decency into him, though I doubt it.'

Charles shrugged. 'It's not him I'm worried about—it's the others. I tell you I'm being followed everywhere. Why don't you *believe* me?'

'Why don't you tell me *why*?'

Charles shrieked at him. 'I don't know! You're as bad as the rest; you won't believe me, but I don't *know*.'

Downing seemed to have worked some of the spleen out of his system, but he looked at Charles with sneering contempt.

'I can tell you.'

'Go on, then—tell me.'

Downing said: 'You have been voted the rave of the year. Women are fascinated by you. They think you're wonderful. They even pay you, so that you can get your drivel published. Carrying on these pretty little affairs with married women as you do, sooner or later they get found out. It may, or may not, surprise you to hear that husbands don't like you; I would go even farther than that, and state that you must have more enemies than any other man in London.'

'Quite a Don Juan,' Dawlish murmured.

Downing shrugged. 'A romantic name for a somewhat miserable specimen. Living free at other men's expense he's being haunted by his own foul conscience, and terror that justice might catch up with him. Give me a free hand and I'll see that the whole despicable business gets in the newspapers. He won't do any more damage after that.'

'Publicity would only help to sell more stories,' Dawlish murmured.

'That tripe? Don't talk rot.'

Felicity began to laugh.

'Pat, it—it's incredible! I thought there was really serious trouble, and all it turns out to be is that Charles is being chased by indignant husbands, and *you're* supposed to help him.'

'It may sound funny,' said Downing frostily, 'but I assure you that it isn't.'

Dawlish said: 'Do you know, I'm beginning to agree with you.' His voice was harsh and uncompromising. 'You can clear out, Downing. Charles is staying here for the night. If you come after him again, you'll find yourself in trouble.' He went across to the door and opened it. 'It's half past four, and I want some sleep. Good night.'

'I'm not going without Horden, and you needn't think I am.'

'Scram,' said Dawlish.

Felicity said: 'Pat, don't you think—'

'I think I've had enough of Mr. Downing for tonight. If he doesn't go I'll throw him out.'

Downing shrugged his shoulders, and sauntered across the room. He passed within a yard of Charles, and appeared to ignore him—but as soon as he was past, he swung round and aimed a blow at Charles's face. Charles, on guard, dodged back.

'That's enough!' snapped Dawlish.

Downing shrugged and went into the hall. Dawlish followed and closed the door behind him.

'This is your big mistake,' Downing said.

'Could be, and it could be yours. Think yourself lucky that you're not charged with assault and carrying a lethal weapon.'

Dawlish opened the front door, and at the same time switched out the hall light. He watched until Downing's dark figure merged with the shadowy shapes of trees and shrubs. Then Dawlish went after him, stepping on to the grassy banks of the drive. He followed, ten yards behind. The grass deadened his footsteps. Now and again a tree got in his way, but most of the time he could see Downing, against the light-coloured gravel of the drive. Downing walked briskly, showed no sign of wanting to turn back. He reached the gates and went out, turning left towards the cross-roads where he said he had left his car.

The cross-roads were a hundred yards away. They were marked by two great beech trees, which blotted out a patch of stars. Beneath them, Dawlish thought he could make out the shape of a car; if one were there, it had no lights on.

Downing slowed down.

Dawlish looked back at the house, noting the light shining from the drawing-room window.

In a job like this you had to take a chance; and he was taking one with Felicity. Charles might really have been followed. The old man hadn't been killed by outraged husbands; murder, cruel and ugly, stalked the night. Why? Was Charles to be framed for that crime? Or was he to be another victim? Why had Downing come? Not simply because of his sister; that was the excuse, not the reason.

Downing opened the car door, and slid into the driving seat. He switched on the side-lights, and the glow seemed bright in that darkness. The car was facing Alum village, a mile away, and Haslemere beyond. Downing started the engine, it took two pulls at the self-starter before it hummed. Then he eased off the brakes, and Dawlish watched the dark shape of the car and the vague outline of the driver—and glanced round again, at the house.

This risk might be the wrong one.

Dawlish noticed that the car windows were open, as wheels crunched on the gravel. Suddenly, hideously, Downing cried out. The cry was cut short. Dawlish strode towards the car, and the faint glow of the headlights showed the shape of a man crouched behind Downing—and Dawlish needed no telling that the man was trying to strangle him.

The engine purred, the car moved slowly forward towards the hedge, and came to a standstill. Dawlish reached the car and opened the rear door.

'Wrong man,' he said.

The assailant swung round, his hands dropping from Downing's neck. He struck out at Dawlish, but Dawlish, fending him off, struck a swift blow at the exposed chin; the man's head jolted back. Downing grunted and gasped for breath, while Dawlish groped for the roof-light of the car, found it—and in the dim glow saw a man with a pale and thin face, and a long nose.

This was the man who had been at Kensington.

CHAPTER SIX

LONG NOSE

Dawlish said: 'Take it easy, Downing; you'll be all right.'

He took the little man's arm and dragged him, still dazed, out of the car. He pulled off the man's coat and then buttoned it round him, back to front, making a makeshift strait-jacket. Then he knotted a tie round him. By the time the man had recovered his wits he was helpless. Dawlish bundled him back into the car, laying him on the floor; it would take a Houdini to get out of that for the next half an hour.

Downing's breathing was harsh and short.

'How are you doing?' asked Dawlish.

A rasping whisper answered him: 'Devil nearly—strangled me.'

'That was the idea. You're lucky he didn't use a hammer. Shift over, will you? I'll take the wheel and we'll get back.'

'You told me to clear out.'

'That was before Long Nose had his go at you,' Dawlish said. 'Many odd things have happened tonight, this is not least of it. Was it you he was after, or did he think you were Charles?'

Downing didn't answer, and Dawlish went round to the other

door and got in. It was a small car, and he was uncomfortably cramped as he groped for the clutch with his foot. The engine started at the first pull of the self-starter. He swung round at the cross-roads, and headed back to *Four Ways*.

Downing didn't speak until they pulled up outside the house.

'Thanks,' he said. 'For the rescue, I mean.'

'I'll tell you whether it was a pleasure or not a little later.'

'You're a queer customer, Dawlish. But you've a lot more nerve than I. I wouldn't leave my wife alone with Horden for two minutes.'

'I don't know much about Horden, but I know he's badly frightened, and I don't think it's you he's scared of. I think Long Nose watched the house, knew Charles was here, saw you leave, took it for granted you were Charles, and had a crack at you. Long Nose might be a husband on the war-path, but I don't think he is.'

'Well, don't ask me.'

They sat in the car as they talked, and shadows moved against the curtains, now drawn across the windows of the drawing-room. Dawlish raised his voice: 'All safe, Fel!'

Downing didn't move.

'So that's why you sent me out?'

'That's it. I thought that if Charles had been followed, his tailer would have a go at him, and in the dark, get you. Thank me for the bruises on your neck. Unless,' Dawlish added mildly, 'you have enemies, too.'

'No known enemies.'

'One day you're going to tell me why you came here tonight,' said Dawlish, and opened the door as Felicity appeared in the hall. She didn't speak as Dawlish opened the back door of the car and dragged the prisoner out. She didn't make any comment when he carried the man into the hall. Downing followed, leisurely, still fingering his neck.

'Darling,' said Felicity, at the door of the drawing-room, 'we haven't any more.'

'Any more what?'

'Spare rooms.'

'The coal cellar will do for this one,' said Dawlish. 'How has Charles been getting on? No passionate scenes, I trust?'

'He's—*sick* with fear.'

'Yes. Downing—' Dawlish paused, still holding his prisoner, who made no attempt to struggle and whose face was turned away from Felicity. 'Don't go for Charles again, or I'll finish what this little joker started.'

He turned towards the kitchen quarters, and as he did so, the light fell on the man's long nose. Felicity screamed.

'*Pat!*'

'What—oh, you—'

'It's the man who was at—'

'Don't tell all the world about it yet,' pleaded Dawlish. 'I'll be along in a few minutes.'

The kitchen was a large, white-tiled room, and there was a comfortable armchair, where Norah spent most of her leisure hours. Dawlish dumped the prisoner into the chair and, to make doubly sure of him, tied his ankles to the legs of it. Then he stood back and looked at the man closely for the first time.

Dawlish said: 'Why did you try to kill Horden?'

The man licked his lips.

'Listen to me. This is a lonely house in a lonely part of the country. You can make a lot of noise here, and no one would hear you. Why did you try to kill him?'

'I didn't!' The voice was husky and weak.

'So it was just a friendly overture?'

'I didn't try to kill him. I wanted to—'

'Scare the life out of him?'

'Supposing I did? He *ought* to be scared.' The husky voice surprised Dawlish, because it was that of an educated man—and it grew stronger with every word. 'I'd do it again if I had the chance. I was going to leave him unconscious, and when he woke up he'd be even more frightened than he is now.'

Dawlish looked meditatively at the man for a few moments and then turned back to the drawing-room.

Charles sat on the sofa in an attitude of utter dejection, hands on his knees, chin sagging on to his chest. Downing stood by the table drinking beer, as if thoroughly at home. Felicity nursed the gun and looked from one man to the other, in silent bewilderment.

'Just a minute, Downing.'

Downing put down a tankard of beer and moved across the room. As the door shut behind him, he grinned at Dawlish.

'What do you want me to do?'

'Follow me into the kitchen after a minute's start. Just walk in, looking as you are now. Don't show any surprise, don't jump, throw beer about, or try to get your revenge on the man who nearly throttled you.'

'I don't know what all this is about, but I'll play.'

Dawlish opened the kitchen door, half closed it again, and shifted Long Nose's chair so that the man was looking towards the door. Then he stood to one side and watched. A moment later Downing came in. There wasn't the slightest change of expression on the prisoner's face—no movement at eyes or mouth to suggest that he knew Downing.

A swift glance at Downing showed a faint smile which touched the dark blue eyes.

'No, I have never seen him before,' he said.

'He tried to strangle you.'

'That's a lie!' cried Long Nose. 'I attacked Horden, not this man! I—no, I couldn't have made a mistake. I saw Horden come in! I was watching, I thought he'd left his car at the corner and—' He broke off and thrust his head forward. 'Are you lying to me, Dawlish? Is this man one of your crazy friends? I tell you I went for Horden.'

'No. Mr. Downing and I are *not* friends.'

The name appeared to mean nothing to Long Nose, who leaned uncomfortably against the chair-back. He had not once complained of being tied up, and appeared to accept his plight philosophically. He closed his eyes, but whether in fatigue, defeat, or weariness of fools, was not apparent.

'Anything else I can do for you?' asked Downing, 'barring, I think, the risk of being taken for a friend of yours again. There are limits to my capacity for taking insults.'

Dawlish grinned. 'They'll stretch! You can stay here because I don't trust you alone with Horden. And you can learn a little of the art of finding facts from men reluctant to talk fast.' He turned to the other man. 'Why did you lie in wait for Horden?'

The little man said slowly: 'Because he smashed up my marriage. If it hadn't been for that smooth-voiced poet, I would still be—' He broke off, and closed his eyes. 'I'll make him suffer before I've finished. *And* I'll make him tell me where my wife is.'

Downing murmured: 'Not such a hard job to get the truth out of him, is it? Now perhaps you'll believe me.'

Downing drank his beer and grinned sardonically. Dawlish cocked his head on one side and watched Long Nose; and wondered. Downing was no fool; in fact, he seemed a man with a good mind and a ready intelligence. These two might be acquaintances. It would not have been difficult to mistake Downing for Charles in the darkness. So they might be in collusion, and the corroborative story of the little man with the long nose worth no more than a snap of the fingers.

Or it might be true; it seemed, on the whole, more likely to be true.

'Why don't you hand Horden over, let this poor beggar free, and go to bed?' asked Downing. 'I've told you it will save a lot of trouble for a lot of people.'

'Yes. That's the weakness of your argument. I've always disliked threats, no matter how well veiled.'

'You'll just have to overcome your rather one-sided prejudice, won't you, if you want to get anywhere.'

Dawlish stood, undecided—and then heard a cry from the front of the house. Felicity came running.

'Pat! There's someone else. A car's coming up the drive. It's—'

'Nicely timed,' said Dawlish. He put his arm round her, and went with her towards the hall. Her hair brushed across his face as he whispered: 'Stay by the kitchen door, sweet. See whether Downing tries to free the other johnny. At the slightest sign, let me know.'

'But who—'

'Ted and Tim on the war-path, unless I miss my guess,' declared Dawlish.

The car purred sweetly up the drive, then swung round in front of the house. A car horn blared out an unmelodious, ear-shattering *Ta-ri-ta-ra! Ta-ri-ta-ra!* A door slammed, and a shrill whistle sounded clearly through the night—a high-pitched call, like that of a bird calling its mate. Footsteps followed.

'When did you send for *them*?' demanded Felicity. 'All right, don't tell me. You telephoned from Victoria.'

Footsteps now sounded in the porch. Dawlish opened his mouth and emitted a short, sharp whistle, an answering call to that which had already come. At the same time he grinned in delight.

Two large men crowded the porch.

One was simply large; tall and broad, although even in that poor light his thin features and hollow cheeks could be seen. The other was a massive giant, with an engaging ugliness.

''Lo, Pat. What's it all about?'

'Bad men and harassed lovelies.'

'Just our pint of beer,' declared the lean man. 'You'd be surprised if you knew the trouble I had getting Ted away. It wasn't his fault, I will say that. But Joan was sticky. She protested doggedly about chasing round the countryside with that big lunatic, Dawlish. She sends her hate.'

'Joan's all right,' said the man named Ted, 'her protests are entirely due to an over-developed sense of protection. Like the mother who said "See what baby's doing, and tell him he mustn't do it". He peered along the passage to the kitchen door. 'Do I perceive my hostess waiting at the threshold?'

'You do indeed, but secretly engaged. Now, listen carefully. We have three guests besides yourselves. One is in an impro-vised strait-jacket, the others are free. They're all here because of Felicity's penchant for a poet. Murder has been done, and more may follow; altogether it's one of the oddest shows I've ever come across. We are likely to be busy. I gathered—more in manner than in words—that in this we have the great Bill Trivett's blessing. In short, you are about to embark on a most promising business.'

'Bee-ootiful!' declared the lean man.

'Are you both free for a matter of days that might become weeks?'

'Could be,' said the large man.

'Am,' said the lean one.

These were old friends of Dawlish, who had often worked with him, and were both loyal and reliable as well as men of resource.

'*Pat*,' whispered Felicity.

Dawlish turned and hurried towards her, and she said: 'They're moving about inside, and I think—'

But she stopped, for the door of the kitchen opened. Long Nose remained where he had been, with the coat still on back to front. Downing, tankard in hand, appeared and raised an inquiring eyebrow.

Dawlish said: 'I'll introduce you in a moment,' went into the kitchen and lifted Long Nose from the chair.

The coat fell open; it had been unbuttoned.

Long Nose butted Dawlish beneath the chin, hard enough to hurt, and at the same time kicked. Dawlish lost his balance and fell back against the table. Long Nose, with astonishing agility, swung round and made for the back door; but it was locked and bolted, and he had no time to unfasten it. Downing watched, without moving, and the two large men came along the passage, without haste, but with obvious interest. Long Nose turned and glared at Dawlish.

'You won't always think you're so clever.'

'I hope not. Tim, you know where I keep the bracelets, don't you?'

'Yes. Won't be half a jiff.'

The lean man hurried upstairs, while the giant stood near Downing and looked large and powerful enough to push Downing over with one movement of his hand. Soon the lean man returned; in his hands were two pairs of police handcuffs. He slipped one loop round the prisoner's left wrist, the other round the leg of the table. Then he pushed the chair nearer, so that Long Nose could sit down.

'All safe,' he said.

'We'll now go and see Charles,' said Dawlish.

Felicity said: 'I think I'll go to bed.'

The men went into the drawing-room, where Charles leaned back in a chair, in an attitude of utter dejection. He did look up; but he took no further notice of the newcomers, and thereafter stared blankly towards the wall, his eyes filled with a haunted unrest. The big men looked at him as they might look at a specimen in a biological laboratory and then made, as one man, towards the beer.

Dawlish said: 'You people had better know each other. The genius is Charles Horden. The other is John Downing. Downing, these are friends of mine—Ted Beresford, holding the bottle; Tim Jeremy, holding the tankard.'

'How do you do?' murmured Tim Jeremy in his deep voice. Beresford nodded.

Downing said: 'Yes, I've heard of your buddies. But if you had twice as strong a bodyguard, you'd still wish you hadn't touched this business. When they hear the truth, they'll agree with me.' He sauntered across the room and held out his tankard. 'May I?'

'He has one point in his favour,' said Dawlish. 'He can outdrink you, Tim.'

'That's a challenge I cannot allow to pass!'

Dawlish said: 'Now, Downing, let's hear why you really came after Horden.'

'It's always a bore repeating things. If a man's not convinced at the first time, he rarely is at the second or third.'

'I'm not convinced.'

'Don't blame me.'

'Why did you release Long Nose?'

'Not, as you probably think, because I'm a friend of his. But I can sympathize, and I don't see why you picked him out for the rough stuff. He tried to strangle me, not you. I don't like being mistaken for Horden, but I've no objection to a man trying to put the fear of the devil into him.'

'That may be your bad luck before this is over,' said Dawlish. He turned to the others. 'And now I'm going to put you both in the picture.' He talked for four and a half minutes, but he said nothing about the murder of the old man, or his own first encounter with Long Nose.

When he had finished Downing said wearily:

'And everything I've told Dawlish is true.'

Charles said in a spiritless voice: 'You're crazy—absolutely crazy. There isn't a word of truth in it. *I* can't help it if so many damned women fall for me, can I? *I'm* not responsible if they come chasing after me at all hours of the day and night. Look at your own sister!'

'You'll keep her out—'

'Your trouble is that you're a moral coward,' snapped Charles waspishly. 'You won't face up to anything unpleasant. Your sister's been trying to make me take her money for *months*. She thinks I'm worth staking. I haven't touched it, but—'

'That's a lie.'

'It's the truth. She even wants me to leave the country. She thinks I'd be prepared to live on her, luxuriating in expensive Continental hotels. Well, I'm not. I wish I'd never seen her. Far from being the little angel you think she is, she's a—'

Downing moved swiftly towards him, fury in his eyes. Beresford shot out a hand and took Downing's arm, pulling him back.

Downing growled: 'If you didn't use her money, what did you do with it? Come on, tell me! She gave it to you. Where did it go?'

CHAPTER SEVEN

A MATTER OF MONEY

Charles drew a deep breath.

'I passed it on.'

Downing said: 'Make what you like of that, Dawlish. Fay's paid him two hundred and fifty pounds in the past twelve months. And he's got the nerve to say he hasn't used it himself! She's not the only one who's paid him, either. The chap out there says that his wife put up nearly five hundred. And there are plenty of others. He's ruined a dozen women, and he'll go on doing it unless he gets a nasty shock. He's going to get that shock. He'd have had it tonight, if you'd listened to reason.'

'Charles,' said Dawlish.

'What?'

'Have you taken money from other women and passed it on?'

'Supposing I have?'

'I'm not supposing; I want to know.'

Charles licked his lips. 'Yes. It's being used for a good cause, doing far more good than if it were spent on clothes and silly fripperies. Idiot women! They think that all that matters in life is a round of theatres and night clubs, furs, model dresses, trips to

Paris and a morning parade of Bond Street. They're nothing but parasites. If I had my way, I'd put them to work. There's plenty they could do that wouldn't tax the brains they haven't got.'

Downing's voice quivered: 'That's the kind of talk he hands out when he's finished with them.'

'I've never used them! I've never asked one of them for money! Don't blame me if they haven't any sense.'

'You make me sick,' said Downing. He turned to Dawlish. 'Well, I've said my say, and I've told you what I intend to do. Want me any more?'

Dawlish said: 'No.'

'As you've got your bodyguards here you needn't fear that I'll come back tonight,' said Downing. 'Make sure that Horden has a nice comfy bed, won't you? And don't forget to give him a hot-water bottle. You mustn't let him get cold feet.'

He went towards the door.

'See him off, Tim, will you?' Dawlish said.

Jeremy asked a silent question with his eyes, which meant: 'Am I to follow him?' Dawlish shook his head. Tim accepted that decision without argument; he did not come back into the room until the car was half-way down the drive. Then he returned and finished off his beer. He looked curiously at Charles.

Beresford said: 'Make head or tail of it, Pat?'

'Not yet.'

'If you'd tried, you might have got the truth out of Downing,' suggested Jeremy. 'Not mine to argue or to criticize, but don't you think—'

'Downing told the truth as far as he knows it,' said Dawlish. 'He also kept something back—we'll find out what it was in good time. Charles—'

'Well?'

'Have you told the truth?'

'Yes.'

'Where does this money go?'

Charles said: 'I can't tell you. I'm under oath not to tell you, but—but it's for a good cause.'

'These people who scare you—are they outraged husbands?'

'I don't know who they are.'

'Could they be?'

Charles moistened his lips again. There was more colour in them, and in his cheeks than there had been. His eyes were bright, and yet they looked glazed; was that just tiredness, or was it an unnatural brilliance?

'I simply don't know. It's no use asking me questions, I can't give you the answers, and I'm not going to guess. Downing's just an unimaginative fool. If he only had some real intelligence he'd understand. *I can't help being attractive to women.* The more I insult them the more they worry me! If I hadn't found out how to use their money—'

He broke off abruptly. Tim Jeremy framed the word: 'How?' but didn't utter it, for Dawlish shook his head.

Charles said in a thin voice: 'Dawlish, can I stay here for a few days? If I could only get some rest I'd feel better. I must get some rest.'

'You can stay.'

'Thank you, I'm grateful, I am indeed.'

'Have you seen the man with the long nose before?'

'What man?' asked Charles dully. 'A lot of men have long noses.' The description obviously meant nothing to him. 'All I know is that I've got to have some peace of mind, or I shall go mad. The strain is bad enough, without this additional worry. If only they wouldn't ask me to do so much! If only they'd realize I'm not physically strong. If you have the gift, you're bound to be physically weak, you can't have it both ways. Can you?' He spoke in a soft, propitiating voice as if he were pleading with the gods. 'I don't want the gift, I hate it. I abhor it! But I've got it, and I must serve. *I must—serve.*'

He raised his hands and let them fall, sitting motionless, dedicated, doomed.

Beresford shifted his leg. Jeremy let a tankard droop dangerously in his hand. A cigarette burned low in Dawlish's fingers; he felt the warmth, but did nothing about it. A strange silence fell upon the room, gradually broken by Charles's laboured breathing. It was uncanny. At first he breathed softly, as if he were falling asleep with his eyes wide open. Then gradually it became an effort for him to breath. His body moved, his chest heaved, the light in his eyes seemed to radiate to every corner of the room. His mouth worked, but he didn't speak—until suddenly he groaned:

'No!'

Then he collapsed, and before any of them could move to help him, rolled on to the floor.

Charles Horden lay in bed, and three large men looked down upon him; three unusually silent and sombre men. Beresford broke the silence with a slight cough, and:

'He looks just a kid, doesn't he?'

'How old?' asked Jeremy.

'Twenty-five.'

Jeremy scratched the end of his nose.

'What do you make of him, Pat?'

'I don't know.'

'Meaning, he could be a phoney, and this could be an act to impress us?'

'Could be, yes. Or it could be that he nurses a lot of queer ideas and thinks he's psychic. He's certainly had a bad run recently, he's worn out physically and not far from a mental breakdown. That collapse was genuine. I'm inclined to think he is, too, but—' he shrugged his shoulders. 'The most dangerous of all men are the fanatics. I think Charles is a fanatic. There's plenty to find out.'

'Better not disturb him,' Beresford said.

'We couldn't; he's flat out.'

Dawlish led the way downstairs. The high spirits of his two friends had been dampened by the scene with Charles. They looked about the disordered room, the littered ash-trays and the empty beer-bottles. A tiny clock struck the hour of five. Beresford yawned.

'Yes, bedtime,' said Dawlish. 'One of you had better kip on the other bed in Charles's room. The other, make do in an armchair in the kitchen.' Dawlish grinned. 'In the morning I've another little surprise packet for you, but if you'd like it now—'

'We'd like it now.'

Dawlish told them of the murder briefly and factually, then left them to settle down for what was left of the night. In his own room, he stood smiling down at Felicity for what seemed a long time. It was nearly half past five before he got into bed. Felicity, warm and drowsy, stirred but did not wake.

Odd that Felicity, who hated his envolvement in dangerous affairs, should have brought him into this.

Had she sensed the strange quality which was in Charles Horden? Had she intuitively realized that here was mystery; mystery which must soon be probed; and had she believed that Dawlish was the man to probe it, whatever the dangers and the risks? What was the situation now? A possible 'genius', almost certainly psychic, on whom women lavished love and money, the one rejected and the other passed on to some mysterious cause; angry, revengeful husbands on his trail, introducing an element of theatrical farce; and a man battered to death in the house where the genius lived. Mix them all up, and what did you have?

Dawlish didn't try to guess.

Felicity said: 'Pat.' It came to him now through a maze of sleep. She called him urgently, shrilly, in fear, in hope, in alarm—but she was always calling him. This time, her voice was gentle but insistent, and she added a soft touch at his shoulder. 'Pat, wake up.' He didn't want to wake up. He was filled with blessed sleep, and knew that if she went away, he would go off again and stay there for a long time; he hadn't slept anything like long enough. But if Felicity wanted a thing, she knew how to get it, and she certainly wanted him to wake. 'Pat darling, wake up.'

He opened one eye.

'Go away.'

'It's nearly ten o'clock. You must wake up. You can't lie there all day, there's so much to do. And I'm worried about Charles. Do you remember Charles? I'm worried about him.'

The soft, insistent voice took on a new note, and he knew that she was trying to stimulate his mind, to bring him back again to that mood of pretended jealousy, which was only half-pretended. It was good to hear.

'Send him away. Forget him.' He opened the other eye. 'You have just one man to worry about, and his name isn't Charles.'

'Would you like a cup of tea?' asked Felicity.

'No. I want to go to sleep.'

'I thought you'd like one; here it is.'

Dawlish groaned and sat up, ran a hand over his stubble and leaned forward to kiss the hand that held the cup of steaming tea.

'I thought your boast was that you could wake at the slightest sound.'

'Not friendly sounds. Only dangerous ones. Where's everyone?'

'Tim's asleep. Ted's up. He's worried about Charles, too. He keeps making odd noises.'

'Ted always did.'

'No, idiot. Charles.'

'He's dreaming.'

Dawlish sipped his tea and looked out of the window, and saw that it was a bright morning, the tops of the trees swaying in a gentle breeze. Beyond the garden lay the hills of Surrey and the spreading pasture land.

'Remember me?' she asked.

'Didn't we spend the night together some time?'

'How clever of you to call it to mind! Seriously, Pat, Ted thinks you ought to see Charles. And I think you ought to get a doctor to have at look at him. He's feverish, if I know anything about illness. And there's everything else, too. We can't keep Long Nose here indefinitely. Tim's taken off the handcuffs, and we've fed him, but—'

'Sympathy for Long Nose?'

'No, for Tim. Darling, I know you hate me saying so, but you ask a lot of Tim and Ted. Too much sometimes. There will come an end to their simple acceptance of your word as the be-all and end-all, if you use them so imperiously. How they do it beats me, but you only have to crook your little finger and they rush to do what you want; but don't overdo it.'

'No, dear.'

'And don't be flippant; this is serious.'

Felicity produced, and held out, a newspaper. 'Look—you're in it again.'

There he was indeed, decorating the front page, if decorating was the right description of a photograph that made him look like a truculent bruiser beside another photograph of Charles which did him more than justice. The headline ran: POLICE SEEK AUTHOR, and a sub-heading: *PAT DAWLISH FINDS MURDERED MAN*.

Dawlish said: 'Now, who let that out? Not Trivett, certainly.'

'One of the small-fry policemen probably.'

'I doubt it. Trivett was hot on the "don't-talk-to-anyone" line. Someone else knew about the murder and knew that we were there.' He skimmed the story; it was mostly true, ending up with the statement that the police were anxious to interview Charles Horden. He put the newspaper down, and finished his tea with apparent relish.

'I hope you've no false ideas that this late tea is going to ruin my breakfast?'

'None at all. Norah's getting it. Are you going to tell Trivett that Charles is here?'

'I don't know.'

Dawlish flung the clothes back, and in five minutes stood by Charles Horden's bed, with a thoughtful Beresford, up and dressed, beside him. Charles's cheeks were flushed, his forehead was hot and his silky hair damp. He was restless, turning his head from side to side and muttering—but what he said was inaudible. Dawlish bent down and put his ear close to his lips, felt the hot breath, but couldn't catch any words.

'I've tried that,' Beresford said. 'Nothing doing, old boy. Question is, fetch the local doctor, or do you think we ought to have a police surgeon, or—'

'We telephone Jim Farningham pronto, and ask him to drop everything and come.'

Beresford looked worried.

'I saw Jim only three days ago. His assistant is off ill, and he's having a hell of a time. You know what it's like with general practitioners these days. It's not as if he were still at the hospital. He'd come like a shot if we asked him, but ought we to ask him?'

Felicity's warning rang in Dawlish's ears.

'I mean,' said Beresford, who looked embarrassed, 'is there anything Jim can do that another doctor can't?'

'I think so.' Dawlish smiled. 'I'll call him myself. How long has Charles been like this?'

'On and off, for the past couple of hours. I've done the nurse act, and Felicity's helped—sips of water and sponging his forehead, but it needs more than that to get his temperature down. Don't want him to die on us, do you?'

'Ugly thought. Anyhow, we can leave him now.'

Dawlish led the way out and back into the bedroom, where he picked up the telephone; he could call the exchange from here or downstairs. He put in the call to Putney, the London suburb where one, Jim Farningham, had recently taken over a large practice.

'Any news from Trivett?'

'Not a word.'

'Or sign of Downing?'

'No, nothing. Norah's been the only one we've had to deal with. She doesn't approve of us.'

'She never did, you eat so heartily. I—hallo! Is Dr. Farningham there, please? . . . Yes, I'll hold on . . . Dawlish, Patrick Dawlish.' He knew that Beresford was still doubtful about the wisdom of calling Farningham, who in past years had often made a fourth in their remarkable partnership. 'Hallo, Jim!'

Farningham said: 'You're an unmitigated scoundrel.'

'I know. Are you still an overworked G.P.?'

'By some miracle, my assistant's back, and I can spare the day if it's really important.'

'Even the fates help! What's to be done for a patient with a temperature probably around a hundred and three, until you arrive?'

'Ask Felicity,' said Farningham. 'I've a couple of calls to make before I can start for *Four Ways*, and you make it sound urgent. I'll be seeing you, and—oi!'

'Yes?'

'Ted and Tim?'

'Both here.'

Farningham gave a resigned sigh, carrying undertones of the deepest satisfaction.

At a quarter to eleven he had breakfasted with the others, while listening eagerly but without luck for a telephone call from Trivett.

'Long Nose is the major problem. What are you going to do with him?' asked Beresford.

'Hand him over to the police.'

'Why? Downing isn't likely to make a charge about what happened last night. Without Downing's support they can run you in for keeping a man here against his will. Why not let him go? One of us can follow him.'

'Because he was at Wyman Street last night, and the police ought to know.'

'Why this sudden worry about the police?' demanded Jeremy. 'You've often done a lot worse than keep a man away from them for a few days. They don't have to know that you saw him at Wyman Street. If he's mixed up in this business, he's more good to us foot-loose and fancy free than in a cell at Scotland Yard.'

'They don't have cells at Scotland Yard.'

Dawlish looked out of the window. A car came along the road. Trivett? It passed the gate. The trouble was that dozens of fragmentary thoughts were passing through his mind;

to express them all intelligibly would take too long. But for Felicity's warning about straining the loyalty of Ted and Tim, he wouldn't have thought twice about this now. As it was, he said.

'I think we ought to hand Long Nose over, as good tactics. I'd like to keep Charles away from the police for a bit, but must see how the land lies with Trivett before I do. Odd fact, Bill probably knows that he's here, but hasn't inquired. He doesn't do things without a motive, and he may want to turn a blind eye our way. Ted, will you stay here? Tim, will you come with me?'

'Where are you going?' asked Felicity quickly. 'You can't ask Jim Farningham to come, and then disappear.'

'Can't he!' grinned Jeremy.

'I'll be back. And I've an appointment at Lincoln Square for twelve noon, and it's going to be a devil of a job to make it.'

Felicity said, suddenly serious: 'Be careful, Pat.'

From that he knew that she was afraid of unknown, unseen things. Was there need for fear?

CHAPTER EIGHT

FAY

Long Nose sat in the back of the Bentley, with Tim Jeremy. Dawlish sat at the wheel and hardly noticed the traffic he passed or the scowling people who watched him speeding by. He turned into Lincoln Square at two minutes to twelve, and first drove past Number 19, then pulled up three doors along.

The Square might have been almost any Square in the West End of London. The roads about it were wide and spacious; the pavements uncrowded. There was the usual fenced off central garden with its patch of grass, its few trees and flowering shrubs, trying its best to live up to the April sun. Flights of stone steps led to the large front doors. There were thirty houses on each side; it was one of the larger Squares.

Having raced here, Dawlish now sat thoughtfully at the wheel.

'Meditating?' asked Tim.

'Could be, or it could be waiting for a loiterer.'

Tim looked round about him.

'If there is one, he's certainly taken to it in a big way.'

Two or three people walked past at a brisk pace; taxis and

private cars, using the Square as a short cut, passed in quick succession. After three minutes Dawlish got out.

'Just keep an eye open, Tim, will you?'

He walked to Number 19, wishing that Felicity had not put the idea in his head, that he might be exploiting his friends. The years had encouraged him to take them for granted; to explain only when a full explanation was either vital or easy; to assume that they would follow his lead, unquestioningly. And in fact, they always had. But Felicity had the oddest way of being right; she must have seen some sign to suggest that he couldn't ride roughshod over them for ever. Only now did it occur to him that he had done just that in the past.

Forget it.

He stood outside Number 19. It was exactly like the other houses, with large windows, a black-painted door, glistening brasses. He watched the curtains closely, but none moved; he did not think that anyone was standing there and watching for him. Would Fay Downing be here? Or had her brother talked to her, and had she gone out, to avoid him?

A car turned into the Square and came towards him. His foot was on the first step as he glanced casually towards it. It was small, and travelling slowly. The man next to the driver stared at him, and the driver appeared to be looking right and left in search of a house number. Dawlish mounted another step, with another quick glance at the car. It was now twenty yards away. There was something odd about that car—what was it? The window was down, yes—and the windscreen was *open*. On a bright but chilly April day you didn't have your windscreen open. Dawlish saw that—and jumped forward, into the porch of Number 19. As he did so, there was a sharp report.

A bullet smacked into the stone, not a foot away from him. As the car passed, he was a clear target. He dropped down on to his knees as a second shot flashed out. The bullet ripped into the door. He heard footsteps approaching—and he also heard a roar, a familiar roar: Tim Jeremy's voice. The car was almost past now, but crawling. A third crack, and more chippings flew from the wall. He shouted:

'*Don't open the door!*'

He waited until the small car had disappeared from sight, then stood up, slowly.

'All right, all safe,' he said.

He hurried down the steps and saw his Bentley moving off in pursuit of his assailant. A few people stood and stared, not sure if they had witnessed a shooting incident, or a television stunt.

A maid opened the door.

Dawlish gave a wide, reassuring smile.

'Hallo! Hope I didn't scare you, but there's been some shooting in the street, and I thought a stray bullet might come this way.'

'Some—*what*?'

'Shooting. You know.' He pointed a finger at her, and wagged his thumb. '*Pop-pop-pop.* It's probably a police chase after smash-and grabbers who have guns.'

He stepped past her, and she was so flabbergasted that she didn't ask him what he wanted. She stared into the street, and he looked about the spacious hall, noting the evidence that the Downings were wealthy people.

The maid said: 'I—I'm sorry, sir. Can I help you?'

'Miss Fay is expecting me.'

'Are you Mr. Dawlish?'

'Yes.'

'She asked me to take you right up, sir,' said the maid.

So that was one question answered as he had wanted it to be answered. The maid led the way up a flight of stairs, stopping at the door of a room Dawlish knew must face the back of the house. He still didn't quite know what to expect; and what he found was the most normal thing in the world.

A charming girl was sitting in an armchair by the window, with a magazine open on her lap. The room was half-study, half-library. In one corner stood a tall, large, lacquered screen, a beautiful piece tall enough to conceal anyone who cared to stand behind it. The screen was so placed that it was impossible for Dawlish to see between it and the wall. He did no more than glance at it.

Fay Downing stood up.

'I wondered if you'd come,' she said. 'Will you have a drink?'

'Delighted. May it be a pink gin?'

'Of course.'

The door closed. It seemed to close on more than the maid; on the outburst of shooting and the wild chase that was now going on; on Charles and his fantastic gift; and on murder. This room was peaceful; the girl had natural grace as well as beauty.

She said easily: 'You're very punctual.'

'Five minutes late.'

'Is five minutes considered late?'

He laughed, taking stock of her. She didn't look frightened; not as she had done the night before; but it could be suppressed. She was wary, too. But her hands were steady and she sipped her drink calmly.

He said bluntly: 'Why were you so worried about Charles last night?'

'I thought he was on edge when I'd seen him in the afternoon. He's such a nervous type.' The reply came smoothly, almost like a recitation. 'But it doesn't really matter. I've finished with him.'

'Poor Charles!'

'He can look after himself; he's not the idiot that he sometimes seems,' she said. 'I didn't realize what a fool I was making of myself. I thought he was desperately in need of help.' She laughed; but didn't sound amused. 'I had a silly notion that I was helping a genius. I've always thought that the best writers and artists should have patrons, and shouldn't have to worry about money and commercial affairs. I was wrong about him—he's a fraud. So it doesn't matter. Anyhow it's rather late in the day to proffer help.'

'Oh; how's that?'

'Well, he's wanted for murder.'

'Is he? I thought the police just wanted to talk to him. I don't think he killed that old man.'

'He probably knows something about it. In any case, I've finished with him. If it's been a waste of your time to come here, I'm sorry.'

'Not at all. A great pleasure,' murmured Dawlish pompously. For the first time he sat down. She stirred, as if she wished he hadn't; she wanted this interview to be short-lived. 'So you're letting Charles down when he's most in need of help.'

'That's a silly, sentimental way of putting it.'

'How did John put it?'

'This is *my* decision,' said Fay, but her breath grew shorter. 'My brother had nothing to do with it. I've just come to the conclusion that he's been right all along, and I've been wrong. It's as simple as that. I'm afraid there's nothing more I have to say.'

'Not even a little of the truth?'

She coloured furiously. 'It's all true!'

Dawlish laughed. 'You make a poor liar, Fay. Charles needs all his friends now.'

'There's nothing I can do to help him, I'm afraid, beyond giving him money. He'll probably need some, to pay his legal expenses, won't he? But I'm not interested in him any longer.'

Dawlish said: 'Well, perhaps it's a good thing. That he's now unlikely to hear about it, I mean. He—'

Fay cried: 'What do you mean?' She jumped up, eyes flashing, hands stretched out in a gesture of mingled anger and dread—dread that something had happened to Charles. Dawlish watched her, without speaking, and she drew nearer and repeated in a tense voice: 'What do you mean? Why won't he know?'

'He's ill. Very ill.'

'No!' she cried. 'No, it's not true; it couldn't be true! You're lying to me; you're trying to make me—'

She broke off, and drew back; she'd forgotten herself completely, all her carefully prepared tactics shattered.

'When I left him he was running a temperature of a hundred and four,' Dawlish said. 'I've never seen a man look worse. Still, you've finished with him.' He spoke with brisk finality as he rose from his chair. 'I needn't worry you any more.'

He went towards the door.

He knew that she was staring after him, torn with anxiety and irresolution. Would she let him go? Would she screw herself up to the point of that? He touched the handle of the door, opened it—and then she called in a strangled voice:

'You're lying to me!'

'Does it matter?'

'Please don't go,' she said.

He turned, and found her in the middle of the room. She looked fragile, like a Dresden figurine, but for her eyes and the dread in them. Those eyes searched his, as if she hoped to drag the truth from him.

'What is the truth about Charles, Mr. Dawlish?'

'He is very ill. I think it is possible that he won't recover, and some think it's improbable that he'll ever speak again. He doesn't appear to have a friend anywhere. All of them have deserted him, now that he's in difficulties. He's also under suspicion for a murder which he didn't commit. Not a happy position, is it?'

She had to force herself to speak.

'I'm sorry. I was wrong before about him; I shouldn't have trusted him, I'm convinced of that. But I should like to help him. Is there anything I can do?'

'No.'

'There must be!' The cry was anguished.

Dawlish said gently: 'You've made up your mind to stop believing in him. You've lied to me. The one thing that might help Charles now is the truth; nothing else will serve. Your brother had persuaded you to cover that up, so—' He shrugged his shoulders. 'Charles will have to manage as best he can. He'll be well looked after in hospital—the police will see to that. You may hear from them; they'll want to take evidence from some of the people who've known him lately.'

Fay said: 'I can't tell them anything.' She shivered and looked past him, as if she didn't want to meet his eyes but was afraid of avoiding them in case she missed something. 'It's an ugly business, and there isn't anything I can say.'

'There's plenty I can. If I hadn't warned you last night, you would have gone back to the Wyman Street house, wouldn't you? And you would have run right into the police. As it is, you're not known to them, except possibly as a friend of Charles's. They want one little word from me to make them come here—they simply want telling that I saw you at the house last night.'

'You wouldn't tell them!'

'Wouldn't I?'

The screen moved.

John Downing stepped from behind it. There was an ugly glint in his eyes.

'No, you wouldn't tell them,' he said slowly, 'not if you've an ounce of decency in you.'

Dawlish said lightly: 'You've peculiar ideas. You've decided to lie yourself out of the spot you've made for yourself. You've decided to influence your sister into behaving worse than any little guttersnipe who's never had a chance to learn what decency is. Criminal types are commonly expected to desert their friends when it suits them; the rest of mankind usually try to help. Don't talk to me about decency.'

'If you go to the police—' Downing's voice was hoarse.

'I shall tell them everything I can, about your sister and about yourself, unless you tell me your story. I'll give you until four o'clock.' Dawlish turned on his heel. 'I'll be back.'

Tim Jeremy sat at the wheel of the Bentley, and Long Nose sat beside him. A steel bracelet fitted snugly round Tim's left wrist, the other round the passenger's right. Tim heard Dawlish coming, and turned his head. Several people stood at the far end of the Square, talking to a policeman in uniform. Tim opened the door, twisting round in order to do so.

'So you didn't lose our boy friend.'

'Not quite. He made another dive for safety, and I thought I'd better manacle him. He is the most persistent beggar I've ever come across. No luck with the gun-play boys, I'm afraid. They had some engine in that car.'

'Pity. Notice what they looked like?'

'Squirts.'

Dawlish grinned. 'They were all that. And they didn't want me to see Fay Downing. I wonder whether Brother John had anything to do with it, or whether our friend here has any friends. Do you think you can look after him for a bit longer?'

'It's a pleasure.' Tim was out of the car now, and the prisoner followed him. Their coat sleeves hid the handcuffs. Tim climbed into the back, and dragged the other with him; the man with the long nose did not utter a word of protest. Tim put a cigarette between his lips and lit it for him; the man nodded, but didn't speak. 'I've been trying to persuade him to tell me who he is, but he won't come across.'

'He will, in time.' Dawlish eased off the brakes. 'Have the police questioned you?'

'Yes. I referred them, with great presence of mind, to a certain Mr. Trivett.'

'Nice work,' said Dawlish.

As he drove, he kept seeing pictures of Fay's strained and anxious face in his mind's eye. He wondered what pressure her brother had exerted to make her swing round. The one certain thing was that Fay was in love with Charles; and perhaps a second was certain—that Charles wasn't in love with her.

Dawlish drove slowly towards Scotland Yard. As he did so he glanced over his shoulder. The pale face of Tim's companion was set in an effort to prove that he didn't care where they brought him.

'Mind waiting?' Dawlish asked Tim.

'Do I keep the boy friend?'

'For the moment.'

Dawlish drew up near a line of parked cars, got out, went up the stone steps, and was greeted by a tall and bulky sergeant, who first frowned and then grinned.

'It's Mr. Dawlish, isn't it?'

'What a memory! How are you, Skinner?'

'Very well, sir, thank you. I suppose you want to see Mr. Trivett. Go straight along, sir—it's the New Building; we're using both now. You know your way, don't you?'

'Yes, thanks.'

Dawlish took a lift to the second floor and, half-way along a wide passage, reached un unmarked brown door which he knew well.

As Dawlish tapped and entered, Trivett was putting a telephone on its cradle. He eyed him without smiling.

'Well, well, this is a surprise.'

'You never know what's going to happen next, do you?'

'I wouldn't say that—where you're concerned.' Trivett laughed. 'Sit down, you beggar. And don't tell me why you've come.'

Dawlish sat down with great deliberation.

'Did I hear aright? *Don't?*'

'I don't want to know.'

Dawlish put his head on one side and studied the handsome face. Trivett's smile was mostly in his eyes; it was a smile of enjoyment, and the enjoyment came from the fact that he had Dawlish guessing. Dawlish offered cigarettes, and they lit up.

'What is it that you don't want to know?' asked Dawlish. 'About the man who came to see me last night?'

'That's it.'

'Hum. What about the man whom I saw at the Wyman Street house? A little chap with a long nose, remember? He threw a paper-weight at me, which I dutifully handed over to you. It ought to have some prints on it, as well as mine.'

'It has. We don't know them. What about the man?'

'You see my difficulty. Do you want to know about him or don't you?'

'I do! Don't say that you can—'

'Produce him. Indeed I can. He's outside with Tim. And both Felicity and I will swear that it's the same johnny. Also—'

'*Where* is he?'

Trivett leaned forward eagerly.

'Outside in the car, and Tim's handcuffed to him, so you needn't worry what will happen next. Then there's the other man, by name, Downing. Short, stocky, very aggressive, with a strong face, nice blue eyes and an enormous capacity for beer. Do you want to know about him?'

'What is there to know?'

'He came to see me last night. He thought I knew where Charles Horden could be found. Stupid fellow! He told a rigmarole about Horden being a lady-killer, and a horde of jealous husbands out for revenge. All nonsense; but it's his story and he told it well. Do you want to know more about him?'

Trivett nodded with apparent vigour, but as Dawlish was about to elaborate, slipped smoothly on with his side of the conversation.

'We didn't tell you the identity of the murdered man, did we?' he remarked, leaning forward for a file of papers. 'He's Arthur Wray, the uncle of the man Horden. His wife arrived at Wyman Street just after one o'clock; she'd been visiting a sick relative and had some difficulty getting home. Nasty business, breaking the news to her. It was a complete surprise, as far as we can judge. She says she knows of no reason why anyone should have wanted to kill her husband. She is quite sure that her nephew wouldn't have killed the old man, and puts her case pretty well. She's passionately fond of Charles—most women seem to be.'

'Yes,' murmured Dawlish.

But he didn't go on, for he was immediately aware of certain facts: among them, that Trivett guessed where Charles Horden was, but did not want to know for certain, and was neither prepared to find out, nor to be told. Charles was wanted for questioning; was an obvious suspect; and Trivett was turning an eye as blind as a bat's.

Why?

CHAPTER NINE

BLIND EYE

Dawlish said: 'So the motive for the murder is unknown, the most likely suspect has vanished, and—'

'Who do you think is the most likely suspect?'

'I read my newspapers. There is mention of a certain nephew of the dead man. Remember, I told you that he'd asked me to help him, being in some kind of jam and worried in case someone tried to bump him off.'

'That doesn't make him a suspect, does it?' asked Trivett. 'I'm surprised at you, taking the newspapers at their face value. We'll have a word with Charles Horden when the time comes, but he's not our main suspect by any means. There were finger-prints on the handle of that hammer—prints which were super-imposed upon the blood-stains, and were probably those of the murderer. They're not Horden's prints. They're not identical with those we found on the paper-weight. When we've found the man who made those prints I think we'll have found the murderer.'

'I see,' murmured Dawlish. 'What about my man with the long nose? He wasn't the johnny who handled the hammer, and so—'

'I want to know what he was doing there; that stands to reason,' said Trivett.

He wasn't a hundred per cent with Dawlish; he was thinking about something else part of the time; and he most certainly did *not* want to interview Charles Horden. It was not an attitude you normally expected from Trivett or from the C.I.D. This was deliberate policy, thrashed out and agreed by the pundits of the Yard.

'Do you know his name?'

'He's a silent customer. He's made two attempts to get away, and he may complain bitterly about being forcibly detained by me all night and most of the morning. But I wanted to hand him over to you, not the local people.'

'And you also wanted to make him talk. You've got your teeth into this job, haven't you?'

'Felicity's teeth.'

'Well, it's something that she isn't worrying you to drop it every five minutes,' said Trivett righteously, ignoring the fact that he had so often done the same thing. 'Didn't your long-nosed man talk at all?'

'He claimed to be an irate husband whose wife has been lured from him by the villainous literary genius the papers imply is the chief suspect.'

'Oh, *does* he? Pat, how much do you know about this Charles Horden?'

'Only what I've told you. I haven't even been able to check anything since last night, nothing more than the fact that he's a writing man of sorts, with big ideas and possibly a kink, and certainly a way with women. What do *you* know about him?'

'Not much,' said Trivett. 'Not enough. I don't think he's done anything before which brings him within the police orbit, and he did this at second hand, as it were. But I'm very curious about him and some of his friends. He's a reputation as a mystic—and as a medium. Interesting business, spiritualism. *Very* interesting. I've exposed some pretty ugly fakes in that line, but I've never been able to rid myself of a feeling that there's something in it. Ever given it much thought yourself?'

'Planchette boards and ectoplasm—no, I can't say that I have.' Dawlish lit a cigarette, and was so preoccupied that he forgot to offer one to Trivett. 'If you mean do I believe in ghosts—' he laughed. 'I don't disbelieve in them. That's as far as I'll go.'

'It looks as if we've the same approach—friendly doubters,' said Trivett. This conversation would have sounded normal enough after dinner at his flat, but seemed oddly out of place at Scotland Yard, where Trivett was the official detective. Yet he was serious, and he would not talk like this without a purpose. 'If I had more time, I think I'd probe into this particular mystic a bit deeper, Pat. The trouble, as far as I'm concerned, is that at the Yard we have to deal almost entirely with the fakes. They're not much more than fortune-tellers, and some of them get a good rake-off. Why don't you do some investigation?'

Dawlish said: '*Hum!*'

'I'd be very interested,' Trivett said. 'There's a lot of it about, you know. The most unlikely people are believers, and—well, you've only to read a book on *yogi* and see what some of the Indian fakirs get up to, to know it's not just a sham.' He laughed. 'Listen to me! Way off the track! And I've a lot of work to do! Where do you say this long-nosed chap is?'

'Third time of telling: outside, with Tim.'

'I'll send a man down for him,' said Trivett, and stood up, to signify that the interview was over. 'Let me know if you hear of anything else that might be interesting, won't you? And I think you could do worse than probe into this medium business, if that's what it is. Felicity thinks Horden needs help; that'll give you your motive.' He led the way to the door. 'Still at the *Mayfair*?'

'We shall be at *Four Ways* tonight,' said Dawlish gravely. 'Thanks for the pep talk.'

Tim Jeremy sat in the seat next to the driver's, alone.

Dawlish opened his door and said: 'You drive, Tim; I'm not safe at the wheel this morning.'

Tim slid across the seat and Dawlish got in next to him.

'So you've realized what a shocking driver you are, at last. What's Trivett been saying to you?'

'I beg you—don't mention Trivett to me,' said Dawlish, and grinned. 'Care to drive to the club? I could do with a snifter. I am going to be very difficult and need much moral support during the next few days.'

'No change,' said Jeremy. They drove in silence past the Houses of Parliament, and in silence parked the car in Carlton House Terrace and went into the Carilon Club. This holy of holies, one of man's last preserves in London, closed about them with an atmosphere at once sacrosanct and deadly. Voices were muted; a thick pile deadened the sound of their footsteps. They went up one majestic flight of marble stairs and crossed a room filled with vast easy chairs filled with balding men behind newspapers.

Out of this room they stepped into a smaller one. Here also was silence; but there was also the bright glitter of a cocktail bar. The bar-tender leaned towards them.

'Nice to see you again, Mr. Dawlish. And you, Mr. Jeremy. What's it to be?'

'Whiskies, Bert. Doubles.'

'Well, thank God for that sign of humanity,' murmured Jeremy.

'Sorry, old boy. Blame Trivett. Thanks.' Dawlish lifted and sipped his whisky reflectively. 'Ah! Tim, I have come across some odd shows, but none odder than this. I tell you that Bill refused to let me tell him that I had Horden at *Four Ways*.'

'What an egotistical beggar you are, don't we come into it?'

'Of course you do. For "I" read "we".'

Tim grunted.

Dawlish went on, a little dashed: 'He knows, of course, and won't admit it. The name Downing didn't mean a thing to him, but when I was about to mention Fay, he branched off into another subject, which was as good as saying: "I don't want to hear about it, don't tell me." He then recommended that if I wanted a nice quiet subject to study, I might take up spiritualism.'

Tim gulped his whisky.

'Now you know why I behave as I do,' pleaded Dawlish.

Jeremy said: 'I knew, anyhow. You can't talk and think at the same time; the cerebral matter just won't stand it, and this will take some working out. What do you make of it?'

'Have a shot yourself.'

'Well, it *looks* obvious. Trivett thinks there is something much deeper, even than the murder, going on. He knows that Horden is mixed up in it, and believes there's a fake mystic hanging around somewhere; can't spare the time to investigate, and thinks it will keep you occupied. He may also think that you'll get results on a job like this where he can't. Police don't find it easy to keep track of spiritualists.'

'There's another possibility. That he would like to tuck us away on some sideline, to keep us out of mischief.'

Jeremy grinned. 'Could be. But he wouldn't expect you to fall for that one.'

'Trusting Tim! Thanks. I don't know. But I do know that

if you told a police constable to see Trivett about the Lincoln Square shooting, then Trivett must have heard about it some time before I arrived. He didn't say a word. Nor did I. I left it to the last minute, thinking that he might, and then couldn't get anything out. I was flummoxed. I'll believe a lot, but it's hard to believe that Trivett would accidentally forget to ask me about a shooting affray in the West End. That omission was deliberate. *Why?* He might have good reasons for not believing Horden to be concerned with his uncle's murder. He might have a good reason for wanting me to prod a bit further, knowing that if it got too deep, I'd have a word with him. Reasonable enough—this might not be a police job at the moment. But he'd like to know more about it, and chooses this way of learning. Still, when it comes to deliberately forgetting that the johnny shot at me—how's your gullet, Tim?'

'I can't swallow it, either.'

'Let's have some food,' said Dawlish.

The food at the Carilon Club was unimaginative but well cooked and plentiful. It was a quarter to three before they finished. At ten minutes to, Dawlish went to a telephone booth, and called *Four Ways*. Felicity answered.

"Lo darling. How's the invalid?'

'Well, he's easier. Jim's worried about him.'

'Is Jim Farningham still there?'

'Yes; he wants to talk to you.'

Dawlish heard a short, muffled drone of voices, then:

"Lo, Pat. Is that you?'

'As far as I know, it is.'

'Pat, I'm serious. I may have to get that chap to hospital before the day's out. I'm taking a chance with him as it is. This could develop into something really serious. I've injected twice, and I'll know the reaction in a couple of hours.'

'What could it be?'

Farningham said, worriedly: 'Well, I'm not convinced that it is, but it *could* be meningitis.'

'Would you be happier if you could consult a specialist?'

'I've one in line—Wilberforce is in Guildford this afternoon. He's likely to be free about four o'clock, and he's coming over if necessary. I'm to call him again. On the whole, I think it might be a good thing, but it'll cost a hell of a lot.'

'Tell him he can count on getting it.'

Farningham sounded relieved. 'All right, Pat. Coming down this way? I ought to be back by morning, you know, but I doubt if it'll be wise to leave Horden here with just a nurse.'

'I'll ring through again early evening, and be back some time tonight. Kiss Fel for me. And thanks, old chap—oh, one thing.'

'Hm-hm?'

'Ever had anything to do with such persons as mediums and mystics? From a medical point of view, I mean.'

Farningham exclaimed: 'What! What on earth made you say that?'

'Call it a combination of circumstances.'

'Well, I *have* come across a case that isn't unlike this one,' said Farningham. 'It was an old woman, who'd been a medium for about forty years. The police went after her several times, but could prove nothing against her. She used to have spells of unconsciousness, with a high fever, just like Horden. I didn't know anything about her until she was brought into the hospital as a suspect meningitis. The symptoms were pretty much the same as Horden's, but—well, she came round after two days. All I could get out of her was that she had been on a long journey. She left the hospital within a week, and when I last heard of her she was at the medium business again. I think she's still around. If it weren't for that case I'd have had Horden away by now.'

'Sounds as if you're on to something there,' said Dawlish.

'Ted did say something which made me wonder. Anything else now?'

'No thanks. Here's hoping you're right.'

Dawlish rang off and passed the gist of this conversation on to Tim Jeremy, who made solemn sounds, but reserved comment.

They left the club at twenty past three, and this time Dawlish took the wheel. He sat at it for a few seconds, watching the terrace and the Duke of York Steps. No one appeared to take the slightest notice of them. He drove slowly towards the West End, and remembered that he had forgotten to tell Tim they were due back at Lincoln Square. Still driving slowly, he turned down Jermyn Street and then crossed Piccadilly. He kept his eye on the driving mirror; no one followed them. He took a long route to Lincoln Square, and pulled up at a corner.

'Dull,' declared Jeremy. 'No one about with guns.'

'Yes. Mind another spell of duty watch?'

'My dear chap!'

'We haven't been followed, yet if the fellow who let fly this morning really wanted me, he could have picked up the car by now. He'd have a pretty shrewd guess I'd go to the Yard and then on to the Club. Why hasn't he tailed us? It could be because he knew I was due here at twelve this morning and has since been tipped off that I'm due back at four.'

'It's nearly that now.'

Dawlish slipped his hand into his pocket and drew out the automatic which he had taken from Downing the previous night.

'I'm the guinea-pig, you do the work. If they try again, I'd hate 'em to get away.'

'They won't,' Tim said grimly.

At Lincoln Square, Dawlish got out and walked briskly back

towards Number 19. The scene was exactly the same as it had been that morning; only the people and the cars nearby were different. Nothing happened. He had a queer feeling of insecurity and danger—the kind of feeling that made his mind travel back over the years. It was like creeping forward, on patrol, into no man's land; or behind the enemy lines. Any moment there might be a challenge, or a bullet might come winging towards him; and he made a big target, not easy to miss. His heart hammered when he reached Number 19. He glanced up at the windows; a curtain moved. So this time he was being watched from the house.

He walked up the steps.

He felt terribly vulnerable, as if a gun were trained on him from every window. He rang the bell. The ground on which he stood was blandly open to attack. There was no protection anywhere, nor did he know, if attack there was to be, from which direction it would come. He hadn't worked on a dangerous job for a long time; perhaps that was why he couldn't rid himself of the jitters, and every moment seemed an age. There were no sounds of footsteps; all was silent. A car approached slowly. He gritted his teeth and prepared to drop down as the driver looked at him—but the car passed without incident. He smiled grimly, as at one danger passed, knowing others were to come, and rang the bell again. Why hadn't the maid answered? Ah, here she was. He heard her walking quickly, heard the lock click back as she pulled the catch. She was a hell of a time!

She opened the door; the same girl, but without the agitation which she had shown before.

'Hallo again! Am I expected?'

'Yes, sir. I'm not sure whether Miss Fay is in the study. Will you please wait in here?'

She led the way to a front room, long and charmingly

furnished, with a colour scheme of wine-red and blue. All was redolent of money. John Downing had been angry because Fay had paid two hundred and fifty pounds in a year to Horden; yet nothing here suggested that the money itself need have worried him.

Dawlish moved to the window. No one was watching the house, and Tim and the Bentley were out of sight. Tim was having a long day of waiting, and was probably regretting that there had been no greater sensation.

Forget Tim; and even forget Trivett.

His threat had worked; but what mood would the Downings be in? John wasn't likely to allow his sister to carry the interview off on her own. This would be ticklish; they had probably hatched up a story and hoped to convince him that it was true, without giving anything that mattered away. That they had something to hide went without saying. He came back to the question: what pressure had John Downing used to make Fay turn round so completely?

He came away from the window.

The maid returned.

'Miss Fay and Mr. John are waiting for you now, sir.'

'Thanks.'

So the pair of them would be together. Was Fay a dabbler in the occult? Was that why John was so bitter towards Charles? Possibilities crowded on him, the thoughts he'd waited for since seeing Trivett and which had obstinately refused to come. In this day and generation, men seldom hated as bitterly as Downing and Long Nose hated Charles Horden, simply because of misplaced affections. But supposing Charles was on the fringe of the occult; supposing men watched their womenfolk gradually fall under its spell, which could be evil, without being able to help themselves—wouldn't that explain a great deal?

The maid opened the door of the study.
'Mr. Dawlish,' she announced.
He went in.
A man stood by the fireplace, covering him with a gun.

CHAPTER TEN

CAPTURE

Dawlish had seen the man before, sitting next to the driver of the small car. Probably this was the gun used in the morning's shooting affair. He was a small man—shorter than John Downing, with a slim figure and sloping shoulders. From the porch he had seemed almost sinister; now, as he smiled, it would be easy—but foolish—to forget the automatic in his hand. He covered Dawlish's stomach with it—avoiding the mistake of training it too high.

'Good afternoon, Mr. Dawlish.'

'Fancy seeing you again.'

Dawlish moved towards the fireplace, but the man motioned towards a chair. Sitting, he was able to see behind the screen; no one was there.

'I'm alone,' said the other. 'And I'm only half your size; it shouldn't be difficult, should it?'

'I left my chain waistcoat at home,' said Dawlish. 'I'll remember it next time.'

'You're the supreme optimist. What makes you think there'll be a next time?'

'Surely unnecessary to point out that if you'd planned my swift demise and a scurry to hide the body, I'd have had it by now!' Dawlish waved his hands. 'You have my word that I have no gun. Mind if I smoke?'

'Carry on.'

'Have one?'

Dawlish opened his cigarette case.

'No, thanks. You're a cool customer, Dawlish. I've heard from many people that it's difficult to dislike you, and that makes the task harder. But duty has to be done, hasn't it?'

'An ambiguous word, but it brings comfort to a great many. Fire away.'

The small man laughed.

'In good time! There are several things I want to learn from you, Dawlish. You went straight from here to Scotland Yard this morning. What did you tell the Yard?'

'We discussed bad men in general. Names were barely mentioned. Having told the Downings that there was an armistice until now, I kept my side of the bargain. Theirs seems not to have been kept so punctiliously. What have you done with them?'

'They're all right, for the time being. Didn't you tell your friend Superintendent Trivett about Fay Downing and her brother?'

'Not to say *tell*. They were mentioned in passing, but the name "Downing" seemed to strike irresponsive ears. I've no doubt time will remedy that.'

'They won't learn from you.'

'Oh, you never can tell,' said Dawlish mildly. 'Communications by agencies other than human have been known.'

He watched the man closely; and saw the narrowing of his eyes, the smile becoming set and wary. He didn't relax his watchfulness, and the gun, held loosely in his hand, still covered Dawlish, but he was discomforted.

At last he said: 'So you've got as far as that.'

'Well, one does pick up odds and ends, you know.'

'Did Horden talk?'

'Only to say that he wished people would leave him alone and wouldn't work him so hard. I'm afraid that Charles is a much-misunderstood man,' said Dawlish earnestly. 'Genius is a double-edged sword isn't it? It preys, and is preyed on. Do forgive the mixed metaphors. I believe the poor chap's on the borderline of a mental breakdown at the moment. He's resting, I believe.'

'We know he's still at your cottage. He can stay there for the time being, but we'll get him when we want him. Who else knows what you know about Charles?'

'I'm afraid I can't help you there. Personally, I never attempt to crack the average man, or woman's scepticism.'

'I wonder if that's true?'

'Scepticism?'

'I mean I wonder whether it's true that none of the others know what you've stumbled upon. You've a great reputation for stumbling on the truth, haven't you, Dawlish? Some men have all the luck, and you certainly get more than your share. Did Horden go into a trance last night?'

'He blacked out. The others called it collapse; I reserve judgment. I shouldn't try to move him yet; he's running a high temperature and is in bed. My wife is anxious about him.'

'Oh, he's running one of *those*,' said the man by the fireplace; and he laughed much more freely. 'That's all right; he won't be able to talk sensibly for three or four days. We can safely leave him. Thanks, Dawlish; that's eased my mind a lot!' He moved to the desk, keeping his distance from Dawlish, and pressed a bell-push. The door opened suddenly.

Another man entered—a faded-looking middle-aged man with tired, servile eyes.

'As arranged,' said the man with the gun. 'Dawlish, don't get up, don't move, don't try to stop my man. I'm going to put you to sleep. You'll wake up, this time—provided you go to sleep quietly. If you struggle—' He shrugged his shoulders. 'The door is specially padded and is nearly soundproof. I doubt if a shot would be heard beyond the landing. I'm quite prepared to deal with the task of getting rid of the body—it's not so difficult as a lot of people seem to think. Just sit back and take what comes.'

The faded man took out a black cardboard box and from that took a hypodermic syringe; it was already loaded. As he approached Dawlish he gave a timid little smile.

'Would you mind pushing up your coat sleeve?' he asked mildly.

'Not at all.' Dawlish pulled back his coat and bared his arm to the elbow.

'Just hold your arm out,' said the other. 'It won't hurt—just a tiny prick, and it's all over. You won't feel anything for a few minutes afterwards, but then you'll begin to feel sleepy. There'll be no pain, I do assure you of that. And you won't have a head-ache when you wake up.'

The man held Dawlish's arm lightly with one hand and brought the needle nearer. Dawlish gave him until the last moment—then twisted his arm, grabbed the doctor's wrist and pulled him in front of him. The man at the fireplace shouted: '*Dawlish!*'

Terrified eyes in a pale face were close to Dawlish, but he didn't hold the doctor there for long. He gathered all his strength and pushed him backwards. The man with the gun, dodging swiftly to get a clear line of fire, was knocked off his balance. It dropped to the floor. Dawlish leapt from his chair and drove his left fist into the sallow, reeling face, picked up the gun, and backed towards the window. The two men were sprawling beside each other on the dark carpet, the syringe near them, its needle broken.

'How things change!' murmured Dawlish. 'Thoughtful of you to arrange a sound-proofed room, I do appreciate that.'

He sat down again in the easy chair, leaned forwards and picked up the syringe and laid it on a small table nearby, and covered both the others with the automatic.

'I keep winning guns in this business; it'll save a lot of expense. Now, George, what's all this about?'

If it were possible for hate to show in a pair of eyes, it glowed in the sallow man's then. He rose slowly to his feet. His lips were parted and his teeth clenched, and there was fury in him. He shrugged his coat into position—and then suddenly shot out a foot and kicked the weaker man in the side.

'Definitely not sporting,' Dawlish said severely. 'It was your own fault. If you do that again, I'll really hit you.'

The sallow-faced man didn't speak. The other picked himself up and moved towards the door.

Dawlish said: 'Sorry, Doc; you can't leave just yet. Go to that corner opposite the door and sit on the floor facing the wall. I don't want to hurt you, but I'll have to if you try any tricks. Just sit quietly, and you'll be all right.' He looked at the sallow-faced man as he spoke, and added: 'And answer my questions. How often have you done this kind of thing?'

The 'doctor', already sitting down, didn't speak.

'He won't be able to hurt you again. Answer me.'

'Quite—often, sir. I assure you—' the man sounded really

distressed. 'I assure you that it *is* quite painless; it wouldn't have hurt you.'

'Who do you work on?'

'Well, Mr. Garcia brings me my patients.'

'And this is Mr. Garcia.' The expression in the sallow-faced man's eyes told Dawlish that was true. 'So we hail from Spain, do we? Are your patients usually men or women?'

'Well—'

'If you tell him anything more, I'll make you wish you'd never been born,' said Garcia.

His English was perfect; there was no trace of accent; it was undoubtedly his native tongue.

'Senor Garcia won't hurt you or anyone else any more,' said Dawlish mildly.

The 'doctor's' watery eyes were pleading; there was terror in them.

'Please don't make me answer, sir! I—I know what it's like when you displease Mr. Garcia, and—and I'm sure I only want to serve him loyally. He's been a very good employer to me; he saved me from ruin and—and if it weren't for Mr. Garcia, I should have killed myself before now. *Please* don't make me answer.'

Dawlish looked from him to Garcia; saw the sneer which had come to the man's sensuous lips; and smiled back at the 'doctor'.

'All right, take it easy. I know your patients have been mostly women, anyhow. Young and attractive women, too,' said Dawlish. 'And Fay Downing's been among them. I don't quite get the hang of everything yet, but the picture's becoming clearer. Going to talk freely, Garcia? Or shall I go straight to the police?'

Garcia said: 'You can do what the hell you like.'

Dawlish shrugged his shoulders.

'All right.'

He stood up and went to the telephone. He had no intention of telling Trivett about this yet; it might be something else which the Yard man did not want to know. He dialled a number slowly, thoughtfully: the number of Ted Beresford's flat. He watched Garcia out of the corner of his eye; the man was making no attempt to turn the tables, seemed to accept this with the same philosophical calm, now, as Downing and Long Nose had done; that didn't mean that he wouldn't make an attempt. The ringing sound burred in Dawlish's ears. It would be his bad luck if Joan Beresford were out. *Brrr-brrr; brrr-brrr.* Garcia grinned; as if he knew that this was a stall; and that there would be no answer. *Brrr-brrr.* Then the sound stopped and Joan Beresford's voice came sharp and clear.

Dawlish said: 'I want to speak to Superintendent Trivett, please.'

'*What?*'

'Yes, that's right. This is Dawlish.'

'Pat, you idiot, you've dialled the wrong number,' said Joan. 'What on earth *are* you playing at? And why did you have to start this *now*? Ted and I are planning to go away for a few days next week; everything's set, and now you've spoiled it. There are times when I dislike you intensely.'

'Bill? Hallo, old chap. I'm speaking from 19 Lincoln Square. Yes, you'd better send someone along, pretty fast; there's been a bit of a mess. I—'

Joan caught her breath.

'Pat, what do you mean?'

'You might tell Tim Jeremy that he can come in,' said Dawlish. 'He's at the corner, waiting patiently in my car. Get a move on, old chap. 'Bye.'

'Pat! Do you want me to tell Tim?'

'Yes, that's right. 19 Lincoln Square, West 1. 'Bye.'

Dawlish put down the receiver, turned to look fully into Garcia's eyes; and saw that burning hatred again.

Garcia now believed that he had talked to the police; believed that it was all up. But—the safety line was tenuous. Dawlish wanted these men out of here, somewhere where he could persuade them to talk. He wanted Tim to come—and Tim would get that message in ten minutes. Tim would read the real message: help wanted. But would he be able to get in? How many other men were here? The maid wouldn't present much difficulty, but if there were others Tim might get badly hurt and make the situation worse. You could spoil a triumph by being too clever; had he been too clever?

Garcia said unsteadily: 'The police won't get anything from us. It's a waste of time. Dawlish—'

'Shut up.'

'Don't be a fool. Let us go. You'll be all right if you do. I give you my word that we won't try to avenge ourselves. It's a waste of time bringing the police; neither of us will talk. It'll be worth— worth a fortune to you.' Garcia licked his lips; it was good to see Garcia begging for mercy. 'I can't pay you now, but I can get the money; this is a paying rack—'

He didn't finish, but his tongue ran along his lips again.

'You can name your own price, Dawlish. We only want five minutes.'

Garcia ran his hand across his mouth, and his hand was unsteady. He fingered his lips, puckering them, talking confusedly.

'Dawlish, it's worth a *fortune*. You'll be crazy to turn it down. Look! I've a couple of hundred pounds in my pocket now.'

He dived his hand into his pocket—and Dawlish fired.

The bullet passed a foot from Garcia's head, thudded into the wall and brought a gasp of alarm from the 'doctor'. But that and the roar of the shot and the flash didn't stop Garcia. He snatched, not a wallet, but a knife from his pocket; he swung round and leapt at the 'doctor'.

Before Dawlish could reach him, the knife plunged down.

You could cover up a lot of things; you could take Garcia and the doctor away from here and question them, and not take too much of a risk. You could, in extreme circumstances, release a man whom you felt sure had committed murder. But you couldn't let a thing like this pass and try to handle it yourself.

Dawlish towered over Garcia, his cold rage reaching murderous heights. He turned away abruptly, kicking the knife out of Garcia's reach. Garcia leaned limply against the wall. He was so determined that no one should squeal that he'd killed in front of an eye-witness. There wasn't a hope for him, and he must have known that; yet he had preferred to take the risk, invite the final penalty, rather than let the 'doctor' betray the truth.

Dawlish went to the telephone, dialled Whitehall 1212, and watched Garcia closely. The sneer disappeared. Garcia actually moved forward, his hands raised, as if he couldn't understand this; and it must have slowly dawned on him that he had been tricked. An operator answered.

'Superintendent Trivett, please,' said Dawlish.

'You—didn't call—them?' sighed Garcia.

Dawlish said: 'I proposed to deal with you myself. I don't, now . . . Hallo, Bill . . . I'm at 19 Lincoln Square. Murder. Yes, I've got the man . . . I'll be here.'

He replaced the receiver.

At the ting of the bell, the window behind him crashed in; he leapt round. He saw a long wall, set at right angles to this room, and a man leaning out of a window, gun in hand.

He felt a thud at the side of his head, and lost consciousness.

CHAPTER ELEVEN

VOICES

There were voices, vague and distant—a man's and a woman's. Dawlish wished they would stop. His head ached and he felt sick. Every time they spoke, it seemed as if someone had tapped him lightly on the head, creating fresh pain. There was light, which hurt his eyes even though he kept them tightly closed. Those damned voices went on; meaningless words were uttered; it was just a jumble of syllables. He knew that he was lying on something hard; he didn't remember what had happened until a word of the conversation took on a meaning—an ominous meaning.

'Yes, he's dead.'

Nonsense! He wasn't dead.

More words: the woman's.

'How *is* Pat?'

'He'll be all right—he was lucky. The bullet caught him a glancing blow and knocked him out. A scratch, really. Concussion at the worst, and a bad headache for a day or two at the best. Don't worry about him.'

The man was Trivett. Trivett did not seem greatly perturbed, and spoke as if Dawlish hardly mattered. Dawlish opened his eyes slightly, and the light dazzled him, but he persisted, and saw vague figures moving erratically. Trivett and Beresford's wife, Joan. Her face gradually became clearer; she had seen Dawlish was conscious and came across the room. Trivett was bending over something in the corner—the 'doctor', of course. There were two other men present. As Joan reached Dawlish, a third entered; Tim Jeremy.

Joan dropped to her knees and took Dawlish's hand.

'Pat, how are you?'

'Where's Trivett?' muttered Dawlish. 'Sorry about this. Did you get Garcia?'

Jeremy's face loomed up, enormous, astonished.

'Garcia? Garcia—?'

Trivett came across, and sudden pain shot across Dawlish's head; it passed into numbness, and the voices became jumbled and meaningless again. He felt a sharp prick in his right forearm and had a sudden vision of the 'doctor', telling him to roll up his sleeve. Pity he hadn't. If he'd done that he would have been a prisoner, but at least he could have learned more about this business. What chance was there now? The thoughts came vaguely, and concentration was difficult and painful. He felt gentle hands touching him, felt himself being lifted—and at the same time his mind seemed to go slack as sleep came over him. They'd doped him, of course; he might be out for a long time, and it might mean the end of his part in this case. Trivett could turn a blind eye to a lot of things, but not to this. Why had Trivett turned that blind eye? Why? Why? *Why?*

He woke. He was comfortable and without pain. He could smell something unfamiliar—a sharp, penetrating smell; antiseptics, of course. He was in a hospital ward or a nursing home. He opened his eyes. The light wasn't bright—just a glimmer from a shaded lamp. He couldn't see anything, but he heard a creak and turned his head slowly, wondering what had happened to make it so stiff and unmanageable. Then a face came close to him—a dear, familiar face.

Felicity's.

'Oh, Pat. I'll never forgive myself!'

There was nothing vague about that voice. He smiled lazily and moved his hand, groped for hers and felt the warm, tense pressure of her fingers. She was very close; her lips brushed his forehead.

'What's the matter with my head?'

Felicity's voice was carefully controlled. Invalids must be kept calm.

'It's bandaged.'

She held a glass to his lips, and her hand wasn't altogether steady.

'I'm doing fine, darling. Be up in a day or two. Your Charles still all right?'

'*Damn* Charles!'

Dawlish said: 'But you were right—you'll never know how right you were—we had to help him. How is he?'

'Much better. But you're not to worry about him, or any of them; just rest.'

'Tell me about Charles.'

She told him, and her voice seemed to fade towards the end of the narrative.

The specialist had come to *Four Ways*, had agreed with Farningham that Charles's condition was probably the result of a trance and an agitated, over-excited mind; he thought a serious illness was unlikely. Charles's fever had subsided, and he was now sleeping quietly. The specialist had left at six o'clock— just before Joan Beresford had telephoned.

The voice stopped being Felicity's; became just a voice, mumbling in the distance. Vaguely, Dawlish thought: 'It's the dope.' Still more vaguely he wondered if something had happened to his head and the wound were more serious than Trivett and a police surgeon had suspected.

It wasn't. Except for a dull ache, his head was all right next day. The bandages were replaced by lint and sticking plaster. There was no reason at all, said the doctors, why he shouldn't travel home, provided he wasn't jolted about too much; a couple of quiet days and he would be back to normal.

He talked to Trivett before he left the hospital; was told in turn that Garcia, the maid and the other man at 19 Lincoln Square were missing; as were the Downings. Trivett didn't question him about Charles Horden. Dawlish didn't volunteer any statement. On the way to *Four Ways*, sitting in the back of his own car with a pillow behind his head, Felicity by his side and Tim driving, he thought of little else.

Taking it easy for twenty-four hours proved even more arduous than Dawlish expected. Tim and Ted, too, chafed at this enforced inactivity. Only Felicity enjoyed it.

Farningham paid a flying visit, pronounced Charles out of danger, and hurried back to Putney. The police ignored *Four Ways*. No one lurked in the woods near the house, no one appeared to watch them. Charles lay in a profound sleep, normal enough, except for its long duration; there was no telling when he would come round, possibly not for several days. The newspapers, on that fine April morning, carried the story of the murder at Lincoln Square and the mystery of the missing Downings; and because Dawlish was mentioned again, connected it with the murder at Wyman Street.

*   *   *

At nine o'clock on the second morning, Beresford came out of the bedroom which he had shared with Charles, tapped to make sure that Felicity wasn't in the room, came in and said: 'Well, the boyo is awake, Pat.'

Free of fear and petulant agitation, Charles looked more handsome than ever, as Dawlish stood massive, unshaven and bulky in his dressing-gown, grimly aware of the contrast.

'I'm very grateful,' he said.

'For what?' asked Dawlish gruffly.

'For you allowing me to rest here. I remember all that happened, of course. I have had these resting periods before, and I always feel immeasurably better for them. I am not so frightened now, I feel much steadier—but had you not looked after me, I might have been forced to wake up. That would have been dangerous. I collapsed because recently I was twice brought round from a sleep too early, and too soon. They do not fully understand this.'

'Who are they?'

'My friends.'

'They haven't behaved much like friends.'

'I don't mean the people who have been threatening me,' said Charles. 'I mean those for whom I work. They are so desperately anxious to get results, yet if they would only realize it, if I could work in my own time and at my own pace the results would be immeasurably better.'

'I'd still like to know who they are,' said Dawlish.

'Although I have worked with and for them, in their circle, for some time, I don't really know them,' said Charles frankly. 'There is one man, strong-willed and powerful, called Garcia. I cannot like him. It is he who usually steps up the pressure; I think the others would let me rest more often.'

'Rest from what?'

It was difficult to make the question sound quiet and friendly.

Charles said: 'You surely know! From trances. I distinctly remember talking to you about them, and about my gift. It is a gift, in a way extraneous, and outside myself. I am not responsible for it, and have no idea of the results, although I am told that I am extremely successful. You see, Mr. Dawlish, it is a *natural* phenomenon. I speak to a layman, of course, for to the student and believer it is not phenomenal at all. There is another dimension—beyond the narrow spheres in which the ordinary human works. You would call it psychic, and if a word has to be used, that is as good as any. I am but the instrument. Thank God I don't have to *know* more than the elementary principles.'

Dawlish said: 'Let's get this straight. You join your friends in a seance, go into a trance, and get results which bring benefits to them but about which you know nothing.'

'That is so.'

'And the only one of these friends you know by name, is Garcia.'

Charles nodded.

'And apart from these seances, you live a normal life, making your living by writing?'

Charles nodded again.

'These people who've threatened you—who are they?'

'I have already told you that I don't know.'

'What have you done to anger them?'

'I don't *know*.'

'You know what you did to anger Downing.'

'Oh, *Downing*. He really doesn't matter. He is a boisterous extrovert, a biased sceptic who has the idea that I live on women. I *don't*. I've told you before that they are attracted to me, even infatuated. Your wife was not one of these, Mr. Dawlish, although I felt that she was sincerely interested. She showed deep intelligence during the session for questions after the meeting in Haslemere. It was my fear, and my knowledge of you, which persuaded me to beg her to see me.'

Dawlish said: 'These women fall for you, and you take money from them. Never mind the obvious conclusion. What do you do with the money?'

'I pass it on to Garcia.'

'What does he do with it?'

'He finances the Circle, and it has a great deal of work to do,' said Charles. 'Although I don't like Garcia, I am convinced that the Circle does good work. The members are always short of funds—all good causes are, and it pleases the women to think that they are my patrons. It harms no one.'

'Why do they shower gifts on you?'

'I have often wondered,' said Charles, gently. 'I believe my type of looks appeals to the maternal, protective instinct in them. They feel that I should be sheltered from the brutalities of life.' He laughed. 'Why should I object? In fact I live frugally. I earn sufficient to keep me in reasonably good health and circumstances. Money as such doesn't greatly interest me, though as a measure of worldly success it *is* encouraging.'

'And you earn your living by writing and by giving lectures. Anything else?'

'Nothing else, Mr. Dawlish.'

'What do you write and talk about?'

Charles smiled again. 'You greatly intrigue me, Mr. Dawlish! Had John Downing asked that question, I shouldn't have been surprised. Forgive me, but you have much in common with Downing. The same forthrightness, the same—is simplicity the word?—and yet I feel there is much more in you than appears on the surface. Your wife can doubtless tell you that I write and talk about a certain class of literature—the literature of the occult, of superstition, of legends and of folk-lore. It is a fascinating subject. I beg you to believe that I am not withholding facts from you. I feel that I owe you so much that I can only pass on everything I know. My enemies? I would tell you of them, if I could. My trances? I am completely unaware of what transpires, and of the results. I only know that they must be extremely successful, or the Circle wouldn't press me so often to serve. It is not the work that worries me, but the pressure of it. If I had had a week or two of rest, Downing would not have worried me. I am, indeed, sorry for him.'

'And not for his sister?'

Charles frowned; it was just a wrinkling of that alabaster forehead.

'Fay troubles me at times. Oh, I remember dismissing her as unimportant before I went to sleep, but there is something in her which harasses me. I've no doubt that she is genuinely fond of me. I was without friends, except Garcia, and he scoffs at my fears, so—I talked to Fay about them. She knew that I was in danger, that efforts had been made to kill me, she had seen my terror, and—she understood. She wanted me to go to France, and offered to pay all my expenses. She thought that I could escape the terror by running away from it, but—that might only make it worse. It is only partly physical, Dawlish. It comes from the mind. But—I *must* have help.'

'Can't you convince Garcia and your friends?'

'No,' said Charles. 'No. They believe that it is a pretence to avoid serving them. Garcia persuades them of that. I see the others only when we meet at the Circle, and have little opportunity to reason with them.'

'Are they all men?'

'There are two women among them.'

'Where do they meet?'

'At various places. Garcia always tells me where the next meeting is to be, and comes to fetch me.' Charles shrugged. 'Each man has his own particular gifts, and can't be blamed for lacking those he doesn't possess. But I *have* enemies, Dawlish. I am not romancing; I have told you the truth. Garcia is a cruel and ruthless man. The doctor is far otherwise. Kind and gentle, he is a very real friend to me. And he is frightened of Garcia; this I know well. Well, Mr. Dawlish, I hope I have satisfied you.'

'Not entirely. You live at home with an uncle and aunt, don't you?'

'Yes.' Charles frowned.

'Why did you give my wife a key that day? Why couldn't one of the others have let us in?'

'I knew that my aunt would be out, and my uncle had to spend a day or two in bed. I'm sorry if—'

Dawlish said harshly: 'Did you know that your uncle was to be brutally murdered?'

Charles caught his breath; surprise and horror showed in his eyes. There was a long silence, until Dawlish rasped:

'Did you?'

'No, Mr. Dawlish. That—happened?'

'Didn't your psychic gift tell you?'

Charles said softly: 'No. No, I had no knowledge. My aunt—'

'She's with friends. Do you want to see her?'

'If it is necessary and I can help, yes. But I have to say this, Dawlish. There are things of great importance, and—'

'You mean, let your aunt get along on her own. You're much more important.'

Charles closed his eyes.

'Whenever you wish I will go to her. For the rest—I hope I have satisfied you.'

Dawlish said: 'I must admit that most of what you've said makes nonsense to me.'

'How can I prove to you that it is *not* nonsense?'

Dawlish said: 'That's easy. Give us a demonstration as soon as you're fit. Show us what happens in these trances. That'll convince me.'

CHAPTER TWELVE

THE PROFESSOR

The two husky men stood looking down at the fragile man in bed. Dawlish was motionless; Beresford drummed the fingers of his left hand against his leg—the leg that he always held out stiffly in front of him, and which made him limp slightly. Charles's eyes remained shadowed. The sun, slanting through the window, touched the pale gold of his hair.

Beresford's drumming became a tattoo.

Dawlish's eyes were filled with challenge.

Charles spoke quietly. 'I do not think I can give a demonstration, Dawlish. Not here. No one here is a believer. I can overcome a great deal of scepticism, but I must have some help. If there were one of you really convinced, then I would try.' He opened his eyes suddenly, startling them with a strange, piercing brilliance. 'There isn't a believer, Dawlish, is there?'

Dawlish said brutally: 'So you need your accomplice. Who is it? Garcia?'

'I have no accomplice; this is no confidence trick. But I cannot use the gift in an atmosphere of unrelieved hostility and disbelief.'

'Do you have to know the believer?' Dawlish's voice remained harsh and aggressive, as if he were trying to break down the younger man's resistance.

'No, that is not necessary. I shall know if there is one in the circle. If you care to arrange a sitting, Dawlish, and make sure that there is a believer present. I shall be aware of it, without at first knowing who it is. Of course, I can promise you nothing, but I do not think you would be disappointed.'

'When will you try it?'

'Whenever you wish,' said Charles. 'You want only to be convinced that I have—a gift, and to know that the gift could be used. Isn't that so?'

Dawlish nodded. His voice, when it came, was lighter.

'I may not be able to find my man today. How long do you want to stay here?'

'For as long as you will allow. Eventually, Garcia will find me, of course, and I have no doubt he will compel me to leave, but if I could stay here a week, I should be much stronger and much happier.'

'That's settled then. Now, what about breakfast?'

'A light breakfast, please—by lunch time I shall be ravenous, but it is never wise to eat too heartily immediately after waking.'

'I'll fix something,' Dawlish promised.

He went out; Beresford followed him, stiff-legged, and Tim Jeremy and Felicity appeared as if by magic. They asked in low-pitched voices:

'Well, what happened?'

'Is he all right?'

Dawlish drew them into the bedroom.

'Ted, what did you make of it?'

'Uncanny,' growled Beresford, scowling. 'Never could stomach that stuff. Beyond me, but—well, he's a convincing, and callous, little beggar.'

'Callous?'

'His aunt.'

'H'm, yes. The fact is that I want to keep him here, and he knows it.'

Beresford shrugged.

'Well, there's one thing, Pat.'

'Yes?'

'*Is* he a man?'

Tim exclaimed: 'If you think he's a ghost—'

'Idiot. He looks more like a woman to me.'

All eyes were on Dawlish.

'I wouldn't like to stake much on whether he's masculine, feminine or neuter; but damn it, two doctors—'

Beresford shrugged. 'Wouldn't be the first medicos to be diddled. What about this trial? Think you can fix someone?'

'Fix *what*!' howled Tim.

'We do want to know about it,' said Felicity, with suspicious mildness. 'Don't just talk as if we're not in the room, Pat.'

'You're seeing Ted's reaction, which is more informative than words. Charles claims to be clairvoyant, although he didn't use the word. He talked round the point a bit, but he says he's used by certain friends to join a certain Circle and to convince doubters and sceptics. The Circle is presumably spiritualist—a seance.'

'Convince doubters of what?' asked Tim dubiously.

'For a start, that he has this gift. For another, that the gift can be used for some purpose or other that he can't or won't define. His vagueness is the thing I find most convincing. If he were putting up a bluff, I think he'd have something more detailed for us. Agree, Ted?'

'He's not average norm,' growled Ted.

'He's getting nearer—he says he can manage a light breakfast, Fel, and will be ravenous at luncheon!'

'Tim dear,' said Felicity, innocently, 'go and ask Norah if she'll get a tray ready, will you?'

'You mean you're scared of her.'

'I don't *want* her to walk out on us,' said Felicity, 'and the authentic masculine touch might—just might—ward off the danger. Be a dear.'

'Come on, Ted,' said Tim morosely. 'We're not wanted.'

Felicity went to the dressing-table and picked up a comb, but made no attempt to use it.

'Pat, what *is* it all about?'

'Don't ask me. Taken on its face value, Charles is a clairvoyant, and he works with friends who include a certain Mr. Garcia. That puts it in the running for high stakes and crime. I wouldn't like to say whether Charles himself is consciously mixed up in one or the other. He also thinks you are a woman of intelligence and have a receptive mind.'

'There are times when I wish I'd never heard of him.'

'But this isn't one of them! Fel, isn't our neighbour, the Professor, a member of your Literary Club?'

Felicity stared.

'Yes, he is.'

'Didn't you say he had heard Charles's lecture and was impressed by it?'

Felicity nodded, her eyes alive to the point Dawlish was driving at.

'How *do* you do it, darling! The Professor is the one man I'd like to bring into this, but I just didn't think of him. We'll go and ask him together—'

She hurried across and opened the door, as a voice pitched high in fury rose from downstairs.

'Oh, *damn!*' said Felicity.

They listened intently, as Norah's tones shrilled even higher. She was sick and tired of it; one guest was all right, even *two* at a pinch, but when it came to everyone wanting breakfast in bed, *and* to be waited on hand and foot, it was more than flesh and blood could stand. Working one's fingers to the bone, one didn't expect gratitude, dear me no, but a little consider*ation*, surely wasn't too much to ask!

'Oh, well,' said Felicity. 'I'll be cook; you'll have to be housemaid.'

'Think she'll go?'

'I think she's been on the point of it for a couple of days. She's all right while everything's normal, but now—well, it *has* been rather much. I'd better see what I can do with her.'

'Tim seems to be trying.'

Jeremy's voice could be heard like gentle background music, punctuated by sharp retorts from Norah. Felicity hurried downstairs, while Dawlish went into the bathroom much subdued, pulling the bathmat straight and lining up his sponge and toothbrush in a neat row, in propitiation to the domestic gods about to pour the vials of their wrath on his luckless head.

When Dawlish reached the breakfast room a silent trio sat at the table, not noticeably eating less, but undoubtedly gloomy.

Felicity said: 'She's going immediately after breakfast; the most she'll do is the washing-up.'

Dawlish grunted and sat down.

The unreliability of domestic help infuriated him. You couldn't reason with Norah, with any of them—or very few. It wasn't a tragedy, but it meant that Felicity would be house-tied; it added a nagging nuisance to life at a time when any distraction was dangerous.

They heard Norah stumping up the stairs.

'Carrying her Last Tray,' said Jeremy, with an attempt at flippancy. 'You'd be surprised at her vocabulary, Pat. I was.'

'No chance of getting anyone else?'

'Not at short notice,' said Felicity. 'I'd like to—oh, forget it!' She threw her hands up in a gesture of release. 'It's absolute nonsense being cast down and gloomy because of this. *Nothing* is going to keep me away from the Professor.'

'And who is the Professor?' asked Beresford.

Dawlish told him what he knew . . .

The Professor was, in fact, a nickname.

When Dr. Anstruther Corbett had first come to the district, his wife had been alive; since her death he had been more or less a recluse, his only concession to social life his membership of the Literary Club. He was known to be a man of letters; he was also known to be a student of the occult; both these facts tending to a certain uneasiness in the manner of the villagers when speaking of him.

'I don't think he's been inside anyone else's house but ours since his wife died,' said Felicity.

'Sounds a sourpuss to me,' said Tim. 'Servants and what not?'

'No, he does for himself. Rumour has it that the place is like a pig-sty.'

'One sympathizes,' said Ted with feeling.

'Any use *you* having a word with Norah?' Jeremy asked Pat. 'We might as well all have a shot while we're about it.'

'You could try,' said Felicity. 'Listen, there she is coming down. What's she been doing upstairs all this time?'

'Making the beds, I hope,' said Dawlish.

'More coffee?' Felicity asked, with forced brightness.

Ten minutes later Jeremy and Beresford began to pile the

breakfast things on a tray, and Dawlish and Felicity went into the kitchen. Norah was at the sink, and when Dawlish spoke she swung round, startled. The word that occurred to him, was 'transfigured'. Her eyes were shining and oddly radiant. She was a plain woman, but something had touched her with the brush of loveliness. She dried her red hands on a flowered apron fastened round her stolid middle, as Dawlish said:

'Norah, don't you think—'

'I'm sorry I lost my temper, m'am,' said Norah quietly. 'It's been a lot of extra work, and I'm not so young as I was. No one likes to be put upon, but I can see now that it wasn't meant, so if it's all right with you m'am I'll stay.'

'Miracle,' said Dawlish.

'Worked by Charles,' said Felicity, dryly.

If the outside of the Professor's cottage was anything to go by, pig-sty was not far from the truth. It had not been seriously cultivated for years. The grass had been scythed, but bushes, hedges and flower beds had run riot, while most of the garden was a tangle of weeds.

As they walked up the overgrown path they saw that the red-tiled roof had mellowed with age, lichen growing over it as thickly as a creeper. The front door and the window-frames, barely seen through over-heavy clumps of wistaria and clematis, ought to have been painted years ago.

'It's worse than I expected,' said Felicity. She added: 'He probably won't open the door.'

Dawlish raised the iron knocker cautiously, and had a feeling that if he knocked too hard, something would break. The quiet rat-tat echoed over the garden and beyond.

As the door opened, Felicity took Dawlish's hand.

The professor stood there, blinking at them through

steel-rimmed glasses. He was a small man, whose mildness and meekness of manner in no way belied an unadvertised strength.

'Ah. Good morning.' His voice was soft. 'It's Mrs. Dawlish, isn't it?'

'Yes,' said Felicity. 'Dr. Corbett, I wonder if we can have a talk with you? We'd very much like your help.'

'*My* help?' Heavily lidded eyes blinked. 'How could that be? But come in.' He stood aside for them to enter. There was no hall, most of the ground floor of the cottage being given to one large room.

Felicity shot Dawlish a startled glance. This room was beautiful; the colours in it rich and harmonious, the rugs of great rarity and great beauty. At a guess, not a piece of furniture was less than two hundred years old. There was charm here, and the evidence of careful, tending hands. The brick fireplace, part of the original cottage, was piled with logs.

'Please sit down,' said the Professor. 'Is it a little early, or will you have something to drink? I should be happy—few visit me, very few, and I get little opportunity for dispensing hospitality.' He laughed shyly. 'And I confess I seldom desire to; there is so much to do.'

Dawlish said: 'We'd love a gin-and-orange, if you have it.'

'Yes, yes.' The Professor fussed placidly with glasses and bottles. He brought the drinks over and sat down. 'Now, Mr. Dawlish, if I can be of help, please tell me how.'

How did you ask a man if he were a believer in Charles's sense of the word?

You didn't, openly.

Dawlish smiled.

'Do you remember the lecture which Mr. Charles Horden gave a month or two ago?'

'I do indeed,' said the Professor pleasantly. 'Yes, yes, a

remarkable lecture; for a young man he showed an astonishing grasp of his subject. And I so admired his courage; he made it clear that he believed in life after death and the possibility of communication with the spirits of the dead, and very few *young* men will admit to that in these days of scepticism and unbelief.'

'I think you are right, there. As a matter of fact, Horden is staying with us, and would like to give a demonstration of his powers tonight. He is a clairvoyant. But he says that it's impossible unless he had at least one person in the Circle who really believes.'

'Certainly it is. *One*? I should have said more than one.' The Professor leaned forward and stared unseeingly towards the window. 'So he is staying with you. I confess I would like to meet him and talk with him. Yes, indeed!' The Professor gave a little, deprecating laugh. 'I nearly screwed up my courage to speak to him after his lecture, but he was surrounded by charming ladies. One could not risk cutting short such evident pleasure.'

'Will you come?'

'Gladly.' The Professor blinked rapidly. 'I confess that I am surprised that you should be prepared to investigate, but— well, I'm quite satisfied, quite satisfied.' He didn't say what he was satisfied about. 'The young man undoubtedly possesses a quality which few are endowed. I could feel the radiations, but—I have wondered how he puts it to use. If you spent as much time as I have in studying this fascinating subject, Mr. Dawlish, you would understand me. I make no criticism. I just don't *know* anything about the young man, except that he fascinates me. But the history of the subject is remarkable. There are the genuine clairvoyants and the charlatans, of course. The charlatans do not greatly matter. They are a danger to credulous people, that is all, and properly the butt of police investigation.

No, the danger is from those who *have* the gift and misuse it. Misuse it,' he repeated softly. 'Why do you want him to demonstrate his powers Mr. Dawlish?'

'I'm curious. And I think he may be in the hands of some unscrupulous people who make him prostitute this gift. I can't be sure until I know that he has it.'

'Oh, he has it. And I will gladly join the Circle. Tonight, did you say?'

'Can you come to *Four Ways* tonight?'

'Indeed I will, and believe me when I say that I am quite excited at the thought of meeting the young man.' He laughed nervously. 'And the time?'

'Will you have dinner with us first?'

'Thank you a thousand times, but I live frugally, and am on a strict diet. I seldom eat after six o'clock in the evening. If you will forgive me, I will come after dinner. Shall we say—'

'Half past eight?'

'Excellent.'

He stood, smiling on them, until they had closed the gate.

'Pig-sty!' Felicity snorted. 'If that is an example, I wish my house were one!'

Dawlish laughed, and they walked briskly towards *Four Ways*, which they could see at the top of the low hill overlooking the village. The road was narrow, with high hedges on either side. Their footsteps rang clearly on the flinty surface—as clearly as the sudden shrill whistle, like a bird's call, which came from somewhere ahead of them.

Dawlish stopped abruptly, Felicity took his arm. They listened intently, and the sound came again.

'Tim or Ted about,' said Dawlish tensely.

'A danger call,' said Felicity, and suddenly she shivered.

CHAPTER THIRTEEN

WARNING CALL

Work it out—Ted or Tim was beyond the right-hand hedge, and thought it necessary to warn him. This was an old signal from their early adventurous days. So they knew danger threatened, and couldn't deal with it from where they were; which put it on the left.

The call came again.

The sun was bright and and morning warm, but Felicity looked cold.

Dawlish said: 'Go back a bit,' and went with her to a bend in the road, where she was out of sight of anyone farther along. 'Stay there, sweet.'

She didn't argue, and didn't speak. He went forward again, walking briskly, heart thumping.

The third call had come from his right. He scanned the left-hand hedge, thick with hawthorn and bramble; no hope of seeing through to the other side.

Here and there the hedge was low.

He took an automatic from his pocket and flicked the safety-catch, then suddenly ran diagonally towards a low spot in the hedge and jumped. He cleared it; and as he reached the other side, he saw a man crouching low. The man swung round, gun in hand.

Dawlish heard the roar of the shot. From a crouching position, he fired, and his bullet rustled the hedge as the man jumped to one side. He fired again. The man started, turned to run, but loosed another shot. It tore through Dawlish's coat. But it was the man's last attempt. He ran as fast as short legs could carry him over the uneven meadowland. Dawlish aimed low; the shot rang out, the man pitched forward and the gun flew from his grasp. It was over as swiftly as that; and Dawlish was on him before he had recovered his breath or tried to get back the gun.

Dawlish picked up the second gun, then gave the shrill call three times in quick succession—all clear.

His captive was middle-aged and wizened, with an ugly pink scar over his left eye. The bullet had gone through the fleshy part of the calf. Dawlish helped him to tie a handkerchief tightly round the leg beneath the knee.

'Did Garcia send you?'

'Supposing he did?'

'Where is he?'

The man said, through twisted, bitter lips: 'You'll never get Garcia.'

Dawlish said thoughtfully: 'You drove the car at Lincoln Square, didn't you?'

'Supposing I did?'

A loud '*Yoicks!*' came from the road, and Tim and Felicity peered over the hedge.

'Want any help, Pat?'

'I certainly do,' Dawlish bent down and hoisted the little man shoulder high. 'Here, take him. He's hurt his leg.' Dawlish shifted his burden into Tim's outheld arms, and drawing back far enough to make a running jump, cleared the hedge again. By then Tim had sat the little man on the grass verge and was busy turning the handkerchief bandage into a tourniquet. 'Thanks, Tim.'

'Not at all. Lucky thing Ted and I spotted the little beggar creeping after you. The old brain does work occasionally, you know. Where are you going to put him?'

'I rather thought the loft above the garage. Let's make a chair for him.'

Jeremy said: 'I could nip back for the car—or Felicity could. Much easier that way.'

'I suppose—' began Dawlish.

He raised his head abruptly; and the others looked at him, startled, knowing that he had heard something which they couldn't yet detect. Soon a steady crunching became audible to them all.

'Cyclist,' said Jeremy briefly. 'Let's put him over the hedge again. We don't want an audience.'

'Too late,' said Dawlish.

They watched as if in a trance a very large policeman, on what, in comparison, appeared to be a very small bicycle, bearing down on them.

'Pity,' said Jeremy. 'Have to hand our captive over to the law, I suppose.'

'Of course,' said Felicity.

Dawlish said: 'Hush,' and bent over the wounded man. 'You've a choice—being dealt with by us or by the police. Please yourself—which is it?'

The man looked shiftily from one to the other of them.

'No point in bringing the cops in,' he muttered sulkily.

'Pat—' began Felicity.

'Hold it, my sweet, and this will work out.' Dawlish straightened up and beamed at the constable. 'Morning officer!' The man drew nearer and slowed down. 'Had a nasty accident here, I'm afraid.'

'Sorry to hear that, sir.'

'We were fooling about with guns—it seemed safe enough. My friend tripped up and shot himself in the leg.'

'*Very* sorry to hear that,' said the constable, and climbed off his machine. 'I heard shooting, that's why I came up. Not far from your house is it, Mr. Dawlish? Going to get him there?'

'Yes, we'll look after him.'

'Looks like a hospital job to me.'

'Oh, it's not as bad as that.' Dawlish looked at the little gunman, who gulped and shook his head. 'I've a doctor coming this afternoon, anyhow; but I don't think this needs more than first aid and rest. Tim, will you go back with Felicity and bring the car?'

'Of course,' said Felicity.

'Be back in no time,' said Jeremy. 'See you later, officer!'

He took Felicity's arm, and they moved off quickly. Dawlish noted uneasily the gleam in the man's little eyes. It wasn't a look of fear now. Dawlish turned slowly, passing a handkerchief casually over his mouth as he emitted a shrill bird call.

The constable unbuttoned the flap of his breast pocket and drew out a notebook.

'Might as well take particulars now, sir. Save time later on. You say it was an accident?'

'Ah, yes. My friend—'

'If I could have the gentleman's *full* name, sir, I'd be pleased.'

The policeman felt in his breast pocket, as if for a pencil, and didn't find one. He put a hand to his side pocket, which bulged. Dawlish waited until he started to draw it out again—and then hit him. Fifteen stone went behind the blow, as it toppled the policeman backwards against the hedge, bringing a savage curse from the wounded man—it also showed a gun, half in, half out of the policeman's pocket.

'How many more of you?' asked Dawlish softly.

Almost as he spoke, he heard the hum of a car engine.

'Quite enough to deal with *you*,' said the man in uniform viciously. He rubbed his chin as he straightened up. 'The whole lot of you. Then we'll go and collect Mr. Horden.'

Tim and Felicity were still out of sight. Dawlish took out his automatic, moved forward and pulled the other's gun from the tunic pocket. Then he opened his mouth and gave the call again. Tim had been warned. The approaching car seemed to be travelling very slowly. Garcia's men were in it, of course. The plan showed up, simple, clear as daylight, yet in its way so cunning. First the little man, sent as a decoy, then the policeman, to disarm suspicion; now the main party, in the car.

Dawlish was on edge for the sound of shooting; he could picture Felicity and Tim standing by the side of the road to let the car pass; and although they had been warned, what could they do if they were attacked? The seconds ticked by, each one agelong. The pseudo-policeman grinned, the wounded man stared along the road, as if he were fearful that something would go wrong at the last minute.

Then the shots rang out—three in quick succession, travelling loud and clear on the wind.

'That's fixed them,' breathed the policeman.

Dawlish hit him again, a shrewd short-arm jab, driving upwards to the point of his fleshy chin. The man's head jolted back and his eyes rolled. Dawlish ran in the direction from which the shots had come, dreading what he might see. The car had stopped; there was no more shooting, no sound of voices.

Then he heard three shrill bird calls. They poured relief into him, and made him quicken his pace, so that he was moving at the double when he reached the corner.

Tim, gun in hand, covered two small men who stood by the side of the car; Felicity was going through their pockets for weapons.

'We can't keep them all,' said Felicity calmly, 'and if we hand some of them over to the police, they'll talk about the others. What are you going to do, Pat. You can't possibly let them go; they might—'

'Police job now,' said Dawlish. 'We want to keep our eye on the ball, and the ball is Horden.'

He stood by the window of the drawing-room brandishing a tankard of beer, his relief so intense that it showed in his face and his voice. Outside in the garage were three of the prisoners; the man with the wounded leg—the wound cleansed and padded—was on a couch in the morning-room.

'Garcia's no fool. I doubt if these people have anything in their pockets to give his present address away—if they have, the police will find it. The main job is to find out what actual job Charles does, and I'd be astonished if any of the quartet know.'

Beresford, leaning comfortably against the cushioned back of his chair, said: 'You could try to find out.'

'We've tackled tougher nuts,' said Jeremy.

'They're not so tough.' Beresford took a pull at his beer. 'I think they'd crack in ten minutes or so. Let me have a go at 'em.'

'Us,' amended Jeremy hastily.

'We'll have to deal with the local Roberts for a start,' said Dawlish. 'Don't forget the reason these boyos came to see us today—simply to put us out of action. They made a mass attack and really meant business, so they wanted results quickly. I'll give you three guesses why.'

'He's going all psychic on us,' groaned Jeremy.

'They're afraid we might pick something up from Charles Horden, now that he's come round,' said Beresford.

'*Must* we guess at the obvious?' Jeremy asked.

Dawlish grinned. '*You* must. Put yourself in Garcia's position. He is a kind of manager for this Circle; he exerts pressure on Charles, dragoons him into putting on his show, and arranges that the sceptics will be present and ready for conversion into believers. I think the key to the problem is—for what purpose have they to be converted? You can take it for granted that it isn't for the good of their souls. The crime, and it's certainly big-money stuff, depends on Charles putting up a good and convincing performance of second sight. Charles says he doesn't know *what* he does, but obviously he does all that's necessary. Now, if Garcia thinks twice, he'll know that we've reached that point in our reasoning.'

'Left it about a mile behind, I should say,' said Jeremy, but he looked thoughtful.

'And he'd be at the next point—that we'll probably try to make Charles give us a similar show, and so find out all about it. So the moment Charles comes round, Garcia is ready to weigh in. We took evasive action, and it worked. But if we try to tackle the prisoners ourselves, we'll have a pretty tough job on our hands. It'll delay the performance; or it could, because now there's another safe bet—that Garcia is waiting for a report. When he doesn't get one, he'll either send someone else, or come himself to investigate. And if we've his johnnies incarcerated here, he'll have a shot at getting 'em back. If he knows they're with the police it'll shake him badly. And if he also knows that we have a strong police cordon round the house—which we can have, for the asking,' added Dawlish dreamily—'it won't be any use having a go at us tonight. So—we hand the boyos over to the authorities and we ask for police protection. Come to think, there's humour in that.'

'Ha! ha!' said Jeremy politely. 'What's so funny?'

Beresford grinned.

'Think, mutton-head! Charles is here, and the police want to interview him. Trivett has reasons for turning the blind eye, but—'

'Charles gives his performance,' Jeremy finished for him, 'and the police stay on guard outside to protect him. Beautiful!'

'But supposing the police want to come in?' asked Beresford. 'And they will.'

'They needn't see Charles. The one thing we've got to make sure of is, that the Professor doesn't let out the fact that Charles is here.' Dawlish frowned. 'The Professor didn't seem to know anything about the way Charles is in the news; he probably doesn't read a newspaper from one week's end to another. But if he meets a constable outside he might talk. I didn't think of that. Will you watch the cottage, Tim, and bring the old boy here?'

'Hum. Watch from when?'

'After lunch. Remembering that more of Garcia's men may have been watching through long-range glasses, and know that Fel and I were there. When the others fail to report to Garcia, the cottage might become a place of interest for any such watchers. Best to be ultra careful. And if anyone is seen approaching the place, hop in first and tell the old boy that no one must know that Charles is here. Right?'

'Yes, *sir*,' said Jeremy.

Inspector Allen of the Haslemere Police, arriving post haste, knew Dawlish well enough not to be greatly surprised at what had happened. He appeared to take Dawlish's word at its face value; that he and Felicity had been attacked when out for a walk. Allen's sergeant took down a detailed statement, while his men drove the four prisoners into Haslemere, two of them in their own car.

By half past one that episode was over; by half past two Jeremy was on his way to the cottage, with Beresford, who was to return later; Felicity was taking a nap, Charles Horden was reading in his bedroom, while Dawlish sat in the drawing-room with a pad in front of him and a pencil in his hand.

But he made few notes.

He stared across the sunlit countryside and let his thoughts run over the events of the past few days. The sight of a genuine policeman, stationed at the gate of *Four Ways*, did not distract his attention. His face was set in the wooden expression of a man whose mind was assessing, accepting or rejecting, a dozen speculations. He was still there at half-past four, when Felicity came in. She was about to creep out again when he turned and smiled at her.

'Deep thoughts, darling?'

'Deepish, I hope. Plan of campaign gradually forming. I'm also getting worried about Fay Downing. Trivett promised to telephone if she turned up, and there's been no word.'

'Well, he can't complain that you haven't kept him informed this time. Tea?'

'Good idea. On our own?'

'That's what I thought. We can pretend we're a normal, humdrum couple again. Pat—'

'Hm-hm?'

'Are you sure you're glad I brought you into this?'

'Never more so. I can only see a glimmer of what's behind it, but I wouldn't have missed it for the world. What's on your mind? The general oppression, or fear that Charles won't be able to justify himself?'

Felicity said: 'It's that girl.'

'Fay?'

'Yes. I keep thinking about her—even when I'm trying to concentrate on something else. You've just accepted the fact that she and Downing let Garcia take over, and paved the way to the first attack. You haven't gone beyond that, but—are the Downings crooks?'

'We'll see,' said Dawlish. 'I—Hallo, visitors!'

A car had pulled up outside the front gate, and a constable was leaning forward, over the driver, who was hidden from Dawlish's sight. Another constable came from behind some bushes and joined the first; the local police were taking no chances.

Norah came in with tea, and departed, soft-footed.

'They're taking their time with him,' said Felicity.

'Thorough. As you'd expect. Ah, here it comes.'

The car turned into the drive, the high banks hiding it until it was half-way to the house. Then Felicity and Dawlish saw the driver at the same time; it was a woman.

Felicity said: 'Look!' and went nearer to the window. Dawlish whistled softly. Felicity had already guessed who it was; and her guess was on the mark.

Fay Downing was at the wheel.

She looked at the front of the house uncertainly.

'One *very* worried young woman,' said Dawlish lightly. 'Let her in, my sweet, will you?'

Felicity reached the front door as the bell rang.

CHAPTER FOURTEEN

FRIGHTENED FAY

Felicity and Fay came into the room side by side. Felicity's eyes asked questions, but she didn't utter them.

'Ah!' Dawlish sprang to his feet. 'I was hoping to have a chat with you. Do sit down.' Fay was frightened, but he did not think he was the cause of all her fear. 'And your brother, where is he?'

'That's what I've come to see you about.'

Fay's voice was low-pitched and husky; she wasn't far from tears.

Felicity raised a hand, as if to catch Dawlish's eye; and he knew that she was sending him a hostile command to go easy with the girl.

But he was harsh.

'Why? Do you think I've hidden him in the cellar? Or slit his throat and buried him beneath an apple tree?'

'Oh, please! He's in terrible danger.'

'So he got the trouble he said I was asking for.' Dawlish fiddled impatiently with an unlit cigarette. 'One of his shortcomings is that he talks too much, and another is, that too much of what he says is nonsense. The same, if I may say so, applies to you. What's happened to him? Did Garcia prove treacherous?'

Fay moistened her lips. 'Yes.' It was a small voice, on the point of breaking.

'If your brother had had any sense at all he'd have known that Garcia ought not to have been trusted.'

'Pat—' began Felicity tentatively; but he didn't answer and didn't look towards her.

'We thought Garcia was a friend.'

'And believing him to be a friend, you let him stooge for you and your brother, and hold a reception party for me. Do you know what happened at that party?'

'Yes.'

'Who told you?'

'I read the newspapers. Mr. Dawlish, we didn't know what Garcia was going to do; we had no idea. I swear that we had no idea at all. We thought he was going to talk to you, and that might make you give Charles up.'

'And you were in cahoots with your brother?'

'Yes, John had persuaded me that he was right about Charles.' She mumbled the words. 'I'm still not sure.'

'It depends what you thought in the first place,' said Dawlish. 'Garcia took over at Lincoln Square from you, you went to a place of his choosing to wait for him, and afterwards he didn't let you free. Is that it? He kept you both prisoner, and now he's sent you to tell me that your brother's a hostage for Charles. That if I release Charles, he'll release your brother. Isn't that it?'

'Yes!' She jumped up. 'How did you know?'

'My dear girl, there is a depressing sameness about bad deeds. But what made Garcia think you could persuade me to exchange Charles for John, I cannot imagine. Can you offer any practical reason why I should make the exchange?'

Fay said: 'Yes, yes, I think so.' But she didn't sound confident.

'He gave me a message. He said that if you release Charles to him, he won't worry you any more.'

'Thoughtful of him. When did you see him?'

'About two hours ago.'

'Did he tell you that he had sent four men to get Charles back and to prevent us from taking any further interest, and the four are now under arrest?'

Fay shrank back.

'No, he didn't say that. I'd no idea. No idea at all.'

Felicity moved restlessly about the room. It was a mistake for her to be present at a time like this, when Dawlish knew that he had to break down Fay's resistance, had to reduce her to a frame of mind in which she would talk freely.

He said sharply: 'Fay, look at me.' She turned her great eyes towards him, and they were dimmed with tears. 'Who do you love most? Charles or your brother?'

Fay didn't speak.

'You've got to make up your mind. Who?'

She said: 'I don't know; I just don't know! John has been so good, he's looked after me most of my life; but Charles—I'm in love with Charles.'

Silence followed; even Felicity stopped moving. Tears welled up in Fay's eyes. Now that he studied her more closely, Dawlish could see signs of strain and sleeplessness. Her face, sweet and quite beautiful in an elfin way, was pale and drawn beneath light make-up.

She said: 'I can't help it if he *is* bad. I'm in love with him. I'd do anything for him. *Anything.*'

'Such as hand him over to Garcia, in return for John?'

She did not speak at once, and Dawlish could imagine the struggle which had gone on in her mind as she had driven here, could understand the torment she was undergoing now. Then she said:

'Garcia promised that no harm would come to Charles. It's in Charles's interests to leave here, to go to Garcia. That's what—Garcia said.'

'And you believed him?'

Fay didn't reply. Dawlish moved forward, towering over her.

'Come on. Let's have the truth. Did you believe Garcia?'

She closed her eyes.

'I wanted to. I swear I want to, but—I wasn't sure. I just wasn't sure.' The last words were hardly audible. 'I wanted to help both—both Charles and John.'

Dawlish said harshly: 'If you really want to, you can.' He paused. 'Will you?'

Felicity crossed the room and began to rearrange a bowl of tulips which did not need rearranging. Fay stared at Dawlish, and hope smoothed away the lines of weariness and anxiety.

'Yes, yes! I will, of course I will.'

'Just tell us the truth—everything from the time you first met Charles and Garcia. If you hold anything back you may spoil the only chance of helping either Charles or John.' Dawlish glanced at Felicity and grinned. 'Could there be tea, my sweet? Fay looks as if she could drink a cup.'

The story took a long time telling. Fay repeated herself frequently; forgot details which she suddenly recalled, and so lost the thread of her story in order to go back and clear up some point she had already made.

It had started a year ago . . .

She had first met Charles at a literary club meeting in London; a small and very arty club, where he had given a lecture and afterwards been besieged by earnest inquirers into the occult. Later, she had been to a seance where Charles had been the medium. Nothing much had happened, except that he had gone into a trance during which strange and rather incoherent voices had floated about the darkness of the meeting-room. It had been judged as not a very successful seance, but for her it had been of overwhelming importance, for she had fallen in love with Charles. So she had written to him, pretending interest in his literary work; they'd had lunch together, and become friends of a sort, if an over-solicitous infatuation on one side, and indifference on the other, could be classed as a friendship of any kind. She had known that many other women felt for Charles as she had done, and that Charles, though apparently spending none of it on himself, had accepted their gifts of money. This acceptance had in no way lessened his indifference to the givers.

She had a certain aptitude for painting, and this, coupled with the writing, supposed a similarity of tastes sufficient reason for their frequent meeting.

She had never attended another seance. She knew that he no longer went to ordinary circles and was doing some special work. It was through Charles that she had first met Garcia. After a few months her brother had discovered her infatuation for Charles, begged her to give him up, and became furious when she had not done so.

She was young—twenty-one—and John had taken the place of father and mother since their parents had died, five years before.

She didn't see Garcia often. She knew that he occasionally visited the Lincoln Square house and saw John—she didn't know what it was about. They did some kind of business together. She hadn't known that Garcia was the man who controlled Charles's special work until today, when Garcia had sent her to see Dawlish.

For the last month or so Charles had seemed worried; more than that, frightened. He would not tell her the cause, only that attempts were being made on his life. She had been terrified for him, begged him to leave the Wyman Street house, to go abroad. She had promised that he would need nothing. She had money in France, for both she and John were wealthy, and had funds in many continental countries, as well as in the U.S.A. Charles had rejected the suggestion, but he had become daily more frightened of these unnamed people, until it had started to affect his health.

He continued with his special work, though he believed that the attempts were made to prevent him from doing that.

Finally he had come to speak at Haslemere; met Felicity; heard of her husband's reputation for uncovering crime, and asked for Dawlish's help.

Meanwhile John, in his anxiety of her, Fay's, association with Charles, had unearthed the names of eleven women, all young, all beautiful, whose homes had been broken up by a similar infatuation. That, and the murder of Charles's uncle and the suggestion that Charles was responsible, had made her behave as she had when Dawlish had called.

She had been on her way to see Charles when Dawlish had first seen her, because Charles was to have met her for dinner that night, and hadn't turned up; that was all.

After Dawlish had left Lincoln Square, Garcia had telephoned and suggested that he should deal with Dawlish. Fay had no idea how Garcia had discovered that Dawlish was interested, but John hadn't hesitated. They'd gone to a West End flat, which they believed to be Garcia's. He'd kept them prisoner for two days and nights. Then, today, he had arrived and told Fay to go to *Four Ways* and persuade Dawlish to let Charles go. If her persuasion were not successful, John would die.

*　　*　　*

'And he meant it,' Fay said. 'I'm sure he meant it.'

'I shouldn't take anything he says as being unassailable,' Dawlish said gently. 'Garcia talks a lot, but doesn't do much. And we've the trump card, in Charles.'

'How *is* Charles?'

'Very much better,' said Dawlish. 'You can see him soon. Now Fay—some questions. Did Charles ever name any one of these people who frightened him?'

'No.'

'Are you sure it wasn't Garcia?'

'I don't see how it could have been. He worked with Garcia.'

'Do you know anything about this special work?'

'Only that it's to do with seances. Charles told me that.'

'Do you know where they're held?'

'No.'

'Or who attends them?'

'No. I assure you, I just *don't* know.'

'Do you know many of these other women who are so interested in Charles? I don't mean do you know them casually, but do you know anything about them, and can you tell me where they live?'

'I know a few of them, but not very well. I can give you the addresses of several, if it will help.'

'It certainly will. Do you know the address of the flat where you and John were kept prisoner?'

'No, only that it's in the West End. We went in Garcia's car, and the blinds were drawn. I didn't notice anything except that it was a big block of flats. It must have been in the West End, or near, because it didn't take us long to get there.'

'Did John know the place?'

'No. There was a chauffeur, and Garcia was talking to John

most of the journey, so he didn't notice much about it. He realized afterwards that he'd been completely fooled by Garcia.'

'Did he say what work he did with Garcia?'

'No. You—you don't know John. He hates being proved wrong. I think he thought that Garcia would help him to break Charles's influence on me; that seemed to be his main reason for having anything to do with him.'

'I see.'

Dawlish leaned back in his chair and looked steadily at her. It had done her good to talk. What she said hadn't helped a great deal, except to confirm that Charles had this overwhelming attraction for women; and that he hadn't used it to his own discredit—that he had been completely convinced of the good work done by his Circle, although he didn't know what that work was.

Fay said anxiously: '*Have* I helped?'

Dawlish said: 'We can tell the police that John is in a block of flats in or near the West End, it'll give them some idea where to look. It clears up a lot of the picture, too. And it throws Charles up in a fairly good light.'

Fay said staunchly, 'He *is* good. I can't help what John says, or all these stories he's discovered, but Charles is *good*. He isn't interested in himself as a person, only as an instrument through which strange forces work. I've never known him vicious, spiteful or malicious—only impatient, because I care for him in a way he doesn't care for me. I want to help him; from the first moment I saw him, I've wanted to help him. Please believe me, Mr. Dawlish, he's a good man.'

As she spoke, the door opened.

Not even Dawlish had heard Charles come downstairs and cross the hall. But he came in now, smiling, normal. He closed the door and walked across the room to Fay. He held out his hands to her, and she took them hesitantly at first; then gripped them tightly. All the anxiety and the weariness seemed to be drawn out of her; it was as if something of the man's inward strength—and now it was great strength—sustained her.

'Charles, I was so frightened for you.'

'I know, I know.'

He drew her closer—and Felicity, catching Dawlish's eye, hurried to the door. Outside in the hall he looked quizzically at her.

'Leave them alone,' Felicity said. 'Whatever it is between them, we're not wanted.'

Abruptly the telephone bell rang.

'Call out and tell 'em we'll answer upstairs,' said Dawlish, 'and then hop round to the window and listen, in case they start speaking first—and watch, in case they listen in!' He hurried upstairs and strode across the bedroom to the telephone. 'Hallo? Dawlish speaking.'

'Hold on, please; I have a call for you.'

He held on, thinking of Fay's story, accepting, rejecting, reserving for further contemplation.

A man said: 'Dawlish?'

The voice was Garcia's.

CHAPTER FIFTEEN

THE TRANCE

'Yes, this is Dawlish.'

'Has the girl arrived?'

'She has.'

'You'd better do what she wants.'

'Don't you mean what you want?'

'It amounts to the same thing. You'll have a parcel in the post very soon if you don't send Horden back to me.'

'I like surprise presents.'

'You won't like this one. It will be John Downing's head.'

The threat came out casually; there was no effort at emphasis, no attempt to curdle Dawlish's blood; but the manner of it made him feel cold, and told him more than he already knew about Garcia. Outside, the constable by the gate stood with his back to the house, ruminating; if he looked round, Dawlish could beckon him and perhaps pass on a message to trace this call. But would Garcia call from anywhere that would be easily traced?

'That would be inconvenient for Downing certainly, but hardly so for me.'

'Great man, aren't you?'

'Not great enough to be worried by the threatened decapitations of men I do not know.'

'What happens to Downing will be an earnest of what will happen to friends of yours. Close friends. Even intimates.'

Dawlish said: 'I don't think I'll worry, thanks. I'm keeping Charles. By the way, and purely as a reciprocal courtesy, I strongly advise you to leave the country. The police—'

Garcia laughed. 'With every port and airfield watched? Do you take me for a fool?'

'As a matter of fact, and since you put it so bluntly, I do.'

'It's your mistake Dawlish.' Garcia paused, then went on hurriedly: 'Get this into your thick head. I want Horden, and I'm going to get him. And I want him by eight o'clock tomorrow night. I'll have a messenger waiting for him at Leicester Square Underground Station. Horden will know the messenger. Don't follow him, and don't try any tricks, or—'

He broke off; and the line went dead.

Dawlish put the receiver down very thoughtfully, hesitated, and then banged the cradle up and down. Garcia's voice still rang in his ears. He couldn't shut out the vivid mental image of his threat. The operator was a long time answering. When she came on, he said: 'Inspector Allen, local police, please.'

'The police station? Hold on, please.'

'Inspector Allen speaking.'

Dawlish said: 'The man Garcia has just telephoned me. I don't know where he spoke from, but you'd probably be wise to trace the call and see whether the Yard can get their hands on him.'

Allen's voice was brisk and confident, and when Dawlish put the receiver down, the thought of Downing's severed head was less insistent.

He went to the window and then restlessly returned and put through a call to the Yard.

Trivett was in his office, and hadn't yet heard from Allen. He listened, his terse comments studiously avoiding the main purpose of Fay's visit and Garcia's call.

'We'll look out all the blocks of flats, but it'll take time, and they may have gone from there,' he said.

'So you've not traced Garcia?'

'We don't know much about him yet, but we're learning,' said Trivett. 'He has a lot of influential friends—wealthy members of the Stock Exchange, big holders in industrial and commercial stocks—some of the best brains in the country.'

'Know any of them?'

'Three or four.'

'Do they happen to have young and pretty wives?'

Trivett said slowly: 'Two of them have.'

'Bill, when are you going to tell me why you're behaving as you are, and what you want me to do?'

'Just keep at it,' said Trivett. 'It won't be long before our trails cross at the place I want them to.'

'Still looking for Charles Horden?'

'Ask me again in the morning.'

Dawlish said: 'All right, keep your little mystery,' and put down the receiver.

Felicity came in, but, after a quick look at him, made no comment. Dawlish glanced restlessly out of the window.

'I wish I knew just what Trivett wants me to find, I've never known him quite so mysterious.'

Felicity said gently: 'Who was the call from, Pat?'

'Garcia.'

'*What?*'

'Large as life and full of spleen, and most remarkably confident. Is there a connection between Trivett's caution and Garcia's confidence, I wonder?' Dawlish shrugged his shoulders. 'What happened downstairs while I was on the telephone?'

'They sat together on the sofa.'

'Did they listen in?'

'I don't think they heard the telephone. They didn't exactly behave like passionate lovers, though.'

'Give Charles time,' said Dawlish. 'Well—what's the set-up for tonight?'

'Aren't you the Boss?'

'I never have been in this house,' said Dawlish, laughing, 'but it's soothing to keep up the fiction. Let's see—police on guard outside. Ted, Tim, you and me, Fay and Dr. Corbett, all at the seance. It's a pity we can't have one or two more whom Charles doesn't know; with only Corbett present he'll spot the believer.'

'Joan's coming; she telephoned while you were day dreaming this afternoon. And, Pat—'

'Hm-hm?'

'Why not let Norah come in?'

'*What?* Hysterics for breakfast?'

'She was strongly influenced by him, wasn't she? She's told me about it. She says she's sure he has "the gift". I don't know whether she means the same kind of gift as he did, but—one thing is certain; she's already conditioned to believe that whatever he says and does is right. It would thin out the blanket of scepticism, wouldn't it?'

'All right, we'll have her,' agreed Dawlish. 'What time is Joan coming? For dinner?'

'Yes.'

'Well, Ted will be pleased about that,' said Dawlish.

He went to the window. The first shadow of dusk was falling over the land. Felicity came to his side, and they stood silently, Dawlish watching the darkening countryside and Felicity looking at him. At last she said:

'It's worrying you, isn't it?'

'Yes. Badly. I can face the normal, but I'm all at sea with this. Charles and Corbett take psychic phenomenon for granted, but I can't. What are we going to see tonight? And what is behind it all? Garcia is a power of sorts among men of great wealth. Some of their wives have been influenced by Charles. The whole set-up makes complete confusion—or is there a simple answer?' He laughed shortly. 'The one thing I'm very sure of is that it's *not* to be found in the occult. Looking forward to the show?'

Felicity said: 'In one way; in another, I'm scared. I have a feeling that something really frightening might happen.'

Dawlish looked round sharply. There were few sounds that his abnormally sharp hearing didn't pick up; but for the second time in an hour the opening of the door and the arrival of Charles took him completely by surprise.

'I hope I haven't disturbed you,' Charles said. 'But if we are to sit this evening, we shall have to start getting ready.'

Dawlish said sharply: 'Who told you we were going to try it this evening?'

'Aren't we?' asked Charles.

'Yes. I still don't know how you found out.'

'Does it matter?' asked Charles levelly. 'If you are asking whether anyone has informed me—no, they haven't, Mr. Dawlish. You must grant me a little perspicacity. I hope you will allow Fay to join the Circle; and perhaps your maid. I believe their presence will help me to give you the practical results you want.'

Dawlish said: 'As you wish.'

'Thank you. And I hope one of you will soon be free, so that I can tell you what is needed.'

*　*　*

Felicity said: 'He is uncanny.'

'A rum beggar, certainly. He jolted me about one thing. What are we going to do with Fay?'

'I've taken it for granted that she will stay here until everything's over,' said Felicity quietly.

The drawing-room was dark. Not just with the darkness of night, but pitch. The heavy curtains had been drawn across, and every outlet covered. There was no light in the hall; no gleam anywhere. The only sound was the muted breathing of the people gathered together. Upright chairs had been brought in from the other rooms and placed in a wide circle. Charles sat with his back to the fireplace, invisible; Fay was on Dawlish's right, nearly opposite Charles; there was no possibility of collusion between them. Ted and Tim were on either side of the clairvoyant, Joan next to her husband, then Felicity and Dawlish, Fay, the Professor and Norah.

Dawlish tried to think of ordinary everyday things; and found himself thinking of the Professor, who had walked briskly up the drive a quarter of an hour before the appointed time, greeted Charles affably, but shown no particular interest in him, approved the arrangements, and begged that there should be no light at all.

Even to Dawlish the darkness was unnerving.

Felicity, clutching his hand tightly, was trembling. All were holding hands, and he remembered the last whispered words which Charles had uttered: 'Hold my hands tightly; whatever I do, or say, *don't let me go.*'

Since then there had been no sound.

There were no props; no planchette board and pencil or crayon; no hidden lights, no cloaks, or shrouds—nothing but the group of people sitting in the pitch darkness holding hands in a muffled silence, which made their muted breath sound like the breaking of waves on a distant shore. Now and again as someone shifted, a chair creaked.

Charles said: 'Please.'

Felicity started—Dawlish heard the others move, like an uneasy sigh.

'Please understand.' It was Charles's normal voice, but low-pitched, pleading. 'I ask again, most emphatically and solemnly: don't, *under any circumstances whatever*, let me go.'

No one responded.

Tim and Ted, their hands enormous, their grip like steel, had no fear that Charles's narrow wrists could escape them.

Silence—

Outside, a cordon of police were stationed near the house at Dawlish's express request, reinforced by an order from Trivett. Trivett had sensed what was going to happen here, no doubt about that; Trivett wanted it to happen. There were a dozen policemen, and it would be impossible for anyone to break through the ring and come to attack the silent group— that Circle which sat in darkness.

'*Please*,' whispered Charles.

It was an anguished sound. Dawlish stared towards it, but could see nothing. Charles was dressed in his ordinary clothes, had nothing in his pockets. Dawlish had been through them; had felt the linings, had made sure nothing was hidden which might help Charles to produce effects and fake a demonstration. Nothing *could* be faked; not even by Corbett, who had asked that he also should be searched, because he wanted to help convince the unbelievers.

Charles groaned; no doubt about that sound, it was a groan, as of a man in physical pain. The Professor drew in his breath.

Charles groaned again.

Well, anyone could groan; sounds would prove nothing. It

was a convincing sound nevertheless; heard anywhere else it would spread alarm immediately.

Charles began to breathe more heavily, deep breaths which seemed to shake his body. It was easy to imagine him writhing, to imagine his lips parted and his eyes staring in agony. This went on for a long time; minutes which seemed like hours. Felicity stirred, and her hand grew colder in Dawlish's grasp. So did Fay's; Fay's grip was tight enough to hurt, but he didn't try to ease it.

Charles whispered an unintelligible word; at least it came from the direction of his chair and the fireplace, but it might have been anyone's voice; it had no depth, was a hollow sound, an unreal whisper.

He said: 'Can you hear me?' and drew the words out so that they were like a sigh, repeated it twice. 'Can—you—hear-me?'

Was he speaking? Was it his voice? Could anyone alter their voice, to make it sound as if it were agony to utter a word? Dawlish had an impression of a man suffering intense physical pain; a creature tortured. But there was just a group of people sitting in a circle and holding hands.

'*Ye-es*, I can hear you.' That *was* Charles.

And then the light came . . .

It was a faint glimmer at first; hardly light, just luminosity above Charles's head; not far above, for the first thing Dawlish *saw* was the golden hair, with its silken curls; it was a small halo of light, and gradually it spread; it did not increase in brilliance, but covered a much wider area, showing Charles's forehead beaded with sweat. It showed his eyes, closed tightly; his cheeks drawn and colourless. It showed nothing else— not even the mirror behind, nor was the light reflected in the mirror, or Ted or Tim touched by it. It seemed to come *out* of Charles.

He groaned; his eyelids twitched; he writhed and rolled his head to and fro. The light spread. His mouth was open, as if he were trying to scream but could not; yes, this was a man in torment. His shoulders moved as he resisted the pain.

Did he *feel* this?

Was it reality or some fantastic illusion?

Charles—no, *not* Charles. That hollow, whispering voice came again, *and it didn't come from his lips.* They were set now; his mouth was tightly closed, as if he were trying not to speak, but the voice came out of the light.

'Save—her. *Save*—her.'

The silence; and the light, which became like a mist and yet did not hide Charles's face, showed it more clear. After his words, his mouth opened and he gritted his teeth and his body seemed convulsed.

Then he stopped, and and the voice came.

'Let me go. *Let me go.*'

Dawlish thought: Hold him, Ted! He checked the words which rose to his lips, tried to see the two big men, and could not. This wasn't normal light, it was just radiance which came from Charles; it showed only Charles.

'*Let me go.*' His shoulders moved; his arms moved upwards. Dawlish heard a grunt—undoubtedly from Ted. It was as if Ted were making a great, but unsuccessful, effort to hold tightly. Charles held invisible hands and his wrist turned this way and that, as if he were trying to free himself; but the invisible grip remained. A chair creaked.

Charles relaxed, his hands fell to his side, out of sight; only his face showed.

'*Save her—save her—save them all.*'

'*Save—them—all.*'

'*Save them.*'

The voice stopped. Charles stood up with a swift movement, but his hands were still held by those invisible fingers. He struggled and fought to free himself, and pulled one hand free. Tim cried: '*He's got away!*' The words sounded like bullets.

'Hold him, hold him—and don't break the Circle. Get him back.' That was the Professor, anguish in his voice. 'Don't break the Circle.'

The free hand stopped moving, seemed to clutch at nothing again; the fingers began to writhe in the air—but they weren't so clearly visible now, the mistiness was greater, the light was dimming. The voice came again, but was unintelligible, just a hollow whispering sound. When it stopped, Charles made another great effort, and held his hands high in the air. His teeth were bared, the sweat poured down his forehead and his cheeks, but he was fading, fading fast.

Dawlish whispered to Fay: 'Is the Professor still with you?'

'Yes.'

'Has been all the time?'

'Yes.'

'Let me go,' said Dawlish.

He drew his hands free, pushed his chair back and went across the room, felt the door with outstretched hand, turned and saw the fantasy fading—and then pressed down the switch. Light blazed out, dazzling the others—but he was ready for it. He saw Ted and Tim, standing, holding like grim death on to the frail wrists—and Charles, erect, lips writhing.

'Put the light out!' cried the Professor. 'Put it out!'

Charles opened his mouth wide and screamed; as if his soul were being torn from his body. Then he collapsed. He would have fallen but for Ted and Tim.

CHAPTER SIXTEEN

BRUISES

'Charles!' sobbed Fay. 'Charles!' She tore herself free and rushed across the room. There the two big men stood stupidly, as if they had no idea what had really happened. Fay raised Charles's head. '*Charles!*'

The Professor came across to them, just an ugly little man with anxiety shining out of his eyes. He put an arm round her shoulders and soothed her.

'He will be all right, he will be all right. Put him on the sofa, please.'

Ted lifted Charles and carried him to the sofa, which had been pushed into a corner of the room.

The Professor turned to Dawlish and said: 'I think perhaps you were right, but I hoped there would be a further manifestation. You have no doubts now about his gift, I trust.'

'*Doubts!*' gasped Tim.

Felicity went across the room and joined Fay. Norah still sat in her chair, eyes wide open, breath coming in short, sharp gasps. Joan Beresford, dark and plump, sat motionless, a strange, strained look on her face. Tim and Ted approached Dawlish and held out their hands—Tim's left, Ted's right. There were red, swollen patches on them; and on Tim's, long deep scratches.

Tim still seemed dazed.

'See that?'

Ted said: 'I wouldn't have believed it. I just wouldn't have believed it. How I held on to him I don't know. I've never felt anything like it. His fingers were like steel. *Look!*'

'Thought he'd broken mine.' Tim's voice held a strange note. 'I tell you, Pat, he was like a demon.'

'And—that light,' said Ted hoarsely.

Dawlish said: 'Yes, I know. I should bathe those bruises and put some salve on 'em. Better try to be normal now, or we'll be in trouble with the girls.' Normal! He had never felt less normal in his life, but he left the two men and stood in front of Norah. 'It's all right, Norah; everything's over.'

The Professor said quietly: 'I should leave her alone, Mr. Dawlish; she will be perfectly all right when Horden has recovered, and I don't think that will be long.'

Charles lay with his head on a cushion, apparently asleep. His forehead and cheeks were still damp, but he showed no other sign of the struggle. Dawlish picked up his limp right arm and examined the fingers and the wrists; there were no marks.

Felicity said: 'Well *some*thing happened.' Her voice wasn't steady. 'What did it mean, Pat? Save her—save them all? *Who* did he mean?'

'That's one practical thing that seems to have come out of it,' Dawlish said.

The Professor was by his side.

'The only one?' He looked up keenly. 'Haven't you had a practical demonstration of the existence of forces which you hadn't previously believed to exist? You might think you imagined the light and the voice; you did *not* imagine the bruises on your friends' wrists. During those few minutes Horden was possessed by a power, or person, different from his normal self—another body, another spirit, call it what you like. He was the husk; the other had taken complete possession. Don't say that wasn't practical. You saw it, you have evidence of it. And everyone here saw it.'

Fay cried: 'He's waking up!'

'There is no need to worry, Norah; you will sleep well tonight, you will feel no unpleasant effects,' said Charles gently. 'I should go straight to bed, and have a cup of something hot before you go.'

'I'll look after her,' said Felicity.

'You're very kind.' Charles turned from Norah and looked at Joan, pale and dark-eyed. 'You also felt the pain, Mrs. Beresford.'

Joan said: 'Yes.'

'I think if I dare to advise you, you should not go any farther along the road of this experience. You are a subject, who would lose yourself completely in it; you have your family, and it would hurt them. I do not think you are strong enough to help the world in its adversity, but I think you would try, and suffer over-much in consequence.'

Felicity linked her arm in Joan's, and tactfully and encouragingly steered both her and Norah out of the room. Fay alone remained, looking pale and wan as she smiled across at Charles; she seemed to have suffered less from the strain than the others.

Ted and Tim came in, their wrists bathed and tended.

'Did I hurt you very much?' asked Charles.

'Plenty,' said Tim. 'I shouldn't like to try conclusions with you in that mood, on your own.'

'Usually I am manacled,' said Charles simply. 'There is a danger that during the trance I might try to harm myself or do harm to others; that is why I am usually made quite fast to my chair and my companions. I thought that this would help to convince you more than anything else, Mr. Dawlish.' He pointed to the swollen wrists. 'You might disbelieve the evidence of your ears and your eyes during the demonstration, you cannot reject a tangible fact.'

Dawlish didn't answer.

The Professor said simply: 'He is convinced, but, like them all, he fights against belief.'

Ted said stubbornly: 'I still don't believe it. What did you mean when you said "*Save her—save them—save them all*"?'

'Did I say that?' Charles frowned. 'I really don't know; I know very little of what happens, and I hear practically nothing. This I can tell you, Dawlish. There is only one solution to the troubles of the world, and the solution is not to be found by men who are practical, realistic and sceptical. The spirit of the world is sick, and I am trying to help to heal it.'

Dawlish said: 'Through Garcia?'

'Will you forgive me if I don't attempt to answer that question?' Charles asked. 'I might be able to make suggestions about Garcia later, but now—isn't it your task to translate anything you heard, Mr. Dawlish?'

Dawlish said to Trivett: 'Bill, I'm coming up to see you, at the Yard—not at the flat. Meanwhile, I think you ought to get the names and addresses of all the women associated with Garcia's friends, and any you can associate with Horden. Then check on where they are.'

'Why?'

'That's what I'm coming to tell you. But don't lose any time. There's a chance you'll be extremely sorry if you do.'

'All right,' said Trivett. 'How long will you be?'

'An hour and a half.'

'I'll be waiting for you.'

The stars were bright and the wind was cold. Only the head-lamps of the car gave light, and revealed the tapering telegraph poles, the hedges and the grass verges. Now and again a car loomed up, but Dawlish avoided towns where possible. Tim sat by his side. They had left the others at *Four Ways*: and the police watch would remain all night; there should be no danger at the house.

Felicity hadn't wanted Dawlish to leave, but hadn't stopped him.

Tim said suddenly: 'It's crazy!'

'It happened.'

'I feel as if I've been in another world.'

'Yes, it's like that.'

'Could it have been faked?'

'I don't think there's a chance in a million. I don't know what the racket is yet, and I'm not convinced that Charles is as innocent as he appears to be, but—he's no fraud at this psychic stuff. And it looks as if Garcia uses him pretty successfully. Question—why?'

'What about this warning? Do you really think—'

'I'm trying not to think, but to let events speak for them-selves. Be as rational as you like, but it was a shaking experi-ence. Taken at its face value, one woman in particular is in grave danger tonight, and others are likely to be in danger soon. Let's see whether events prove that.'

Tim said: 'I hope they don't.'

Dawlish slowed down, until the car came to a halt.

'Why?' asked Tim.

'Can't get my mind clear,' said Dawlish. 'There's something

hovering about the edge that just won't come out and be recognized.'

They lit cigarettes, and smoked two a-piece before Dawlish said:

'No go.'

'No hurry,' said Tim.

'There is. I shouldn't have wasted time.'

It was nearly half past twelve when they reached the heart of London. There was little traffic about, and few lights in the windows. Yet buses and trams were still rattling along, and there were signs of activity at Scotland Yard when Dawlish swung the wheel of the Bentley into the courtyard.

Dawlish left the car and hurried up the steps of the new building, followed by Tim. The door of Trivett's office was open, and a man stood flatly in front of his desk.

'Well, try to find her,' Trivett said. 'The minute there's any news let me know.'

'Right.'

The man, dark and bullet-headed, pushed past Dawlish and Tim as if he didn't see them, and hurried along the corridor. Trivett beckoned them in, as the telephone bell rang. He listened, then said: 'That's all right, then. Is there any news of Garcia? . . . Hmph, all right.' He rang off, as Dawlish and Tim sat down.

'Well, Pat, you've given us a nice job.'

'Anyone missing?'

'Four, so far.'

Tim exclaimed: 'No!' and then lapsed into silence.

'Who are they?' asked Dawlish.

'Women who have known Charles Horden and whose wealthy husbands are among Garcia's friends. I've checked, and found that they're all men of good reputation; no funny business as far as I can find out. The women may turn up of course—two of them are with their husbands, and no one at their homes knows where they are, except that they're eating somewhere after going to a show. The other two left home this afternoon. They were expected back this evening, but as yet there has been no sign of them.'

'Husbands?'

'Didn't report it, didn't want to talk when we questioned them, but finally admitted that they are worried, because this has happened before. One of them blames Horden.'

'And knowing that you want Horden, still didn't report?'

'No.'

'Distinctly odd,' said Dawlish softly.

'Even I see that. Now, Pat, what's it all about? You wouldn't have raised a scare like this unless you had a good reason.' Dawlish said: 'Do you still *not* want to know about the clair-voyant who put on a show at *Four Ways* tonight?'

'I thought that would be it,' said Trivett. 'I'll save you asking questions, Pat. Horden's been giving a lot of special demonstra-tions. He's influenced a great number of extremely odd people—all of them wealthy. It's all been innocent enough—as far as I've been able to find out. I've twice had men at this Circle. The demonstrations have been pretty effective, and, on the face of it, no hint of fraud. But there were always several of the same men there—who could have helped a fake. I wanted Horden to give a show where there wouldn't be a chance of faking anything—I hope you fixed it.'

Trivett seemed fully satisfied that he had taken the right course, nor did he seem to think there was really anything exceptional about it. A hardened Yard man, trying out the claims of a clairvoyant with absolute seriousness and prepared to let a wanted man stay free until it had been done!

'I did,' Dawlish said slowly.

'No possibility of faking?'

'I couldn't see any, I took stringent precautions. The only stranger to me among the circle was a Dr. Corbett; he's the man I asked you to check on this afternoon. He wasn't near Horden, and they didn't touch hands and Corbett didn't move from his seat during the business. I needn't describe what happened.'

'The groans and manifestations of light, the struggles to free himself from anything that held him back, and the hollow, whispering voice?'

'That's it.'

'And the message was about these women, in danger?'

'First an urgent plea to save one of them, then the others.' Dawlish rubbed his chin. 'You know, Charles Horden could be neck deep in this racket. He could know that something is planned against one of the women tonight; it could have been planned days ago. And he *could* have put this across, to try to impress us.'

Trivett said: 'Do you think he did?'

'I don't. I wouldn't rule out the possibility, but I don't think there was anything faked about the seance. There were some indications that he has second sight or is psychic—give it what name you like. Horden wasn't told when we were to hold the seance. But he knew. I'd put Charles Horden in a class by himself, but I know where to put Garcia. He's among the worst types of big-time crooks we've ever come across. Have you learned anything more about him?'

'That he's always been in the Circle, that's all. So it shook you, Pat?'

'It did.'

'I sent the steadiest, most difficult to impress feet-firm-on-the-ground men I've got to the try-outs before, and they were also shaken.'

'What actually was said then?' asked Dawlish.

As Trivett opened a file of papers on the desk, selected two, and handed them across, the telephone bell rang.

'Have a look at these,' he said, and picked up the receiver.

Tim read one, Dawlish the other; they were statements which had been lifted out of the detectives' reports on the seances they had visited. They had written down, from memory, what had been said in that hollow, whispering voice. Dawlish read: '*Be very quick. If you are not too late it will multiply threefold. The grey and the blue are the best. The number is* 195345.' Dawlish took Tim's in exchange for his own. The message was less coherent, as if the detective had caught only snatches of it. '*The yellow is of great importance and there is . . . of it. No one . . . too much.*' There were pencilled notes, saying: 'Believe the omissions were (a) "too much" and (b) "wants", but cannot be sure.'

Tim said: 'Rigmarole to me.'

'I doubt if it is to Trivett.'

'I haven't got my breath back properly,' said Tim in a thoughtful voice. 'If Charles puts up shows like this to order, he's convincing plenty of people. You know, Pat, it would take a pretty tough nut *not* to be convinced.'

Trivett put down the receiver.

'They've found two of the four missing women, one of them with her husband. That leaves us one pair, and one woman, still unaccounted for.'

'Who's the woman by herself?'

Trivett said casually: 'Lady Marrick.'

Tim whistled.

Dawlish ran his finger along the bridge of his nose. He didn't need Trivett to describe Lady Marrick, or to tell him anything about her husband. Sir George Marrick was one of the few money barons of the post-war era. He was known as the wealthiest man in Great Britain; he had made fantastic deals on the Stock Exchange; and recently he had married a girl, half his age, from the theatre—a rare beauty.

'Is Marrick the man who blames Horden?' asked Dawlish, 'and whose wife has disappeared before?'

'Yes.'

'What does he say about her and Horden?'

'He's rational about it. He doesn't think there's any question of seduction or luring her away; he blames his wife for making a fool of herself. Since she's known Horden she's attended a lot of seances, and since she knows he disapproves, has done so secretly.'

'Is Marrick a friend of Garcia's?'

Trivett said: 'No. He's never been at a sitting.'

'I'd like to see Marrick,' said Dawlish. 'Think you can fix it easily? If not, I'll go along and tackle him myself.'

'Why?'

'To find out whether—'

The telephone bell rang, and Trivett, with a shrug, lifted the instrument from the cradle.

'Yes, speaking. Are you *sure*? . . . All right . . . Get the squad cars out and warn the division . . . I'll come myself.'

He banged down the receiver, and sprang to his feet.

'Marrick's had a telephone message, saying that he won't see his wife again. But she was seen, just after half past nine, entering a block of flats in Pelham Court. Care to come?'

CHAPTER SEVENTEEN

GARCIA'S FLAT

Two police cars hummed through the quiet of the night and Dawlish's Bentley followed them. Only a few night prowlers glanced casually at the speeding cars.

'Of all phenomena, this is the strangest,' Tim remarked.

'Meaning what?'

'All resources of Scotland Yard, as they're so fond of saying, put on this job. Trivett just pressed a button and everything worked at once—and all because you told him it was worth it. He's not often as willing to believe you as that, is he?'

Dawlish said: 'Trivett's told us a little, but there's a hell of a lot he's kept to himself. From the beginning this was a smelly business—judging from the way he acted. When he saw me at Wyman Street after Charles's uncle was killed, he didn't appear to take the affair seriously. We just went round to his flat for a quiet nip, as if one murder more or less didn't matter.'

'It's clear enough to me that he was after you for the job, Pat. Knew that if he behaved oddly you'd wonder why and get on with it. He wanted you in from the beginning.'

'It could be.'

'Lay you a fiver that it is. And he knew something big was brewing. He was all set for tonight's show—he knows something of what's behind it, and he's scared. The Yard only mobilizes like this on a big job. It wouldn't surprise me if Trivett isn't under orders to get it settled, never mind how.'

'Hm. Marrick is a power behind the scenes, you know.'

'What kind of power? Money?'

'Not just that. He's a close friend of Cabinet Ministers, and has important overseas connections, vast stocks in all kinds of unlikely foreign undertakings. He's one with many of the big-money American barons—the better kind. There's never been a whisper against him, as far as I've heard. Remember anything?'

'No, not to his discredit. His marriage hit the headlines; many thought it a pity, man of fifty losing his head over a girl of twenty. Hal-lo! Looks as if we're getting hot. I say, Pat—take an eyeful of *that.*'

They swung round a corner. Immediately in front of them were seven or eight police cars, all with their headlights shining on a large concrete block of flats, the white walls dazzling under the blaze. Dozens of men in plain clothes and in uniform were moving about, many of them going towards the back of the flats. Trivett's car pulled up near the entrance, Dawlish immediately behind him. Two men stood in the brightly lit porch, and two red-uniformed commissionaires hovered in the background. These were luxury flats, likely homes for millionaires.

A burly man, who had been in Trivett's office earlier that night, was saying:

'She went into 27a, sir—that's on the top floor.'

'What have you done subsequently?' Trivett asked him.

'Made no approach to the flat, blocked the fire escape, and set a watch from the lift and from the flat opposite. We haven't heard anything inside, there are no lights at the windows.'

'Right. We'll go up,' said Trivett.

'Come on,' said Tim, taking Dawlish's arm.

Dawlish said: 'Hold it.'

Another car, a sleek black Rolls-Royce, turned into the road, and came to an abrupt standstill. Trivett and two other men went into the building; Dawlish stayed near the entrance, while the driver of the Rolls-Royce got out.

He was a tall, powerful-looking man in a dark overcoat and evening dress. There was strength in the man—in his walk, in his carriage, in his square jaw, well-cut lips and handsome, expressionless face.

'The Great Marrick,' murmured Tim.

'We'll go up with him,' said Dawlish.

As Marrick approached the front doors, two policemen drew together, to block his path.

'Yes, sir?'

'I have come to see Suprintendent Trivett. My name is Marrick.'

Marrick's voice was hard and clipped.

'The Superintendent said no one else was to come in, sir,' said the constable respectfully. 'Except these two gentlemen.' He look at Dawlish and Tim. 'I'll send a message up to him, if you like.'

Dawlish stepped forward.

'It'll be all right, constable, Sir George is with us.'

Dawlish took Marrick's arm and led him past the guard. Tim brought up the rear. The front hall was empty now, except for the commissionaires. One of them went towards an empty lift.

'Mind if we walk?' Dawlish said.

He felt the raking glance from impressive grey eyes.

'Very well.'

They went to the carpeted stairs and Marrick added: 'You are Mr. Dawlish, I believe.'

'Yes.'

'What can you tell me?'

'Only what I expect you know—that Lady Marrick was seen to come here earlier in the evening.'

'Do the police know which flat she visited?'

'Yes.'

'Do they think that Horden is here?'

'They know he isn't. Marrick, I'd like to help. I can't unless I know more than I do now. You've kept a lot back from the police, haven't you?'

Marrick said: 'You have a reputation for making wild guesses.'

'And you have a reputation for never taking wild risks. It will be a wild risk, however, if you hold out any longer. Garcia's been trying to get you into this Circle of his, hasn't he? You've been fighting against him and trying to influence others who've joined to leave him. Right?'

'Yes.'

'Has he threatened before?'

'He has.'

They walked steadily up the dimly lit staircase, their footsteps making no sound.

'In what way?'

'He has threatened to alienate my wife's affections.'

'Using Charles Horden?'

'Yes, rather more successfully than I like. My wife is an impressionable woman, extremely sensitive, and likely to be easily influenced by a man with unusual gifts.'

'Did Garcia ask for anything more specific than your membership of this Circle?'

'No.'

'What was his chief line of sales talk?'

Marrick hesitated before he said: 'He tried several. At first, that he was organizing a group of industrialists to corner the world markets. Afterwards he became a benefactor to mankind, and said that the politicians were making a hash of world affairs and that industrialists should get together and see what they could do. Apparently he thought that they would be able to do much better than the politicians.'

'And you disagreed?' murmured Dawlish.

'Only a fool would disagree. The way to work is by influencing the politicians, not usurping their duties. I am not unaware of my obligations.'

'What was his third line?'

'One, I think, almost of desperation,' said Marrick.

He hadn't smiled and hadn't raised his voice. He spoke with the utmost economy of words.

'Garcia said that there was no hope for the future unless mankind forsook the material for the spiritual—that forces higher and greater than man must be harnessed to the fight against the Powers of Darkness.'

'And again you disagreed?'

'Only a fool would disagree with that too,' said Marrick dispassionately. They started up the next and final flight of stairs. 'I do not think the higher forces can be harnessed by Mr. Garcia or by Mr. Garcia's charlatan friends,' he added dryly.

'What did you think was behind it?'

'A wildcat scheme which would have a semblance of plausibility, and the purpose of getting money from me.'

'Some of your friends were converted, weren't they?'

'Yes.'

That came sharply.

'Did they help Garcia to influence you?'

Marrick smiled grimly.

'My friends know that it is a waste of time to try to influence me in that way. But you have commented on a peculiar thing, Dawlish. Not one of them, since joining the Circle, has uttered a word to me about it. I know that they meet regularly, and in secret.'

For Marrick, he was talking very freely. That betrayed the pressing sense of anxiety in his mind, and suggested that he knew of Dawlish sufficiently to trust him; yet behind every sentence there was a hint of reticence.

They were near the top landing now, and could see men standing up there.

Dawlish said: 'How were these friends of yours influenced in the first place?'

'In different ways. The majority through their wives or through a daughter—women were fascinated by Charles Horden, and persuaded their menfolk to go along and hear him. Once they went, they were converted.'

'And you still stood out?'

'You mean, *why* did I still stand out? Because I was convinced that Horden was a charlatan and Garcia a scoundrel.'

Dawlish stopped and put a hand on Marrick's arm.

'The last question: believing this, why didn't you tell the police what you thought?'

'I think we will see what the police have found,' said Marrick, as they reached the landing.

Trivett was there, and a man working on the lock of the door. Half a dozen plain clothes detectives stood around. All was quiet. Marrick made no attempt to speak to Trivett. His quietness was not assumed; it was the nature of the man. He was used to authority; to saying exactly enough to convey his meaning and not a word more.

The man at the door said expectantly: 'It's coming.'

He pushed gently, and then with greater force and the door

swung open. A small, square hall, with dark walls and one or two pieces of furniture showed dimly.

Dawlish and Marrick joined Trivett and the Inspector as they moved forward cautiously. Trivett, wearing gloves, pushed down an electric switch. Concealed lighting flooded the hallway.

'This place is empty.' The Inspector spoke regretfully. 'You can almost smell it.'

'No talking, please,' said Trivett curtly.

They stood listening intently, and there was no sound, no hint that anyone was in this flat, Trivett opened the first two doors. One opened into a sitting-room, the other into a small dining-room; the curtains of neither room were drawn, suggesting that no one had been in them since darkness had fallen. Trivett went along the passage and opened the next two doors—a bathroom and a bedroom. The muffled sound of their footsteps alone broke the stillness.

'Empty,' repeated the Inspector.

Marrick muttered: 'Do you think it is, Dawlish?'

'No.'

Trivett opened the door of a fifth room, from which opened another. Here there were signs of recent occupation. A mink coat hung carelessly across an easy chair; by it was a pair of gloves and a crocodile handbag.

There was a beading of sweat on Marrick's forehead; the controlled tension in the man was becoming unbearable. Now he stooped towards the chair and stretched out a hand for the bag.

'Don't touch that, please!'

Marrick said: 'It is my wife's.'

He ignored Trivett's command, and picked up the bag. He opened it, as if he were used to the fastening—and then his lips clamped together as he glanced inside. Dawlish saw a white card, caught a glimpse of printed lettering. Marrick stared at it, as Trivett came across to him, his voice harsh and peremptory.

'I asked you not to touch that. There may be fingerprints on it. Please do what I say.'

Stonily, as if every movement was an agony he was trained to suppress, Marrick withdrew the card.

'Sir George—' began Trivett.

Marrick said: 'I won't do any damage.'

He moistened his lips and read slowly, as words without meaning:

THIS CAN HAPPEN TO OTHERS

Trivett took the card, glanced at it, and turned away.

'Are you sure these are your wife's things, Sir George?'

'I am quite sure.'

Marrick hesitated, and then strode towards the inner door. It was shut, the key on the outside. He put out a hand to touch the key, but Dawlish, moving swiftly forward, shouldered him aside.

'If I were you, I wouldn't go in first,' he said quietly.

Marrick pushed past him, and flung the door open. There was a light on in the room, which was small, little more than a box room. Two arm-chairs, a small divan, and a table were the only furniture.

A woman lay on the divan.

She was dressed in a black dress, of simple cut; her shoes lay on the floor. One arm was raised almost to her shoulder; the other arm drooped over the side. She was small; almost as petite as Fay; even lying like that, she looked exquisite. But sight of her brought cold horror to Dawlish; he forgot Marrick as he stared in terrible fascination.

The blood drained from Trivett's face.

Marrick uttered a little, gasping cry, and swayed.

Dawlish shot out a hand to support him. Behind them, the burly sergeant whispered in a horrified voice:

'My God!'

The woman's body lay there, but not her head; it had been severed at the neck.

CHAPTER EIGHTEEN

MAN OF IRON

Trivett said: 'Out, all of you, please.' He was still pale, and there was a sick look in his eyes. 'Pat, look after Sir George. Wilson, send up the photographers first, then the others. Get the prints outside as quickly as you can—telephone for a police surgeon, get Dr. Arnold if possible.'

His voice, with its forced calm, brought to the room some degree of discipline, if not normality. Dawlish took Marrick's arm. He expected him to protest, but Marrick allowed himself to be led away, to the chair over which the mink coat hung so casually, and lowered into it. His complete collapse was like that of a man who would never lift his head again.

The burly Inspector called orders.

Trivett came out, and said in a low-pitched voice: 'Get him out of here.'

'Try questioning him, he knows more than he's said.'

'It'll be a waste of time,' said Trivett, but he touched Marrick's shoulder and said: 'I'm sorry about this, Sir George.' The words sounded inane. 'If there is anything at all you can tell us, this is the time—it might make the difference between catching the murderer and losing him.'

Marrick didn't speak, didn't move.

'What else can you tell us, Sir George?'

Trivett had no heart for this. He was still suffering from the shock; that sight would shock everyone who saw it. 'What does that card mean? What others did the murderer mean?'

Marrick didn't show any sign that he had heard him; the iron man had turned to stone.

Dawlish said: 'Marrick, other women may be in danger. Minutes might make all the difference to them. Whom else did he mean?'

Marrick sat there, staring at the floor.

Dawlish said harshly: 'Haven't you the guts to face the fact that you yourself are not entirely blameless? You knew she was in danger and you let her leave the house alone, without having her followed and guarded. Must you repeat the pattern, by now endangering the lives of others?'

Marrick looked slowly, sluggishly at Dawlish.

'I'm told she was a beauty,' Dawlish said. 'And I was also told that it was a love match. Love! Why, you—'

Trivett hissed: 'Dawlish!' Two of the detectives stared at Dawlish as if he had gone mad. Tim watched from the doorway, from where he could see the body on the bed as well as Dawlish and Marrick.

'If you'd taken ordinary care, it wouldn't have happened,' Dawlish said harshly. 'At least have the guts to—'

Marrick jumped up from the chair and struck at him. The savage blow caught him on the cheek and made him stagger back.

Dawlish fended him off, his voice of cold accusation still coming clearly.

'Why didn't you tell the police everything you knew? Out with it! What's the guilty secret, Marrick? *What was worth your wife's head?*'

A man said in a voice of sick horror: 'Stop him!'

The tension was unbearable. Marrick's fury had now taken complete possession of him; he got past Dawlish's guard with a violent blow on the chin. This time Dawlish returned it. Marrick's teeth snapped together and he swayed backwards; before he could regain his balance he fell heavily into the chair, his head resting on the soft, warm mink.

'For an exhibition of sheer savage cruelty, that's about the worst I've ever come across,' Trivett said icily. 'Have you lost your senses?'

Dawlish said: 'If you want cruelty, have a look in the next room. He took a risk with his wife, and lost. Now he's paying for it.'

'He'll pay plenty without help from you. Have you any reason at all for this—accusation?'

'Take a look at him, and ask yourself,' said Dawlish. 'And don't forget that you started this hunt because of a warning from Horden. Don't forget that Horden mentioned others. Use kid gloves on Marrick if you like, but you'll regret it.' He swung round. 'Come on, Tim, let's go.'

Tim said: 'Mind if I drive?'

'Nervous?'

'Of you, in this mood, yes.'

'If I was over-rough, it was necessary to be so.' Dawlish went to the far side of the car. 'Whatever Marrick knows, we've got to discover it—and he knows something of importance. Save your castigation for another day, will you?'

'None coming from me,' Tim said. 'I've never seen you put up a show that wasn't justified yet, and Marrick's behaviour backed you up. Trivett's jumpy about something—but he's not the type to be influenced by wealth, or men with influential friends.'

'He is, in this job.'

'That's where I stick.' Tim let in the clutch and eased the car away from the Rolls-Royce, which was immediately behind it. 'I can't see Bill in that role.'

'Not his fault—he has his orders. He's side-tracked them as best he can, given me a run for my money which I wouldn't have had otherwise, but some V.I.P.s are very much in the offing: He was shaken by that sight tonight, and he—well, why talk about it?'

'What's the next line?' asked Tim.

Dawlish didn't answer, and seemed to browse.

Tim's voice took on a thoughtful note.

'You know, I'm getting some delayed reaction. Although I experienced what actually happened at the seance, I wasn't altogether convinced by that show Charles put on. It did happen, but it needn't have been what it appeared to be, if you know what I mean.' He glanced at his wrists. 'I'm not forgetting this, either. The power of his grip was fantastic, but some people have a tremendous strength in their hands, and it can be developed. If he's trained himself to this, so as to make it look more genuine, that would be a natural explanation without the necessity of any funny business, I can't explain the light away, but— the thing is, finding that woman hit me in the stomach. Did Charles *know* what was going to happen? Or was it a warning out of the air, so to speak.'

Dawlish laughed shortly.

'It couldn't happen, but it did! Things are not what they seem. Tim, you're dead right. It isn't possible to accept what we've seen and heard as proof, and the warning about that woman stinks of fore-knowledge. Yet I'm inclined to believe in Charles. And I'm as worried as hell about the other women he—or his voice!—asked us to think about. So is Trivett, I fancy; but Trivett is still handicapped. Maybe after tonight he'll shake off his shackles.'

Tim shrugged. 'Well, where do we go from here?'

'Marrick's house, of course.'

'*What?*'

'My dear chap, we've only just started on the iron man,' said Dawlish. 'I'd like to have a look round before he gets home, and I doubt if Trivett will send him back just yet.'

Marrick lived at Number 27 Princes Street, which was near Kensington Gardens and was one of a row of all, stately houses in a wide road. There were few street lamps, and fewer lights showing from the handsomely curtained windows. They parked the car at a nearby corner, and walked to Number 27; it was in darkness.

'Do we just knock or do we break in?' asked Tim airily.

'Mind a spot of burglary?'

Tim said: 'Not so's you'd notice. But we might catch a packet, Pat.'

'I think it's worth taking the chance. Back or front, I wonder?'

'Front's quicker,' said Tim.

They approached the front door and stood in the porch, looking up and down the road. No one was in sight. A car passed, its engine whining on a high-pitched note. Dawlish left the cover of the porch and went down into the small area in front of the house. There was a semi-basement and a window with the blinds drawn, on a level with his waist. He listened, and heard nothing; bent down and started to work on the catch of the window. He thought little of the danger. He wanted to get in, and this way was the best way. But he recalled Felicity's warning that he mustn't take Tim and Ted too much for granted. It was one thing to risk a chance like this himself; another to expect Tim to do it. Tim hadn't argued, but was he happy about it? The influences behind Trivett might act harshly later on, and Tim's 'we might catch a packet' hadn't sounded too carefree.

Using his penknife, Dawlish forced the catch of the window.

He didn't open it, but shone a pencil torch on to the framework, seeking some sign of an electric wire; Marrick's house was probably fitted with a burglar-alarm system. Yes, there it was. Dawlish studied the window and the wire. There was only one way to get at it; break the window and work from the inside. He took out a handkerchief, and spread it over the glass.

Tim called: 'Easy.'

He came out of the porch and joined Dawlish in the well-like area: They crouched against the wall, close to the pavement, as plodding footsteps drew nearer.

'A Robert,' said Tim.

The policeman's shadow fell, vaguely, over the area. He flashed his torch on the front door of Number 27, and then passed on. Dawlish and Jeremy gave him three minutes before straightening up.

Dawlish said: 'Tim, let me have it straight, will you?'

'Ever known me not?'

'Would you prefer not to carry on?'

Tim laughed scornfully.

'Idiot! I'm right with you. I suppose Fel has been talking to you.'

'Felicity?'

'The same. She gave Ted and me a ten-minute drill on the

folly of doing everything you ask us to do. I think she thinks that if we cooled off these jobs, you would, too. We promised that we would, on suitable occasions, show a marked lack of interest. This isn't a suitable occasion. Can't blame Fel, you know; she gets badly shaken by these jobs. This one isn't any easier because she started it herself.'

Dawlish grinned, in a surge of relief.

'Tim, hold this handkerchief against the window for a moment will you? It'll deaden the sound of the smash.'

Tim spread the handkerchief out, Dawlish took his cigarette case from his pocket and struck the glass sharply; it didn't break at the first go. He tried again; a hollow booming note sounded.

'Not so loud,' whispered Tim.

Dawlish said: 'Wait a minute.' Using his torch again, he concentrated on the glass, then grinned wryly. 'My error. It's toughened glass, see the yellowish tinge? We can't break that without a hammer or a bullet.'

'So we're stumped.'

'Better try the front door,' said Dawlish. 'As the Robert's passed we'll probably be all right for a bit.'

They went back to the porch, and Dawlish took out his knife, and opened a blade that was in fact a skeleton key. He worked for five minutes, and then drew back.

'No go?'

'Special double lock, and proper tools are needed. It's not going to work, Tim.'

'We could try the back.'

'It'll be as well protected on the ground floor. Like to try some mountaineering?'

Tim laughed softly . . .

A narrow passage led to the back of the house, and a small

courtyard paved with flagstones. Here there were window-ledges and cornices—and there was a garden seat. Dawlish stood on the seat, and Tim joined him. Dawlish made a step with his hands, and Tim climbed on to his shoulder. Tim groped for a window-ledge, and whispered:

'Here's an open window.'

'Prise that wire loose. There's sure to be one.'

'Okay.'

Tim's feet were heavy on Dawlish's shoulders, but Dawlish waited patiently while Tim fiddled with the wire, using Dawlish's knife. Minutes passed slowly. Somewhere in the distance, radio music sounded. There were lights at the back of several houses, but none here. A church clock boomed the hour; one o'clock. Suddenly Tim said:

'Got it!'

Dawlish grunted. Tim pushed the window up, then took one foot off Dawlish's shoulder and wriggled through. They were in.

Dawlish muttered: 'Make for Marrick's room.'

'Look, old chap, if he's got any secrets he'll have 'em locked away in a safe or behind steel doors.'

'Could be,' said Dawlish. 'Let's have a look round. Odd that no one's about. Lonely lives, these iron men lead.'

He used the torch, and they looked into the four main rooms on the ground floor, finding nothing to suggest that Marrick used one for a study. The staircase creaked a little as they walked up—and Dawlish remembered the start of the case; the little man with the long nose, who had been at Wyman Street; it seemed a long time ago. As they crept slowly upwards, keeping close to the wall, Dawlish felt a quickening atmosphere of suspense and alarm. His heart began to thump for the first time since he had seen the headless body.

As they stood half-way up the stairs, Dawlish heard a sound, very faint but not far away.

'Someone about?' whispered Tim.

'Could be. Go a little farther up.'

Two steps higher their eyes were on a level with the landing—and they saw the light under a door. Covering the distance with cautious speed they approached the door and listened intently.

'Perhaps someone else had the same idea,' Tim suggested.

'Could be. Hold it.'

Dawlish groped for the handle of the door. Someone was moving about in this room; drawers opened and closed. He turned the handle and pushed gently. He could see a wardrobe; and as he pushed the door farther open, saw the mirror in front of the wardrobe. There was a reflection in it—the reflection of a woman. He could see that she sat at a dressing-table, brushing her hair—long, golden hair. He opened the door a little wider; it was just possible that she could see the door in the mirror, but she paid no attention. She wore a silken robe, over what appeared to be a nightdress. The room had twin beds; and there were touches of luxury everywhere.

Dawlish stepped inside, Tim followed—and the woman at the dressing-table continued to brush her hair. Her face was hidden from Dawlish, as theirs was from her, but he knew that if once she looked up she would see their reflection. Tim closed the door very gently while Dawlish stepped towards the woman— and he was only a yard behind her when she glanced into the mirror and saw him. She started violently and her lips opened, but Dawlish darted forward and covered her mouth with his hand, stifling her cry.

She was small; blue eyes stared at him in dread. She was lovely, too.

He said: 'If you say a word, you'll get hurt.'

He took his hand from her mouth, and she simply sat there, staring at him.

Tim said helplessly: 'It's *her*.'

'Yes, indeed,' said Dawlish. 'We have the pleasure of meeting Lady Marrick.'

CHAPTER NINETEEN

WILLING VICTIM

She whispered: 'Who—who are you? What do you want?'

She was as beautiful as Fay, and in some ways not unlike her. She didn't move, made no attempt to raise the alarm.

Dawlish said: 'If you keep quiet, you won't get hurt.'

She said: 'You're Dawlish, aren't you?'

'Who told you about me?'

'I read—the newspapers.'

It might be true; but she might be lying. That hardly mattered. The woman whom the police believed to be dead was sitting here, unharmed.

He said: 'You know you're in danger, don't you?'

'Yes.'

There was no doubt about her answer.

'I want you to come with us.'

'Where?'

'Not far. There's no time to dress, just put on a coat and some shoes—we've a car outside.'

'Aren't I—safe here?'

'No. Not tonight.'

She said: 'Why should I come?'

'Because I know where Charles Horden is.'

At mention of Charles's name, the fear faded from her eyes, she stretched out her hands as if in supplication.

'I mean it,' said Dawlish.

'I must see him.'

'You will, if you do as you're told.'

She stood up, and Dawlish watched her closely, but she made no attempt to shout or run towards the door. She opened the wardrobe and took out a fur coat; it looked almost a replica of the one which they had seen at the flat. She put it on, and then slipped her feet into a pair of shoes, eager to obey, a willing victim snared by the bait of Charles. Swiftly she folded some day clothes into a case, and stood waiting.

Dawlish said: 'I'll come later. You go with my friend.'

She nodded.

Tim said: 'My flat, of course?'

'Yes. Lady Marrick, I want you to tell Mr. Jeremy all about this affair from the beginning to the end. If you value your life, you won't hold anything back. Don't worry if it sounds unreasonable, illogical or crazy—just tell him what's behind your fear and why you're so willing to go away with him, why you want to see Horden so desperately.'

'I am willing, because I know I can trust you,' she said. 'Charles said so. Will you tell me one thing?'

'What?'

'Where is my husband?'

'He's all right.'

It was impossible to tell whether she thought that good news or bad.

She turned towards the door, and Tim opened it and took her arm. She only came up to Tim's shoulder. Dawlish went ahead of them and opened the front door, looked up and down the street and saw no one about.

'Hurry,' he said, as they passed him quickly.

Lady Marrick seemed as anxious to get away as Tim. They disappeared round the corner.

Dawlish went back to the upstair rooms, studying them closely. None was locked. One, he saw, was a study. A fire burned red in the grate. There were some papers on the desk, business letters. All the drawers were unlocked.

There was a photograph of Lady Marrick on the desk; it did full justice to her. He studied her features and wondered—why had she gone so willingly? Had she been sitting there, doing her hair, for the sake of something to do? Just to pass away the time until her husband returned? Was she frightened of him, because she had been out when he had asked her not to go? Did she know about the woman at the flat? Had she seen Garcia? What hold had Charles upon her? These were all the questions he would have liked to have asked her before she had left; but there hadn't been time.

She was lovely; apparently fascinated by Charles Horden; and carried away from normal life by these new visions which Charles had shown to her.

As Dawlish studied the photographs, the telephone bell rang.

He lifted the receiver, but didn't answer immediately; just stared at the wall in front of him, recalling Marrick's voice—the hard, clipped voice with the undertone of culture.

He said: 'Yes, what is it?'

'So you're back,' said Garcia.

There were moments when a split second made the difference between success and failure; when a false move could undo everything; this was one of those moments. Did Garcia know that Marrick had been to the flat and seen the body? If he did, he would expect Marrick to be suffering torment, to be beside himself with grief and rage. Probably Garcia knew; so Garcia wouldn't expect a normal reply. He might easily be fooled into thinking that Dawlish was Marrick.

'You—' Dawlish began, and swallowed the word. 'You devil, I—'

Garcia laughed.

'Take it easy,' he said. 'Just keep everything I tell you to yourself, don't say a word to the police or anyone else, and be ready for a shock. I—

'If I have to spend every penny I possess, I'll get you,' Dawlish rasped.

'You'll spend plenty, but not every penny. You'll do what I've been telling you to do, or—next time it won't be someone else.'

Dawlish gasped.

'Next time I'll really finish off your wife.' said Garcia. 'No, it wasn't her. I'll call you again.'

The line went dead.

Dawlish lit a cigarette. He felt satisfied that Garcia believed he had spoken to Marrick. So Garcia knew where Marrick had been, but didn't know that the millionaire had not returned. Why hadn't the house been watched? Probably Garcia was finding a shortage of man power; the capture of the four men at *Four Ways* might yet prove the deciding factor.

Tim would be at his flat now.

There was a sound downstairs. Dawlish sat up and looked towards the door, hearing a click as of another door closing. There followed heavy footsteps across the hall and up the stairs.

Dawlish's right hand dropped to his pocket, his fingers closed snugly about the handle of his gun. The man outside drew nearer.

The door opened. Marrick stood there.

He didn't see Dawlish immediately, just stepped inside and closed the door. He looked a broken man; ten years might have passed between this moment and the time when Dawlish had seen him outside the block of flats. His shoulders sagged, he moved heavily, as if every step were an effort.

Then he saw Dawlish.

He drew back, hands clenched. Surprise came, followed by anger. Then that, too, faded. He looked as if all the life had been drained out of him.

'What do you want, Dawlish?'

Just that—no questions as to how Dawlish had got in; no curiosity; just a hopeless: 'What do you want?' He moved towards the desk, but stopped at the side of an armchair and rested against it.

'Haven't you said enough?' he asked.

'The truth can't be repeated too often,' Dawlish said.

Marrick turned and went to a cabinet, opened it, and poured himself out a whisky. He drank it straight, and poured another. Then he came back and stood with the glass in his hands, his eyes blurred with pain.

'All right—say it again.'

'Obviously it doesn't need saying right now. Marrick, what have you kept from the police? What made you take risks like that with your wife? The police aren't here, no one can hear you except me. Even if I pass it on, it's only hearsay.' He stretched out for the photograph and turned it towards Marrick, whose eyes closed involuntarily. 'What was worth all this?'

Marrick said: 'Nothing. Nothing in the world. I didn't think it would happen. You're right, I gambled.'

'What stakes were so high?'

'Money,' said Marrick. 'Money—power—success. Important, aren't they? I—didn't think she would go out tonight. She promised me that she would not. I ought to have watched her. I left only for an hour. When I came back, she had gone. I employed two men to watch her for me—I suppose Garcia bribed them: I trusted others to do what should have been done by myself.'

'What made it worth it?' insisted Dawlish.

Marrick said: 'Two financial and industrial groups, Dawlish. Mine—and another. We've fought for years, and I've always won. Now they're winning. One after another of my partners have been drawn away from me, through this accursed clairvoyant. These men were once my close friends and confidants; now they ignore my existence. Not one has told me why he withdrew from my group. Of them all, I am by far the biggest fianancial operator in world markets—'

'What particular markets?'

'There is very little I don't touch,' Marrick closed his eyes and paused. The words came out slowly, the spirit was still very low in the man—but there was more than he had shown at first, talk of his business had put a spark of life into him even now. 'Grain, gold, ores, diamonds—the Marrick Trust is a very large one. I think Garcia and his backers know that they can't do without me if they are to corner world markets.'

'So it's cartels—on a big scale.'

'Yes. And if you're going to tell me that they are intrinsically evil, I shall say it's nonsense.' Marrick's voice grew a little stronger. 'I know there is a great deal of opposition to cartels, but—better that markets should be in the hands of a few who can be trusted, than a lot of fools who don't know how to handle them to the best advantage. I have spent my life gaining control of a hundred industrial plants, a thousand commerical undertakings; there is no single individual more powerful on the world markets. And I have never played them dangerously. I have never sought to make quick profits; I've never ruined a man; I've kept some companies paying dividends when anyone else, especially your small man, would have been compelled to declare heavy losses.'

Dawlish said: 'Is there any one thing that Garcia seems to want?'

'What is in your mind?'

'A uranium project—anything of that kind.'

Marrick gave a twisted smile.

'No, Dawlish, nothing like that. This has been a struggle for financial control of vast, global undertakings. It has resolved itself into this: I am on my own against a group of fifteen or twenty others. I still hold the balance, but it's a slender one. Garcia began to threaten action against me and my wife if I wouldn't sell at least enough to give the others fifty-one per cent—or absolute control. I challenged him, and—'

He buried his face in his hands.

Dawlish said: 'You knew the threats were likely to be carried out. You knew of the danger. Yet you didn't tell the police; you preferred to keep the thing in your own hands, and risk everything. *Why*?'

Marrick said: 'Does it matter?'

'Tell me,' said Dawlish.

Marrick looked at him with burning eyes. In so short a while, age had touched him. His hands were unsteady and his voice quivered.

'There are several close friends of mine on the other side of this struggle, Dawlish. Oh, they've left me, but if they lose their loyalty, need I lose mine? A man must have some standards and stick to them. And the standards here—' He paused, then backed away and said in a hopeless voice: 'Several extremely highly placed politicians have interests in the opposition group. If it were once uncovered, it would be a vicious scandal. It doesn't touch any one party, it cuts across all parties. It would drag the good name of this country into the mud, and I thought I could fight it alone. If I won, then in the end they'd have come to my side. At the moment, they are ranged with Garcia. I can't believe that they know he is a rogue, even after what has happened. But they mustn't be named, Dawlish.'

Trivett either knew or suspected the truth; there could be no other explanation; and it rationalized everything Trivett had done.

Dawlish said: 'Well, you've fought hard; but what happens now?'

'I hardly know. I can't think clearly. The shock when I saw her! I cannot believe that it really happened to Estelle. She was— perfection. Dawlish. She—' He broke off abruptly. 'Never mind. I'll fight while I can. Of course I shall fight! But I'm a realist, and I know this has broken me. You were right. The others called you brutal, but you were right. I can't face the future, but I can face the truth—and I know that they've been too much for me.'

'Do you know who is the power behind Garcia?'

'No.'

There was no point in forcing that question; if he knew, Marrick would say so while in this all-revealing mood. He went to the chair and sat down, groping in his pocket for his cigarettes. His glance fell on the photograph, and he flinched and turned his head away.

Dawlish said: 'You've had a lot of shocks. Can you take another?'

'After this, I can take anything.'

'You don't know what it is, and it will be different from anything else.'

Marrick said wearily: 'Why make a mystery of it?'

'This time you need to be properly warned. Marrick, that card—remember? Five words—"this can happen to others". Who were the others?'

'I don't know, but I suppose it was Garcia's way of telling me that he won't stop at what he's done. He was thrusting another burden on to my shoulders. And Dawlish, don't forget that so far as the financial dealings are concerned there is *nothing* criminal. It is simply a struggle for financial power and industrial and commercial control. Garcia has used criminal methods, but he isn't likely to betray his leaders.'

Dawlish said: 'There's something else—he's in a great hurry.'

'It's simply that he's lost his patience.'

'I don't believe a man like Garcia would step up the pressure to this extent if it weren't vital. He—and his backers—want control of something urgently, that's why they've worked at this pressure. But we can forget that for the moment—I've warned you about a shock.'

'Nothing can be greater than the one I've had.'

'I didn't say that it was unpleasant. You've been cunningly and diabolically handled, Marrick. Garcia's worked on your nerves, and he's come near to breaking them. Within the next few hours he'll try to force the final issue. You've got to hold him off a bit longer. It's largely up to you, whether he's got you where he wants you or not.'

'For God's sake come to the point, man.'

'Your wife isn't dead,' said Dawlish. 'The body belonged to someone else.'

Marrick stood up in a single swift movement; anger, pleading, a wild and pitiful hope, flamed in his eyes.

'Don't lie to me, Dawlish!'

'It's the truth.'

'I don't know what you think you'll get by it,' said Marrick. 'I don't know whether you think that by such a pretence you'll make me fight it out any better, but—'

'I came here an hour ago, with a friend. We came, by way of a back window, up the stairs. There was a light in the bedroom along the landing. I opened the door. Your wife was brushing her hair—long, golden hair. She was, she is, a very lovely girl.'

Marrick took a step towards him, his hands clenched, but uncertain, now.

'I spoke to her, and recognized her. She was your wife—and she was very frightened. She knew there was grave danger, and I persuaded her to leave here. She is safe, with my friend. Garcia killed another woman. He dressed her in your wife's clothes. He did it to break your spirit. He has telephoned since, and thought that I was you. Get a hold on yourself, Marrick— it's true.'

Marrick stood, unmoving.

'She's alive. The other woman must be avenged, but she wasn't your wife. You've still got her. You've still a chance to win out completely. And you've got to play the game with one object in view—finding out *why* Garcia and his group are so anxious to get the thing over quickly. That, and discovering who is behind him.'

Marrick's voice, hoarse, unnatural, breaking on a sob, muttered: 'It *can't* be true.'

Dawlish lifted the telephone, and dialled Tim's number.

'Hallo, Tim. All safe? . . . Ask Lady Marrick to speak to her husband, will you? . . . Yes, he's back.' He held the telephone towards Marrick.

Marrick took the receiver with trembling fingers, put the mouthpiece in front of his lips, hesitated and then spoke so harshly that the words were hardly distinguishable. He fought for self-control.

'Is that you, Estelle . . .'

Sweat shone on his forehead as he listened. After a while, he said:

'Yes, I will be careful, and I will come and see you soon. Goodbye, my darling.' He put the receiver down. His eyes were filled with a strange, inner brightness which reminded Dawlish of Charles. He turned away, walked slowly to the other end of the room, then looked at Dawlish. 'I must see her.'

Dawlish said: 'I've taken a chance, and maybe it wasn't justified. I've told you the truth because I thought it would give you the strength you need. From now on you've got to pretend that you don't know she's alive. You saw her, dead. Garcia knows she is alive and that she came back here, but he doesn't know she's gone again. He'll be in touch with you soon. You've got to convince him that she's missing and that you think he killed her. You've got to say that you'll do nothing until you've broken him. That's the line—he's broken you, you'll break him.'

Marrick said thickly: 'Why? What's in your mind?'

'He thinks his trump card is your wife, alive; that after this, you'll give way. But if *you* think she's dead, he's lost his trump card. He'll be forced into a different kind of action; he'll have to bring new pressure to bear on you. I want to know what he's prepared to do.'

'You mean, force him into making a mistake?' Marrick spoke more calmly now. 'It could succeed, but—'

'It must. Behind all this is the reason for his urgency and the identity of his backers. We've got to find both. He's got to take more chances than he's ever done before. When he comes through, tell him I was at the house when you arrived, that's all.'

'Then he'll be after *you*.'

'I can take it.'

'I believe you can,' Marrick said wonderingly. 'You are a different man from the one I imagined you to be, Dawlish. I'll handle Garcia now.'

'And you'll tell me the rest,' Dawlish said. 'Did you try to put the fear of death into Horden? Did you hire men to try to frighten him out of his wits, force him out of the country? Is that the way you tried to break his hold on your partners and on your wife?'

'Yes,' said Marrick.

So the decks were cleared for the final fight. Who backed Garcia? Why was he in such a hurry? How did Charles persuade hard-headed businessmen to desert Marrick, to transfer their allegiance overnight; and what was Garcia after? How much did Charles really know? And what did Downing know—yes, and even Fay?

Marrick said: 'Dawlish, I don't know whether you've seen the consequences of this as clearly as I have.' His voice was clearer, the mask of the iron man was almost back in position. 'You are quite right up to the point that Garcia thinks that my wife, alive, is his trump card. But do you really know what he'll do if he thinks you have taken her away?'

Dawlish shrugged.

'Do you, Dawlish? Or have you a blind spot? He'll work on you as he has on me, and—'

'Yes. And I've a wife. I know how far Garcia will go. I don't think he'll win. For one reason, I've got the police watching my home, and I'm not without friends. But whatever the risk, I'll take it. We've got to find what's at the back of it. You say it isn't uranium, although that's the most likely single factor. It may be that some big syndicate is after control of your markets for international political reasons. I don't propose to guess, I only know that it's of outstanding importance. And your job is to make sure you convince Garcia that you think your wife is dead—make sure also that he knows I was here.'

'He'll believe me,' said Marrick.

Dawlish moved away. He didn't look back, and Marrick didn't speak again.

Dawlish went downstairs through the silent house, and opened the front door. He paused for a moment in the porch. No one was in sight at first, but when he approached Marrick's Rolls-Royce, which was parked outside, a figure loomed from a nearby porch.

It was one of Trivett's men. Two others followed him.

'Mr. Dawlish,' one said.

Dawlish was thinking of Marrick's face; and the brilliance of his eyes.

'Yes?'

'Mr. Trivett would like to see you at the Yard, sir.'

'Sorry to disappoint him, but I've a date.'

Dawlish smiled and turned away from the man, but the others barred his way.

'In that case,' said the first speaker, 'It is my duty to inform you that there is a warrant out for your arrest.'

CHAPTER TWENTY

ARREST?

He could make a dash for it; there would be a fifty-fifty chance of getting away from them. But he'd be on the run, sneaking away in hiding, unable to do half the things he wanted to do. Yet if this were true, and the warrant were out, he'd be in a far worse plight. He had thirty seconds in which to decide; thirty seconds, while the three men from the Yard watched as if they knew what was passing through his mind.

He was tense, rigid; muscles taut.

Then he relaxed.

'More mistakes,' he said. 'What's the charge?'

'I think you'd better talk to the Superintendent about that, sir. We were only to use the warrant if you refused to come.'

'Thoughtful of Mr. Trivett. I hope I don't have to walk to the Yard.'

'We've a car round the corner, sir.'

'Is this house being watched?'

'I believe it is,' said the man who had done the talking, casually. 'I think we've been watching it for some days.'

There was a thrust concealed in that remark; he was

saying, in effect, that he knew Dawlish and Jeremy had broken in.

It didn't take long to get to Scotland Yard. But it was long enough for a hundred thoughts to flash through Dawlish's mind. Was this part of Trivett's tactics, or had someone brought pressure to bear on him, to force Dawlish off the case? What did Trivett think now of the scene at the luxury flats? Cold hostility had sounded in his voice when he had last spoken to Dawlish. Did the police know the truth about Lady Marrick? Had they discovered that the headless body wasn't hers?

Dawlish didn't go beyond that; didn't try to plot out the next stage in the battle with Garcia; time to do that when he knew that he would be free to work.

The detectives didn't trust him. All three followed him up in the lift and along the passage to Trivett's room. The light was on, and Trivett called a sharp command to enter.

He looked up from his desk when the door opened; and his expression hardened when he saw Dawlish.

'All right. I'll ring when I want you.'

'Yes, sir.'

The door closed on the three men. Dawlish waited, watching Trivett, and heard one man walk away; so the other two were standing on guard outside. He grinned as he went to an easy chair, dropped into it, and took out his cigarettes; he had two left. Trivett's expression was bleak; he shook his head at the proffered case.

Dawlish shrugged and lit up.

Trivett waited for him to speak; wanted him to speak first. Two could play that game. Dawlish relaxed and blew smoke rings, and looked everywhere but at Trivett—until suddenly he stared at the Yard man, his own eyes hard.

Trivett said: 'What got into you tonight? You reached a new low.'

'Trusting friend,' murmured Dawlish.

'Where did you go after you left the flats?'

'To Marrick's house.'

'What did you do there?'

'I broke in, went upstairs and waited for Sir George.'

'A criminal offence.'

'So I believe.'

'What did you do between the time you got in and the time you left?'

Trivett's words came sharply. Dawlish tried to see what was behind the interrogation. Assume, first, that Trivett's men had been watching from a house opposite, or at least from nearby; and that meant Trivett had received a report and knew that Tim and Lady Marrick had left. He'd done nothing to stop them, but he knew that a woman was with Tim. He probably wasn't sure of her identity.

'I had a talk with a lady, and she went off with Tim. Great one with the ladies, Tim Jeremy.'

'Who was she?'

Dawlish said: 'At this stage, oughtn't you to be more interested in the dead than the living? Who was the woman we found at the flat?'

Trivett said flatly: 'It was Lady Marrick.'

'Then the woman who went off with Tim was just a friend of the great man's. Nice little thing. Obviously he prefers the tiny type, and likes 'em with long, golden hair. Bill, what's biting you?'

'You are. You broke into Marrick's house. For that we can hold you, put you in dock tomorrow and get an eight-day remand in custody. That means we can keep you out of the way for eight days. We can stop you getting up to more mischief.'

'The idea has its appeal. Good food and no chivvying.'

Dawlish didn't understand this; he couldn't break down Trivett's hostility; and Trivett's manner froze something in him. They were behaving like sworn enemies, not old friends. *Why?* Trivett had started it; it was a deliberate policy.

'What did you say to Marrick?' asked Trivett.

'Much the same as I'd already said to him in the face of your disapproval. Marrick is keeping plenty back. He needed a shock to make him open his mouth.'

'Has he opened it?'

Dawlish said: 'I think I now know nearly as much about this business as you do. I know that it's a fight between two big industrial interests, that the odds are against Marrick, that the bother with his wife was a form of blackmail. I know that some very highly placed politicians have let themselves be drawn into the other side, and that Marrick didn't talk freely because he was afraid of causing a public scandal. From that I guessed the reason for your peculiar attitude. You could resign, you know.'

'Why the devil should I resign?'

'Because pressure had been brought to bear upon you to make you deviate from the path of duty.' The scorn in Dawlish's voice was unmistakable. 'You couldn't act officially, so got me to do your dirty work.'

Trivett said: 'That's one thing you've got wrong. Using you was approved by my superiors. It has been an extremely delicate matter. Once I am satisfied that anyone, no matter how highly placed, has broken the law, I'm free to act. I'll be judge of when to act and whom to act against.'

'Me, for instance. Bill, I've rubbed shoulders with you for a long time, but you've got me beat now. What's on your mind?'

Trivett stood up.

'Perhaps I'm a fool. But I know you're quite ruthless when it comes to getting results. I've seen you in some nasty moods, but never so savage as you were tonight. That gives colour to the charge which has been made against you. I have been talking to Garcia's four men who were held at Haslemere. Each of them says that you have been at these Circle meetings, with Garcia. Each—'

Dawlish exclaimed incredulously: 'And you fell for *that*?'

'Another arrest was made near the flat where we found Lady Marrick's body. He was another of Garcia's men. He says that you arrived at the block of flats an hour before the police; that you left, carrying a parcel. That you took the parcel to the Embankment and dropped it into the river. Add that up.'

Trivett's voice grated.

Dawlish said softly: 'All right, I've added it up. You're saying that I went to the flats and chopped that woman's head off, and dumped it—and you fell for that, too.' He laughed; it was an ugly sound. 'Are you dragging the river?'

'Yes.'

'And until you've proved that I've never been to a Circle meeting, and until you can be sure I didn't decapitate the woman, I'm under detention. I still don't get it. I can understand you believing a lot of odd things, but—why should I murder the woman in order to get results?'

Trivett *couldn't* believe that. But if he didn't, why pretend?

'You might have gone there, found her dead, had some reason for wanting to hide her identity, and chosen that way of delaying us from finding out who she was. You're quite capable of it—and in your present mood, capable of doing it tonight. It depends whether the stakes are high enough. When did you first hear of Charles Horden and the Circle?'

'I heard of Horden a month ago, when he was at a cocktail party after making a speech. I heard of the Circle a few days ago. You're wrong, Bill. And Garcia—' He laughed. 'Yes, Garcia's good. He wants me out of the hunt. So he laid it on with the bright boys at *Four Ways*. If you fail and miss Dawlish, tell the police this story, it will get him out of the way. Nothing about Garcia surprises me. You pretending to fall for it does. But we're wasting time.'

'Are we?'

Trivett went back to his desk, and as he reached it, the telephone bell rang. 'Hallo . . . Yes, I'll speak to them.' He held on, looking into Dawlish's eyes all the time. 'Hallo, Allen.' So this was Inspector Allen, of Haslemere. 'What time? . . . Are you quite sure? . . . He's a tricky customer, you know, he might have foxed you . . . All right, if there's no doubt. Thanks.'

He replaced the receiver, and went on where he had left off.

'I still don't know whether you've told the truth. You've taken a remarkable interest in this business. I thought I was leading you into it, but from the beginning you've behaved as if you already knew a great deal. Let's have the truth.'

'You've had it.'

Trivett said slowly: 'I wish I could believe you, Pat.' It was the first time he had relaxed even slightly since Dawlish had come in. 'The stakes are so high, I daren't take chances. You know, and I needn't minimize the seriousness of it, that a lot of V.I.P.s are in this Circle. Outwardly, all of the members are reputable people. Since Garcia started his tricks, there is at least a possibility that these V.I.P.s are prepared to back Garcia in murder and violence.'

Dawlish said: 'Take the more cheerful view. They've been persuaded by Charles Horden that they're on to a good thing, and Garcia had been after them to put up a cover for his criminal activities. Why pick on me?'

'If you're trying to uncover the truth, well and good. If you're trying to hide something—and you're capable of it—I daren't let you loose.'

'Fall back on the law, Bill! A man is innocent until he's proved guilty.'

'A policeman is wonderful until he makes a mistake, and I might make a fatal one with you,' said Trivett. 'It's no use telling me that we've worked together for years and you've never let me down yet. There's no room for sentiment in this business. Some of the people involved are so high up that any breath of suspicion against them seems fantastic. The obvious explanation is that they have fallen under the influence of Charles Horden. Have you?'

It had been dawning on Dawlish for some minutes; yet it came as a surprise. Trivett's whole attitude was governed by the possibility that he, Dawlish, had fallen under Charles's influence. That wasn't easy to laugh off. Trivett knew plenty about the scope of that influence; knew that it made Marrick's friends disloyal; froze friendship into antagonism; made women forsake their husbands—no, it couldn't be laughed off. Trivett had to consider the possibility.

Dawlish said: 'Not yet.'

'What do you mean by that?'

'I'm more than half convinced that he's got something you can't explain by the ordinary rule of thumb. Whether he's good or bad'—he shrugged—'I don't yet know. I do know there's a lot I can do to help you. Up to you to decide.' Dawlish relaxed and smiled faintly. 'I fancy you'd have Felicity's unqualified approval if she knew that there was a chance of my being lodged at Brixton for a few days.'

Trivett said: 'I don't blame her. What do you propose to do if you leave here?'

'Go for Garcia.'

'How?'

'Dangle a bait and hope to get him hooked.'

'What bait?'

'It's too involved for me to go into details. But I take it that you sent your buddies out so that this could be an unofficial bit of chatter. Is that right?'

'Yes. This won't be held against you, whatever you say. That doesn't mean that I might not decide to hold you.'

'Very well then, I'll tell you what I can. Garcia is trying to persuade Marrick that his wife isn't dead and that if he'll play ball, he'll get her back. Marrick, at my request, is not going to be convinced that she's still alive. He's going to try to switch Garcia's main attention over to me—make me the key to success or failure. You will say that I'm sticking my neck out. Maybe I am, but it seems the only way to get results. And what results! Find out what Garcia is after, and who is backing him in his venture into violence. Find out why the show suddenly became urgent—ah, that got you, didn't it?'

Trivett said slowly: 'Yes. This affair has been going on for some time. The tempo speeded up after the murder of that old man at Wyman Street—*and* after you took an obvious part in the affair. The reason for the higher tempo could be that murder, or it could be you.'

'I wouldn't know the answer,' said Dawlish.

'*Is* Lady Marrick dead?'

'No. And I gave you a gentle hint earlier in the evening that you shouldn't take too much for granted, Bill. I doubted from the first whether it was Lady Marrick—why, if so, take away her head? Marrick jumped to the obvious conclusion, and I tried to cash in. I thought it important that he should talk, and he talked. The whole plot was carefully laid on by Garcia, so that he could hamstring me for a few days. When he discovers that I've managed to make Lady Marrick vanish, he'll be desperately anxious to have me free so that he can take the necessary steps. Any idea where to find Garcia?'

'No.'

'Or John Downing?'

'No. He had been in that room where we found the body, his prints were all over the place.'

'That bears out Fay's story,' murmured Dawlish. 'Question—was Downing really held there under duress, or is he working with Garcia and throwing dust into my eyes and yours—not to mention his sister's. Know anything about Downing?'

'He inherited a large fortune five years ago, and leads what appears to be a blameless life. He met Garcia in the ordinary course of business, as far as I can find out. He's a big stockholder in some of the companies concerned in the struggle—well, biggish. Garcia was probably trying to get him to join the Circle, but if you read the facts at their face value, he wouldn't touch anything with which Charles was associated.'

Dawlish said: 'Face value, yes. Find Garcia, find Downing, and you'll probably know a great deal more than you do now, Bill. Or is that being fatuous?'

'I should say it comes very near to it. Do you know of anyone else involved?'

'Not a single name, William. Getting down to basic, I'd say that I've two chief worries. Putting the bait out for Garcia, and finding out which other women are in danger, if any. Presumably, the wives of the men in the Circle—black business, that Circle. If they're the women concerned, I cheerfully hand over the responsibility to you. But I don't think anyone else can bait Garcia successfully. Try me, Bill.'

It mattered; it mattered desperately.

Trivett leaned forward and said slowly:

'Pat, if I try you, I'm staking my own reputation and the possibility of a disastrous public scandal. Have you told me the truth?'

'Yes. Cross my heart.'

Trivett said: 'All right. Whatever help you need from now on, you can have.'

'Thanks.' Dawlish stood up, surprised by the measure of his relief. 'For a start, ask the Haslemere people to watch *Four Ways* as if it held the Crown jewels. Whoever is there—or whomever I take there—mustn't get into Garcia's hands yet.'

'I'll see to it.'

'Thanks,' said Dawlish again.

But he left quickly, aware that Trivett was far from happy, and only a hair's breadth stopped him from rescinding the decision he had made.

CHAPTER TWENTY-ONE

QUIET BEAUTY

A police car dropped Dawlish in a side street near Piccadilly Circus, and he stood on the pavement for a few minutes, with a cold wind sharply stinging his upturned face. Two or three shadowy figures passed the end of the street, but no one approached him. He walked slowly. Not until now, when he was free of the police, did the full reaction come. He knew how close he had been to being held; Trivett had taken a chance based on the years of their friendship. No time, now, for marvelling that Trivett could have doubts; doubts which meant accepting the fact that Trivett was convinced that Charles could influence anyone; everyone. That was the key to the whole affair; the influence of Charles Horden. It was being used evilly, for there was no doubt about the blackness of the Circle. But did Charles know that? Was Charles a willing participant in the affair; or simply an instrument?

Dawlish quickened his pace, then slipped into the doorway of a small shop. No one was following him. Relieved, he walked briskly towards Tim's flat.

Looking back, few things had impressed him more than the

alacrity—once she had been bribed with the promise of seeing Horden—with which Lady Marrick had gone with Tim. Fay would have gone as promptly; so would many other women, given the chance, if what he'd heard was true.

He reached a point from which he could see Tim's flat. There was a street lamp near it, and he peered about him, to make sure that the flat wasn't watched. He saw no one. He walked slowly past, warily alert. Tim would have called such caution unnecessary, but Garcia might have had Dawlish followed; could have known what had happened after he had gone to the Yard. It wasn't likely; he wouldn't have telephoned Marrick's house had he known Dawlish was there—but if the police had watched, unseen, one of Garcia's men might have watched also, and reported afterwards.

Garcia wouldn't lose much time finding where Tim lived; it was an obvious rendezvous.

The shadows of the night seemed to hold chill menace.

Dawlish approached the house at last. He had a key, went inside, and closed the door with a snap. He stood there, waiting, then opened it again cautiously and peered out. He went as far as the pavement and glanced in each direction—and then he grinned to himself.

All clear!

He whistled softly as he went upstairs, and the whistling became clearer as he approached the top flat—Tim's. Before he reached the landing, the door opened and a light shone out. Tim's shadow appeared, but not Tim; cautious Tim.

Dawlish gave a muted bird-call.

Tim appeared. 'So it is you.'

They went inside. Tim closed and bolted the door.

'You're nearly as jumpy as I am,' Dawlish said.

'I'm worse.'

'Why? Any alarms?'

'No. Put it down to the beautiful Estelle. I'm not often at a loss to know what to say to a lovely, but—she isn't with us, Pat. Speaks like a robot; mechanically. "Yes, please." "No, thank you." The only question she asked was: "Is Mr. Horden here?" When I told her he wasn't, she closed up like a clam. She won't, listen to me, doesn't seem to know I'm there. But her eyes!'

They were in a small hall; this was a modest flat, with three rooms, all leading from the hall. Tim's voice was hushed; he wasn't happy.

'What's the matter with her eyes?'

Tim forced a grin, but it was a sickly effort.

'I keep getting nasty visions. Of her head, leaving her body and floating about the room. I don't think seances are good for me.'

'It'll pass,' said Dawlish.

He hung up the coat, and went into the living-room. This was the largest of them all; roomy, obviously a bachelor's apartment. There were large, hide armchairs; books untidily placed on built-in shelves. A set of golf clubs in a bag which had seen better days stood against the wall by the fireplace, and in one corner a small barrel of beer stood on a trestle, with a remarkable array of pewter tankards on display near it.

Estelle Marrick sat in one of the big armchairs; it engulfed her, made her look even smaller than she was. The end of her nightdress and robe showed beneath her coat, and the walking shoes on her bare feet. Her lovely golden hair fell to her shoulders.

Her eyes—

Dawlish could understand what Tim meant; they were enormous, blue, beautiful. She was as fragile and delicate as Fay Downing; no, that wasn't quite true, she was even daintier than Fay. The women weren't alike; their smallness and daintiness made them seem alike.

She looked round at Dawlish; her voice was gentle and expressionless.

'Have you brought Charles?'

'No, he's in the country. You'll see him.'

She turned her face towards the fire, watching the flames with a wide, unseeing gaze.

Tim shrugged, and forced himself to say: 'Have a drink, Pat?'

'Thanks. Any beer?' He turned to the girl. 'So you haven't told your story to Mr. Jeremy?'

Lady Marrick said: 'There is so little to tell.'

'I'd like to hear it, please. Will you have a drink or something to eat?'

'No, thank you. What *is* there to tell? That I believe Mr. Horden to be the personification of goodness? That I will follow him anywhere and do what he tells me at all times? That I will give him a loyalty which you may say that I owe to my husband? That is nearly all. I went out tonight, because I was told that I would see Charles. He wasn't there; it was a trick. This is also a trick. Why do you harass me?'

Dawlish said: 'This is no trick; I know where Charles is and can take you to see him.'

'Please do that, soon.'

'Why are you so anxious to see him?'

She didn't answer; and he knew that no matter how often he put the question, or what trick he used to get the truth from her, she would, or could, say no more.

Dawlish took a tankard of beer from Tim.

'Lady Marrick, how well do you know the man Garcia?'

'I hardly know him at all.'

'Has he ever asked you to influence your husband in his business affairs?'

'Yes. I have refused, of course.'

'Has he asked you to take your husband to see Charles?'

'Yes. And George would not come.' She smiled faintly. 'He is afraid of seeing what I see when I am with Charles.'

'Has Charles ever asked you to bring your husband to see him?'

'No. Never.'

'Have you ever attended one of the big Circle meetings?'

'No. I have heard of them; Garcia asked me to take my husband to one of them, but I have never been there.'

'Where have you seen Charles?'

'In many places.'

'How did you first meet him?'

'Does that really matter?' she asked. 'I have long been interested in the life beyond the veil, and sought for it, and he has shown it to me.' The lovely, tantalizing smile appeared again—she was as beautiful in her way as Charles was in his. 'Having seen it, I do not want to lose it, and there is no one else who can show me. I am not concerned, now, with worldly things, Mr. Dawlish. I have lost my interest in everything but the other side. I must ask you to believe me, please. I shall not endeavour to influence my husband in his business or in his private life, because he is a sceptic, and there is nothing one *can* do about that.'

'How long have you known Charles?'

'For nearly two years.'

Dawlish said sharply: 'And you're in love with him. Isn't that it?'

The way she looked at him was pitying; not contemptuous or derisive, just pitying.

'You do not understand, Mr. Dawlish. You talk of love when you mean lust, you cannot think of love except of the body. You do not know the other side, and—perhaps that is as well. But you are quite wrong if you think that I am attracted to Charles in that way. It is what he can give me spiritually, what he can reveal to me, that matters.'

Dawlish said: 'Very pretty, if it were true.'

She didn't answer, staring steadfastly into the fire, as if she had lost interest in Dawlish and in everything but Charles.

Was this a pose?

Dawlish said: 'How well do you know John Downing?'

'I know his sister, slightly, and I have met him.'

The answer came lightly, easily.

Dawlish moved across to her, took her hands, and made her look into his eyes.

'Did you know that Garcia is using you in order to bring pressure to bear on your husband?'

'Oh yes, I knew that.'

'Did you know, when you went out tonight, that you might help Garcia to do that?'

'Yes. But you forget, Mr. Dawlish, I had to see Charles and believed I could see him if I went to see Garcia.'

There was little expression in her soft voice; she spoke as if the only thing that mattered was seeing Charles, and she would sacrifice anything and anyone to that end. It would be impossible to reason with her, she wasn't susceptible to ordinary logic or ordinary values; and the one governing factor was Charles.

'Why do you want to see Charles so urgently?'

'I must,' she said, and looked away from him.

Dawlish said: 'Right. You'd better get dressed; we'll go down right away.'

Tim took her case into the main bedroom and soon rejoined Dawlish.

'Well, what do you make of it?'

Dawlish didn't answer, but finished his beer.

'I tell you she's an uncanny piece,' Tim said. 'The more I see of this business, the less I like it. What did Bill Trivett have to say?'

'Awful warnings. I've seen Marrick, and that's more important.' Dawlish told Tim briefly, and added: 'We've got to keep Estelle safe, and we've got to bait Garcia. You know, if there's one thing I really want, it's to sit in at a Circle meeting.'

'Any hope?'

'Could be,' said Dawlish. 'We'll think about it. I'm going to hire a car for tonight's job. You take Estelle, and I'll follow; it's possible that we'll meet some trouble on the road.'

They met no trouble.

It was a little after six o'clock, and still pitch dark, when they reached *Four Ways*. They were stopped by two constables at the gate, and told that there had been no incidents. The police were friendly. Headlights shone on the house, and Dawlish saw a figure appear at the bedroom window; Felicity. She was coming down the stairs when he opened the front door, and drew back when she saw Estelle.

'More visitors,' said Dawlish. 'All quiet, I'm told.'

'Yes, but—' She hesitated, and looked at Estelle. 'I'll tell you later.'

'Nothing to do with Charles?'

'No, he's asleep.'

Estelle said: 'Yes, I know he is resting, and I know he is here. I can feel the quietness and the contentment. Thank you, Mr. Dawlish.'

Felicity, looked startled.

'Lady Marrick—my wife,' said Dawlish gravely. 'Do you want to disturb Charles?'

'No, please not! I will wait until he is awake.'

They went into the drawing-room. Estelle sank down in an easy-chair, and closed her eyes. Before the others fully realized it, she was asleep.

Tim ruffled his hair, and Felicity whispered:

'What's the matter with her?'

'Completely dominated by Charles, if we read the signs aright,' said Dawlish. 'Will you watch her, Tim? Ted will be around soon, and he can take over while you get some shut-eye.'

'Right—but after I've heard the news from Fel.'

They went into the hall and closed the door.

'I don't really know whether it matters if she hears,' said Felicity. 'Darling, Garcia telephoned. He scared me.'

'He has that trick to a nicety. When?'

'About an hour ago. He said he wanted to see you—you can forget what orders he gave you about Horden and Leicester Square Station; all that can wait. He said that Downing will be all right for the time being, but he must see you.'

'And he didn't say why?'

'No. He was afraid of being overheard, I think; he kept it short.'

'Where am I to see him?'

'You're to drive to London tomorrow morning, starting from here at eleven o'clock. He'll see you somewhere on the road. Pat, he—'

'Threatened wild things if I didn't turn up. Heads on salvers, probably?'

'He—scared me,' Felicity said slowly. 'I needn't say more than that. Pat, don't go alone.'

She knew it was useless to ask him not to go.

'Did he make that a condition?'

'Yes.'

'I'll take Tim,' said Dawlish. 'Better wake Ted up, so that Tim can get those forty winks. The only thing I'm anxious about now is seeing Charles and Estelle meet. Call me when he wakes up, sweetheart.'

'If you're tired out when you see Garcia—'

'I shan't be much more tired than Garcia,' said Dawlish, and grinned. 'Keep a hold on yourself, we're nearing the end.'

He went upstairs, loosened his collar, took off his shoes, and lay down on the bed, fully dressed. He was asleep almost as quickly as Estelle Marrick had been.

Dawlish woke up with the sun shining on his face. He blinked at the ceiling, then started, and turned to look at the clock. It was a quarter past ten. He could hear the usual sounds about the house—Norah singing downstairs, someone talking in the drawing-room. He got up, and looked into the other bedrooms—and in Charles's he saw not Charles, but Estelle. She was sleeping soundly, and didn't stir when he approached the bed. He went downstairs, running his hand over his stubble, and Felicity met him as she came out of the kitchen.

'So I wouldn't wake up,' Dawlish said reproachfully.

'There are limits. You needed that sleep. Nothing much happened, anyhow, but—'

'Forgiven,' said Dawlish, 'but only because I have an exemplary character. Tell me all.'

'It was strange. Ted was in the room with Estelle, and she woke up suddenly. He says that she didn't seem sleepy, just woke up as if she'd really been awake all the time, and said: "He is awake now." And when Ted went upstairs, Charles was just opening his eyes.'

'Hum. When did they meet?'

'Soon after that. Charles seemed quite pleased to see her, but that's about all. She didn't ask him anything, seemed satisfied to see him—as if all she wanted was to make sure that he was all right.'

'Odd. Devilish odd. What about Fay?'

'She's still worried about her brother, but she's much more interested in Charles. They're out in the garden now. Ted's keeping an eye on them, and Tim's fast asleep. The police are still outside in force.'

'That's a relief. What chance breakfast?'

'It's all ready.'

Dawlish kissed the tip of her nose, and went upstairs to the bathroom. When he came down again Tim was before him, tucking in as if he hadn't seen a square meal for weeks. Felicity, pale and worried, hovered about the room. Charles and Fay were still outside; he could see them through the breakfast-room window, and they were arm-in-arm.

Afterwards Dawlish went into the garage, where there was a small bench and a number of bottles, mostly of gardening chemicals. One was labelled *Ammonia*. Unstoppering this bottle, Dawlish took three small white silk bags from a box and filled them from it. They were about the size of table-tennis balls, and as weapons he had found them invaluable in the past, partly because they looked so harmless.

By eleven o'clock Dawlish was at the porch. The Bentley stood outside, the hired car near it.

'Taking both?' asked Tim.

'No, I don't think so. Send the other back to the garage, will you? 'Bye, Felicity. And it isn't as bad as you think. Garcia just wants to talk business.'

'I wouldn't trust him for a second.'

Dawlish kissed her. She clung to him for a moment, but he broke free, gently, and took the wheel of the car. Tim sat next to him. Fay and Charles waved from the rose-walk, and Dawlish had the idea that Fay wanted to speak to him; but that must wait. He drove on.

At the gate, the police saluted.

Dark rain-clouds gathered over the sun, and soon a drenching downpour smacked against the windscreen, reducing visibility to almost nil. Going through Haslemere the storm cleared, and as they swung on to the London Road, Dawlish began to hum to himself. Tim sat silent.

Two miles on the other side of Haslemere, at a garage, Dawlish slowed down.

'No petrol?' asked Tim.

'No passenger,' said Dawlish.

'Eh?'

'Felicity is worried enough; there's no need to make it worse. But this time I want to do exactly what Garcia's asked, probably the first and only time.'

Hot words of protest were on Tim's lips, but one look at Dawlish showed him that he intended to have his own way.

'Wait for half an hour, and then hire a car and come to London. I'll call you at the club.'

'If you ever live to call me.'

'What a melancholy beggar you are.'

Tim shrugged as he got out of the car. Dawlish let in the clutch, smiled and waved, and then drove off. By the time he had gone fifty yards, he had forgotten Tim; forgotten everything but the coming meeting.

Had he gambled too wildly? Would Garcia attack him *en route*?

Why was he so ready to accept the risk? He couldn't answer, beyond recognizing a great evil and great danger—not simply to him, but to many.

Tim would call it a hunch.

It was much more; it was conviction. There was much he didn't know and couldn't guess, but an inner compulsion drove him on.

CHAPTER TWENTY-TWO

ON THE ROAD

There was no other traffic on the road. Dawlish stopped on the breast of a hill and looked back; he wasn't being followed. Tim was doing what was expected of him, and the police were leaving him alone; Trivett had probably made sure of that. A big green bus came lumbering towards him, and then a stream of cars; that was the only traffic he saw for the next few miles. It was a good road, running through the hilly country of Surrey. He drove at a moderate pace, until he was on the outskirts of Godalming. Afterwards he put on speed. He scanned the countryside for any sign of Garcia or Garcia's men; but everything looked normal.

Then a car swung out of a side turning, just behind him. It was a large black Packard.

Dawlish tensed himself, took a hand off the wheel and dropped it to his pocket and his gun. He slowed down; the speedometer quivered about the forty mark. The Packard purred up behind him. He could see the driver and another man at the front; the head and shoulders of a passenger in the back.

The nose of the Packard passed the rear of the Bentley.

Dawlish pulled a little farther over. If this were to be a shooting match, he wouldn't stand much chance; it was a risk he had taken knowingly. By the light of the attack at Lincoln Square, what he had done appeared an action of sheer folly. The two cars were alongside for what seemed a perilous moment.

It passed; there was no shooting.

When it was clear of the Bentley, the slowing-down signal was given. Dawlish braked. Both cars came to a standstill. The back door of the Packard opened and Garcia got out.

One of the other men came with Garcia, passed the front of the car and looked into the back; went to the tonneau and raised the boot, to make sure no one was hiding there.

Dawlish said: 'I've played according to directions.'

'You're wise, Dawlish.'

'That's yet to be seen,' said Dawlish. 'Well, what is it?'

'Where is Lady Marrick?'

'Quite safe.'

'I have some instructions for you. See Sir George Marrick. Tell him you have taken her away. Tell him that she is alive.'

Dawlish grinned. 'I think not.'

'You'll regret it if you don't, Dawlish.'

'It's always rash to prophesy, don't you think? One can so easily look a fool.'

Garcia's thin face was set; the glow in his eyes burned with enmity and hatred; and yet he kept his voice steady. It seemed to Dawlish that every ounce of his will-power was bent on making Marrick believe that his wife was still alive.

He said: 'Dawlish, you're not a wealthy man.'

'I get along.'

'You can be wealthy. You can name your own price. I will give you the money before you release Lady Marrick.'

Dawlish smiled.

'I mean real money, Dawlish. You can talk in big figures.'

'It's not my language.'

Garcia said: 'I hope you change your mind. There is nothing to stop us from killing you, now, at this moment.'

'Except the fact that it won't help you.'

'Your friends—'

Dawlish said: 'My friends know exactly what to do if I don't turn up. They're not fools. Take it from me, Garcia, threats won't help you. There's one thing that might.'

'What is it?'

'I want to know how you're using Horden and I want to know what it's all about.'

'Dawlish, you may not believe me when I say that I can do what I like with several women who are quite willing victims. They will do exactly what I say, if I tell them that they may see Charles Horden. You saw that body last night—it can happen to others.'

'So you said.'

Garcia leaned forward.

'It *will* happen to others, unless you do what I say. Make Marrick believe that his wife is alive. He won't believe me. Don't think I'm bluffing, Dawlish. I can do it, and I will do it, if you make it necessary.'

'You're not doing so well, are you? You want Charles Horden—I have him. You want a live Lady Marrick. I have her. You overplayed your hand by showing Marrick that dead body. Why kill the girl, anyway? Who was she?'

'A woman who worked with us and then tried to withdraw. She knew what you want to know, Dawlish, and she had to be silenced. I've warned you.'

'You've tried money and threats, and they won't work. Why not look round to see if you've a trump card in your hand?'

He grinned into the sallow face; the remark puzzled Garcia. The other man, small and dark, stood by the side of the car, his right hand at his coat, as if he were fingering a gun in a shoulder-holster. Several cars passed, and drivers looked curiously towards the group at the roadside.

A dark cloud drew nearer, and a few heavy spots of rain fell.

'Better get in; you'll get wet,' Dawlish said, and leaned back and opened the rear door.

'Don't—' began the bodyguard.

Garcia said: 'Talk so that I can understand you, Dawlish.'

'You've a trump card. Use it.' Dawlish laughed, and the rain came down more heavily. 'Or forget it, get on with your dangerous work. While you're waiting for the hangman, remember a showery day in April when you nearly had the job in the bag.'

Garcia climbed into the car.

The bodyguard said: 'Don't do it!'

The driver of the Packard had slewed round in his seat and was watching intently.

'Your boy friends seem anxious about you,' Dawlish said.

He leaned forward and took a packet of cigarettes from the dashboard pocket; took an ammonia bag at the same time. With a slow, casual gesture, he tossed the ammonia bag into the bodyguard's face. It burst almost before the man realized that anything was coming.

At the same time Dawlish turned, and drove his fist into Garcia's face, sending him smacking against the door. Then he switched on, and as the engine hummed, eased off the brakes. He swung the wheel; his front wing and the Packard's rear wing scraped. The bodyguard was staggering back into the road clutching at his face, tears streaming from his eyes.

As the Bentley scraped past, Dawlish saw the gun in the driver's hand, and tossed the second bag. The bag burst and the gun cracked at the same time. A bullet whanged through the door of the Bentley. Garcia, weak from pain, presented no threat.

The Bentley raced on.

Dawlish took a hand off the wheel, groped for Garcia's shoulder-holster, and slipped the gun out. He smiled dreamily to himself as he drove on.

The Packard wouldn't start to chase for another five minutes; perhaps ten, because the men wouldn't be able to see well enough to drive. Say he had a clear five minutes start. He could get to London first, but Tim's flat wasn't a safe rendezvous; the police would probably be watching, and they wouldn't let him keep Garcia for five minutes. Garcia's men would doubtless be watching, too. He swung off the road, drove along a narrow, winding lane which ran uphill. There was wooded land on either side, and this was common land, not fenced in. A mile from the main road, while Garcia was stirring in his seat, Dawlish turned beneath the trees. Young, fresh green undergrowth crackled beneath the wheels. He drove over bumpy grassland until the car couldn't be seen from the road. Garcia's eyes were flickering. Dawlish got out, and looked in all directions, but saw no sign of house or human being. This was a quiet and lonely place.

Garcia's sagging jaw had strengthened when Dawlish returned to the car. The dark eyes were no longer dazed; all the hatred in him blazed from them, the more venomous because he knew that he was helpless.

'Get out,' said Dawlish.

Garcia obeyed slowly, the hint of danger about him unquelled, unsubdued.

'There's a comfortable log just over there—go and sit on it,' said Dawlish.

Garcia sat on the log as if by his own choice. His spirit remained unruffled although his hair was dishevelled and the marks were clearly seen of two dark, angry-looking bruises—one on his temple and one on his chin.

'Smoke, if you care to,' said Dawlish, leaning against the wing of the Bentley. 'After all, fair's fair. Two armed henchmen on one side, and none on the other *was* a little lopsided for a *téte-a-téte* don't you think?'

Garcia moistened his lips; and the cloudy hatred cleared a little—as if he had begun to see a chance of coming to terms.

'Remember, you still hold the trump card.'

'And that is?'

'In a spot like this it's so hard to see the wood for the trees,' murmured Dawlish. 'Garcia, my little one, you have performed miracles. You have made strong men wilt. You have won the allegiance of men of great respectability. You have lured wives from their wealthy husbands, and for the most unusual of reasons, none other than a conviction that Charles Horden is their rarified soul mate. How do you work it?'

Garcia didn't speak.

Dawlish said mildly: 'People do die. It's happening all day, every hour of the day. And people get hurt. You won't scare me that way; nor can I be bribed by money. I want to know how it works, and I don't think anyone else can tell me.'

'You mean—' began Garcia, and then stopped abruptly.

'That's right. I mean I want to know how it works.'

'You want to come into the Circle?'

This wasn't what Garcia had expected; the surprise showed clearly in his eyes; it was a new situation, and he wasn't yet capable of coping. He took out his cigarettes and lit up.

'That's it, in a nutshell,' said Dawlish.

'Why?'

'Well, I'm human. There's a lot of power in that Circle. It's big enough to fight against the great Marrick, and it's touch and go whether he'll win. And if you get Marrick in, you'll have cornered many world markets, not without a profit. Yes, I'm very interested in that Circle, Garcia. How *does* it work?'

'I can't—tell you.'

'Pity. It was your one hope.'

'And I can't *show* you, while you've got Horden.'

'He can be used,' murmured Dawlish.

'If you'll free him—'

'Not exactly free him, but I might, perhaps, agree to an arrangement, for the sake of another demonstration. You're a queer mixture, Garcia, of cunning and innocence. Have you ever stopped to ask yourself what my interest is in this business? Or have you been deluded by newspaper reports into thinking that I'm a gay cavalier, adventuring for the sake of damsels in distress? I can make use of influence and power, too.'

Garcia said slowly: 'You'll—*join* us?'

'On the right terms, and if I'm convinced that what you're doing will really work successfully. Why not?'

Garcia's face broke up into a snigger. The snigger grew into a laugh. The copse rang to his laughter, now harsh, now shrill, and the birds chattered and were scared and darted across the narrow clearings.

'So funny?' murmured Dawlish.

Garcia gasped: 'I—didn't—*dream!*'

'It took me a lot of time and a lot of trouble to get as far as this into the show. More trouble to convince my friend Trivett of my high-mindedness, but I managed that. He's promised me his full support, and if you know what's happening at my home, you also know that I'm getting it. I kept Charles away from the police when every newspaper was screaming for him—and I took a big risk. If you start looking at this business from the point of view that I'm in it for myself, you get a different angle.'

Garcia laughed again, weakly.

'And one thing that's been evident from the beginning,' Dawlish went on thoughtfully, 'is that you are on to something quite out of the ordinary. It's been going on for a year or more, and the police haven't been able to do much about it. Until you started clubbing people to death, you were clear of police investigation. Why did you kill Charles's uncle, by the way?'

Garcia said: 'The old fool put one across me. He discovered something of what I was doing. He would have told Horden all about it.'

'And how did he find out?'

'He knew Marrick's wife was involved, thought that his nephew was fooling around with her, and went to see Marrick about it. Marrick, hoping to get his help against Horden, told him enough to convince him it was what the old fool called "Bad". But Lady Marrick told me about the visit because she thought it would mean danger to her Charles. She's sold on Charles, isn't she?'

Garcia laughed again.

'*Wasn't* she?' said Dawlish.

'Going to keep *that* up?'

'For the time being. I want you to do a lot of guessing, Garcia; you've made me do enough. Tell me more—was Long Nose working for you?'

Garcia grinned; in spite of the evil that was in him, he was a handsome fellow; not breathlessly goodlooking like Charles, but—Dawlish was puzzled by that grin. The face reminded him of another. He wasn't getting confused because he had seen Garcia before, there was a genuine likeness to someone else. He brushed the thought away, as Garcia said:

'No. His wife was a follower of the great Horden. He assumed the worst. But he had found out that I was mixed up in it, too, and could have been awkward. So I tipped him off that he'd find Horden and his wife together that night. The police were to have been tipped off, too, but one of my men slipped up and sent the tip through two hours too late. The man was to have been framed; that would have kept him out of the way. He was doing the same as you, Dawlish—and the same as Downing.' His lips twisted suddenly. 'One of these days I'll get Downing.'

'Haven't you got him?'

'He got away,' said Garcia slowly, 'I still don't know how he did it, but he escaped.'

If Garcia wanted to whitewash John Downing, he couldn't have chosen a better way. Was Downing really working with him? Was Garcia trying to make sure that he looked like a victim instead of a villain?

'And you don't know where Downing is,' murmured Dawlish.

'Not right now. But I'll catch up with him sooner or later. Forget it, Dawlish. Downing's small fry. Where's all this leading? What do you want to do?'

'Sit in at a Circle meeting.'

'I'll need Horden, I tell you.'

'You can have Horden, once I'm satisfied that all of the others will be there.'

Garcia said slowly: 'And what's to stop you from having the police around when it comes off, Dawlish? How can you prove you're not going to fool me?'

'That's simple. Keep me with you while you're making all the plans to get the boys together.'

'Then how shall I get Horden?'

'I'll telephone for him to come and meet me. He'll come. The others might think it's a fake message, but Charles won't; he can pick out a fake in a flash.'

Garcia said: 'You've got something there. What about Lady Marrick and Marrick himself?'

Dawlish laughed. 'If you can get Marrick to join you, that'll be all the evidence I want about how good you are. So when you're all set, I'll persuade him to come along and see his wife, who'll be at the Circle. If I judge him properly, he'll do anything now, to find out that his wife *is* alive.'

His plot with Marrick was paying good dividends.

Garcia rubbed his chin, and leaned back, nursing his knees; Dawlish had that odd feeling again, that the man was very like someone he knew. It was more in expression and manner than in actual features. He studied the face while the minutes passed and Garcia pondered.

Suddenly: 'I'll try it,' Garcia said. 'You'll hand over your guns, Dawlish, and surrender completely to me. That's understood.'

'From this very minute,' said Dawlish. He took out his gun, and the one he had snatched from Garcia's bodyguard, and laid them on the grass. Crazy? The risk must be taken.

'I'm coming to think that you and I could do things together,' said Garcia. 'But don't forget one thing, Dawlish.'

'And that is?'

'All the time you'll be watched. Before the meeting, during it and after. *All* the time, and if you put a foot wrong you'll have had it.'

'My risk.'

Garcia leaned back and looked at him through drooping lids.

'Deep thoughts?' asked Dawlish.

'Deep enough. You'll tell Horden to come and bring your wife with him. Just a hostage for your good faith, Dawlish.'

Dawlish shrugged.

'All right. Better have Fay Downing, too; that will lure her brother.'

Garcia stared—and then suddenly threw back his head and laughed again. Dawlish thrust his hands deep into his pockets and waited until the outburst died away.

Garcia came forward, picked up the guns, still chuckling.

'You drive,' he said.

'Where are we going?'

'I'll tell you when we get nearer.' They got into the car, Garcia nursing the automatics on his lap as Dawlish let in the clutch. 'It isn't that I don't trust you, Dawlish, but I'll feel happier when I've got your wife and Horden with you. We'll go to the nearest telephone and call 'em.'

'Just say the word,' said Dawlish.

CHAPTER TWENTY-THREE

THE HOSTAGES

He *had* to take risks.

He'd never taken greater; but he doubted whether he had ever played for higher stakes.

As he drove towards the main road, his mind was filled with fear and uncertainty. Risking himself was one thing; Charles— yes, it was worth the risk with Charles. Fay? Yes, even Fay; she was deeply involved and couldn't blame him or anyone for drawing her further into it.

But Felicity—

Garcia sat grinning at his side, and occasionally burst into a snigger.

They reached the main road, and had to wait while several cars passed.

'London direction?' asked Dawlish, and Garcia nodded.

Dawlish turned right and drove steadily, watching the other cars coming towards him; seeing the people in them, all apparently as law-abiding, as humdrum, as he probably appeared to them.

At the next telephone box Garcia told him to pull up.

'We'll use this one, Dawlish. I think you had better tell the others to meet you at your friend Jeremy's flat.'

'Right.'

Here was the final moment for decision. In spite of the automatics, Garcia could be outwitted. If Dawlish cared to change his mind—what? Garcia could be handed over to Trivett. Garcia was the operative chief of the Circle; take him and Horden away, and the Circle would be just another syndicate of financiers, but—who else was behind it? The case wouldn't be really finished until that was known.

Garcia opened the door of the car.

'Don't change your mind,' he said.

Dawlish laughed . . .

Felicity answered the telephone; her voice was subdued, and he knew that she was scared.

'Hallo.'

'Hallo, my sweet!'

'Oh, Pat. Pat, you're crazy!'

'Yes, I know.'

The relief in her voice was so great that it went through him like a physical pain.

'Why didn't you let Tim come with you?'

'So he had an attack of conscience, and told you.'

'He came as far as Haslemere and telephoned Ted, I listened in on the extension. Have you seen—'

'Yes. It was an armistice. Garcia didn't try any tricks.' It was difficult to lie; Felicity knew when he wasn't being sincere, but just now she was so relieved at hearing him that her sharper senses were clouded. 'Fel, I've decided to move headquarters to London.'

'Oh, why?'

'It'll cut out this journey, every time we want to do anything.

I want you, Charles and Fay to come to Tim's flat, after lunch. You drive. Tim and Ted are to follow, just in case Garcia makes trouble on the road, but I don't think he will.'

Garcia gave a sardonic grin.

'What about Lady Marrick?' asked Felicity.

'I've assumed she'll want to come with Charles. Better let her. Now, a message for Tim and Ted. They're to lay back, a hundred yards or so behind your car, and not get any nearer. All clear?'

'Yes. Pat, are you sure—'

'Quite sure. Tell the police where you're coming. I'll have a word with Trivett.'

Garcia's smile faded.

Felicity said, as if that reassured her: 'All right, darling. Be careful. Don't take unnecessary risks.'

No unnecessary risks! He laughed as naturally as he could.

'We'll be all right. I'll expect you about three.'

'Wonderful, darling!'

Dawlish rang off. Garcia, gun thrust forward, asked grimly:

'Why call Trivett?'

'He's watching the flat. I have to call him off.'

'Be *very* careful what you say to him.'

Dawlish shrugged.

Trivett said: 'I suppose you know what you're doing. But don't stick your neck out too far. I've had approval from on high for letting you carry on.'

'Good sense in unexpected places!'

'As to the good sense, I hope you're right.'

Garcia marched with a conqueror's stride into Tim's flat, patted the pocket where he kept the gun, laughed, and sat in an easy-chair as if he owned the place. The puzzling likeness to someone he couldn't place was more marked than ever.

It was one o'clock.

'Can we get some food up here?' Garcia asked.

'Yes, I'll ring for some.' Dawlish called the restaurant in a neighbouring street; luncheon for two would be sent round in fifteen minutes. He rang off. 'Have a drink?'

'Out of a sealed bottle,' Garcia said.

'You're right to be cautious.'

'I'll say I'm right!'

Garcia went to the telephone while Dawlish was opening a bottle of whisky, dialled a number and spoke crisply; he wanted a couple of men to come to the flat at two-fifteen.

They said little during luncheon. Garcia seemed to have moments when he felt on top of the world, others when he wasn't so sure of himself.

At two fifteen precisely, the two men arrived.

Garcia said to them: 'You don't have to do anything, just make sure Dawlish doesn't touch the telephone or leave the flat. If necessary, finish him off—but I don't think it will be necessary. I've one or two arrangements to make, Dawlish.'

'Carry on.'

Garcia grinned. 'Thanks!'

Ted Beresford and Tim Jeremy, in Ted's black Talbot a hundred yards behind the leading car driven by Felicity, sped along the quiet road, lulled to a complete sense of security. When the attack came, it took them by surprise. Shots from an automatic, which burst both front tyres, sent the driving wheel out of Tim's hands. Swift, sudden chaos followed. The car turned over on its side, quivering like a living thing, and came to rest with two wheels in a ditch. Tim lay across the wheel, unconscious; Ted struggled to get out of the car, but hadn't succeeded when another pulled up just behind them. It also was a black Talbot. The passenger from the second car came running, and before Ted realized what this meant, a hypodermic needle was thrust into his arm.

The second Talbot made off, almost at once.

When the police arrived at the scene of the crash, both Tim and Ted were unconscious, but neither was badly hurt.

Dawlish stood at the front window of Tim's flat, just before three o'clock, and watched the corner of the street. The two men were in the room with him; with their guns trained on his back. But they couldn't see his face. It was set hard, but there was a glint in his eyes which betrayed the depth of his feeling. Two cars passed the end of the road; a third turned the corner, but passed the house. At sight of each, Dawlish's lips tightened. The minutes crawled. He stood unmoving—and then suddenly a roomy Chrysler, Tim's car, turned the corner. He caught a glimpse of Felicity at the wheel.

One of the men drew nearer to him, as if sensing that this was a moment of danger.

In the street, three men approached the car swiftly, and one of them opened the door. Dawlish heard Felicity's sharp cry. He clamped his teeth together. The man climbed in, and after a few seconds the Chrysler moved off.

Then Garcia came up behind him.

'Did you see all that, Dawlish?'

Dawlish didn't look round.

'I certainly did. As a partner, I shouldn't say you erred on the side of trustfulness.'

'One must take precautions,' murmured Garcia. 'Your wife will be quite comfortable and in no danger, while you carry out your side of the bargain. The others I shall bring to the Circle meeting. I hope to arrange it for tomorrow night. Tomorrow morning I shall ask you to send for Marrick and use your remarkable powers of persuasion to make him join us.'

'He'll come.'

'What a pity we didn't start working together before,' murmured Garcia. 'Now I propose to leave you here, Dawlish, but must ask you not to go out. I have disconnected the telephone, in case you are tempted to get in touch with any other friends. Beresford and Jeremy are unconscious, but not hurt.'

Dawlish said: 'When they come round they'll tell the police; Trivett will practically be forced to come here.'

'But you're so clever at dealing with him, aren't you?' asked Garcia softly. 'I shall have a man listening to all that is said, so hope you are convincing. I didn't realize before how charming your wife is.'

Dawlish was watched every moment; could do nothing without being conscious of the dark, suspicious eyes of Garcia's men on him. Garcia might be half convinced of his goodwill, these men weren't; they hated him. He tried to read; nothing held his attention. He glanced through several newspapers and read the accounts of the murders; it was stated definitely that Lady Marrick was dead. He sat back in an armchair by the window, while one of the two men sat in a chair opposite him, looking at him over the top of his book.

Dawlish slid his pencil out of his pocket and began to do the crossword in the *Daily Record*. As he worked on it, he wrote an occasional note in the margin of the newspaper, as if he were trying to find out the word he wanted.

Each word was part of a message.

He felt jumpy, and when the guard stood up and came towards him, had to fight against the temptation to cover the partly completed sentence with his hand. He didn't. The man stared at the crossword, was satisfied, and went back. Dawlish continued to write one word at a time. When it was finished, the message read: *Watch George. Show is tomorrow night.* Then he went on with the crossword, until it was finished.

It was five o'clock.

Trivett *would* come.

There was a ring at the front door bell, and the man outside hurried to open it. He came into the sitting-room a moment later.

'Trivett's coming.'

The man in the room turned to Dawlish.

'I'm going to hide behind this chair,' he said. 'Don't let him know I'm here.'

Dawlish shrugged his shoulders.

It was a big chair. Trivett would not be able to see the man crouching behind it, even if he drew near.

The front door bell rang again, and soon Trivett came in, slowly and watchfully.

'Got a new servant?' he asked abruptly.

'Yes,' said Dawlish.

'How long have you been here?'

'Since one o'clock.'

'What have you heard, since then?'

'Nothing.'

Trivett said: 'I don't believe you.'

Dawlish picked up the newspaper casually.

'I believe you've worked all this,' Trivett said. 'That you know Tim and Ted are in hospital—'

Dawlish pretended to start. 'No! They—'

'That Felicity and the others left *Four Ways* and headed here—and haven't arrived.'

Dawlish didn't speak, but tried to make his eyes work for him.

Trivett walked to the window, turned and faced him—and his handsome face had a haggard look. His expression indicated that he didn't believe in Dawlish, that he was afraid that he had made the wrong move. He took his time deciding what to say, and each word came out slowly.

'Dawlish, if you have let me down, it is the foulest thing you've ever done in your life.'

Dawlish shrugged.

'Why dramatize it? If you're not satisfied, you've still got that warrant for my arrest, haven't you? If you think I've done enough harm, stop me from doing any more.'

'I just don't trust you.'

'You're making that obvious.' Dawlish darted a glance at the chair in the corner, then went towards Trivett, holding the newspaper in front of him. At least he wasn't being watched now; but he was almost afraid that the rustling of the paper would make the listener suspicious. He held the margin side up so that Trivett could read it, and went on: 'I thought the chance was worth taking. Garcia's got them all now—the damage is done. I miscalculated.'

Trivett said harshly: 'I believe you've done this deliberately.' But he had read the words; his expression altered slightly, although his tone was still harsh and accusing. 'I think that accursed clairvoyant has got you.'

'I can't stop you thinking. I've taken a risk; it's time you learned how to take one without whining. I'm sick of the business. I've tried to do your job, all that's happened is moan, moan, moan. But do what you like, take me over to the Yard, clap me in jug—and see how much good it does you.'

Trivett said: 'I'll do that, when I want to. Dawlish, there's something that maybe you don't know.'

'What is it?'

'Seven women, all devotees of Charles Horden, disappeared this afternoon. Vanished without a trace. If anything happens to them, it'll be your fault, because you released Horden. You damned fool, what do you think you're playing at?'

'I know *exactly* what I'm doing.'

Trivett said dryly: 'I seem to have heard those words before. Most grown-ups have, though they're sometimes dimmed by the crash that comes after them.' He moved to the door. 'As for me, I've gone as far as I can on my own responsibility. I shall put the situation before the Assistant Commissioner, and act on his instructions.'

'Just as you like.'

Trivett went out, and the door shut with a sharp click.

After dark, the two men on guard told Dawlish they were leaving. They watched every move he made, as they took him out by way of the fire-escape. They were jittery, in case the house was being watched, but no police appeared. A car was waiting in a nearby street. They made Dawlish get into the back, one of them sat by his side, gun in hand; the other sat by the driver. The rear blinds of the car were down. Dawlish judged their direction for the first five minutes and knew that they were heading west; then the driver twisted and turned through the maze of streets, and Dawlish could not be sure where they were when eventually they drew up. The men were jumpy, and watched carefully as Dawlish got out before a large terrace house, probably, he thought, in Kensington. They hurried Dawlish up to the front door, which opened as they reached it, and hustled him inside.

Garcia was standing at the foot of the stairs.

'Welcome, Dawlish!'

'Your words are friendlier than your men have led me to expect.'

'I have to be very careful, and they are only carrying out instructions,' said Garcia comfortably. 'By tomorrow night all will be over. I had to get you away since Trivett was so diffi-cult. I congratulate you on the way you handled that situation, Dawlish.'

'Thanks. Where are we?'

'The Circle will meet here,' said Garcia. 'And I thought it just possible that you contrived to give Trivett a message about the time of the meeting, so I have brought it forward; it will be midnight, tonight. I do hope you can use your influence on Marrick by then.'

'I can try.'

'Before you do so, I have something to show you,' said Garcia. 'Come with me.'

He put a hand on Dawlish's arm and led him up the stairs.

Light streamed through the house clearly and clinically. Two or three men stood at the doorways of the rooms as they passed, as if on guard, giving the whole place the atmosphere of a prison. Garcia, still smiling, still worrying Dawlish by that likeness to someone he could not recall, led the way up the second flight of stairs and then turned left. Dawlish thought of the position of the house, the stairs on the left—against what he would have considered the wall of the house next door. Were they going into another house? Had two been converted into one? Details like that might hold a life or death significance when the final moment came.

'Come in here,' said Garcia.

He led the way into a small, dark room; there was one window, from which a dim light came, as if through frosted glass. Garcia drew him towards it and Dawlish saw that it was a type of glass which he had come across before—you could see through it in one direction, not in the other.

Urged by Garcia, Dawlish looked down into a large room. There was nothing really remarkable about the room, except that it would have been more in keeping with a hotel than a private house, for there were dozens of lounge chairs and coffee tables. On the tables were empty coffee cups; on some glasses— he could see that the glasses were half filled.

A dozen women were down there.

All of them sat in little groups—except one, who was alone. That was Estelle Marrick. Felicity and Fay sat with a third woman whom Dawlish did not recognize. All of them behaved normally; two or three were laughing, all seemed to be talking.

Garcia murmured: 'They are the hostages, held against your good faith, Dawlish. Most of them are beautiful women, most of them are wealthy—or have wealthy husbands. I don't *think* you will do anything foolish, but if you should, then—it is easy to kill, isn't it, Dawlish?'

Dawlish said: 'You should know.'

He found it hard to tear his gaze away from Felicity, but he had to. Garcia was watching him closely. He turned again towards Estelle Marrick. She was as aloof from the other women as she had been from him and Tim the night before.

'Now you must get in touch with Marrick, and bring him here,' said Garcia.

Marrick came.

CHAPTER TWENTY-FOUR

THE CIRCLE MEETS

Marrick stood by the window, with Dawlish and Garcia, and stared towards his wife, who hadn't changed her position, but sat with her eyes closed, as if she were asleep. He didn't move. Garcia seemed prepared to let him stand there for a long time. Dawlish groped for cigarettes, and was lighting one when Marrick turned.

'I hope you are satisfied,' murmured Garcia.

'What devilry are you up to now?'

'You should have believed me when I told you that she was alive,' said Garcia. 'You would have saved yourself a lot of anxiety, Marrick. As I've told Dawlish, all of those women are hostages. If either you or he fail me now, I'll kill them all. Mass murder isn't new, isn't difficult—I told Dawlish a little earlier how easy it is to kill. Imagine the result if those doors are closed and a little poison gas were to be released. Have you any choice, Marrick?'

Marrick licked his lips.

'I am going to let you come into the Circle tonight,' said Garcia, 'and you will join us, Marrick.' He laughed. 'Dawlish has seen the wisdom of it, too. I shall be glad to leave some of the work to another, and I think Dawlish could do it well. I don't think I ought to stay in this country very much longer—not, at least, under the present régime.'

The present *régime*.

Dawlish took the shock, showing how it affected him only by a slight narrowing of his eyes and tensing of his hands; and the light was too dim for either to be noticed. But within his mind, all those nebulous fears grew together into one great menacing danger.

'These are days of great changes,' continued Garcia softly, 'but Britain has always been a difficult nation to change easily. The people aren't stirred as easily as many on the Continent, and we have never really made much progress here. But we shall—oh, we shall!'

'Change to what?'

'Come with me,' said Garcia.

He opened another door, which Dawlish hadn't seen before. It led to a room overlooking another large chamber. It was empty, except for a ring of chairs and desks and a rostrum at one side. Over the rostrum was a red flag, and on the flag, the hammer and sickle.

The risks had been justified; the burning calculation remained. How was he to handle it?

'One of the handicaps under which we have laboured is shortage of money,' said Garcia. 'Another—the fact that there are so many isolated outposts of the old system all over the world. Marrick and his erstwhile friends gradually cornered vast resources. We needed them. We had to get them without letting the Western Powers know what we were doing. The Western capitalistic

Powers have one blind spot, as you know—they permit and encourage individuals to wield the influence of money. They permitted cartels and great price-rings and combines, not knowing that when the time came, those could be taken over more easily than if there were many smaller groups. We've merged everyone into two groups—Marrick's one, *mine* is now the other. Mine? *Ours*, Dawlish. In order to win a complete battle, we had to move fast and yet stealthily.

'By using Horden's strange influence, we brought your erstwhile friends to our side, Marrick.

'We did it very simply. Horden went into a trance. The voice spoke—and we imitated that voice and made statements about future movements of certain commodities—gold and the like—and then we engineered those movements, so that to your friends it was evident that Horden had pre-knowledge.'

Dawlish remembered the papers which Trivett had shown him at the Yard—the apparently meaningless words which Charles had uttered to the Circle.

'Imagine the temptation!' Garcia went on. 'With his help they could gradually corner many world markets—and they have. Meanwhile, we brought them all into the Circle, forged together in the loyalty of greed. We worked, also, on certain politicians in all parties—and so we have access to much dynamic information, and we have done all this by convincing them of Horden's supernatural powers.

'We have, of course, made our position stronger and our tactics perfect, by using the influence which Horden exerts. Once we had the women fast, we were certain of the men.

'The women you see in the other room are the wives or daughters of a few key men who are still outside our Circle and whom we must draw in. We have arranged to hold them until after tonight. Then their menfolk will either join us, or their women will disappear. Few men are dependent on one person for his delight. A man may lose his wife and yet have a son or daughter, parent—mistress—always someone who matters a great deal to him. The shock of losing one makes sure that he does not willingly risk losing the other.

'I am sure that you both understand me.'

Garcia laughed; softly, savouring his own brilliance.

'The reason for the quickening of the tempo, the sense of urgency, was threefold. First, because Horden's uncle had seen you, Marrick, and you told him a little of what was happening—enough to be dangerous. You would doubtless have reported to the police long ago but for Horden's influence over your wife—*and* but for your own confidence in yourself. How do you feel now that it's shaken out of you?'

He didn't wait for an answer.

'The second reason is that the police have shown a much greater interest, of late, and several of the men in the Circle are being closely watched. Throughout all Government Departments we've some pretty good agents, in spite of the silly purge the Government started some time ago. The Western democracies do things so half-heartedly! They do not really know the meaning of the word 'purge'. Half of our success has been due to this absurd tolerance.

'The third reason for the urgency, and perhaps the most important, is the fact that we are in a position *now* to seize three of the atomic piles in this country. It has taken a long time for us to get into that position, and the happy chance of the illness of three of the people concerned in the security measures has given us the opportunity to strike *at once*.

'Now, the position is quite simple.

'You, Marrick, can join us—and we can use your remarkable gifts for money-making, your remarkable organizing ability *and* the influence which you have in so many parts of the world. Or you can refuse. In that case, you will be liquidated—with your friend Dawlish here. On the one hand, you will have very great power, backed up by a political force greater than any ever known to man. On the other—death. What is more, in order to persuade you to take the right course, we shall use your wife. I have discovered in the past that the most effective power to exert over a man is the threat to his womenfolk. It is astonishing how effective it is. Don't you agree, Dawlish?'

Dawlish was thinking: 'Liquidated.' Of course, Garcia had not been fooled. Garcia had pretended to be, so as to get what he wanted.

But Garcia didn't know about the message to Trivett.

Cold fear gripped Dawlish.

Trivett had been warned to be ready *tomorrow* night.

Liquidated—he himself; and a civilization.

'Don't you agree, Dawlish?' Garcia asked softly.

There was more light in this room than the one next door. Armed men stood at the doorway, three guns covered Dawlish. Garcia was prepared for all emergencies.

Dawlish said: 'Oh, yes, of course. Very neat. I don't quite see why you were so desperately anxious to get hold of Marrick. In the early days, when you were acting by stealth, yes. But if you're ready for a *coup*, Marrick's approval or disapproval won't make much difference.'

'It will make a great deal of difference. He, and only he, can make sure that we obtain quick control of the raw materials, the general resources, in so many of those isolated outposts of capitalism that remain. True, if he stands out, the rest will consist of little more than mopping-up operations. But they will take time. As our immediate objective we have the domination of Great Britain. That will leave Western Europe virtually at our mercy.

The Commonwealth, its ties already strained, will break up. The rest of the English-speaking world, strung out and very weak in a military sense, will be aligned against us. But we are not fools, Dawlish, we wish to avoid a shooting war, so wasteful of wealth and material. We are ready with non-aggression pacts and offers of spheres of influence for the remaining Western democracies. We won't, of course, be accepted as sincere. But what will their position be? The key to all Western pacts—United Europe and the Atlantic Pact—is Great Britain.

'In this country we have been careful to put up stooges as our official Party leaders. They have done a wonderful job. No one officially associated with the Party in any way has been used in this plan. No one, except ourselves, suspects the real motive behind it.

'The *coup* will succeed.

'America and the isolated dominions of this country will be compelled either to fight a war for which they haven't the proper bases and which they cannot win, or to make an arrangement with us. They will probably realize that we shall be prepared to let them alone for a long time. Without their overseas markets, they will gradually weaken. *We* shall be the only overseas market, and they will eventually come to terms. Capitalists *have* to find markets.

'This is the inevitable step to world domination, Dawlish, and not a single fool in England has realized it. Unless, perhaps, you had an inkling—some blind sense which warned you of the importance of what was happening? I think you must have, otherwise you would not have taken such risks as you did.

'I checked most carefully on your history, your record and your reputation. I knew that you were quite incorruptible. You are one of those men, I think, who will accept any sacrifice, see anyone suffer, rather than accept the loss of your principles, your sense of honour and duty. When you made your approach to me, I was almost overcome, Dawlish! I knew it was a ruse. Even that interview with Trivett—how transparent! But I didn't know any other man who could get Marrick here. And I needed Horden for tonight's revelation of the truth. You see, Dawlish, every man in the Circle is committed so deeply that he cannot now back out.

'Tonight they will be told everything.'

Garcia stopped; then laughed . . .

'I might talk of using you for future work, but you would be the first to begin an underground resistance army,' he continued. 'We shall have a great deal of that kind of trouble, but it won't last, we shall be able to put down all revolt with utter ruthlessness. It has been done in the past, and it will be done again.'

He went on softly: 'Tonight—yes, you can see what happens tonight. Horden will go into his trance and the voice will come— and the voice which *we* use, pretending it is his, will make the final revelation. That flag and the hammer and sickle will be hidden until he is in the middle of the trance. He will tell the gathering of the new rulers of the world, and a misty light will appear and the flag will loom out of it. *Very* convincing. Then by concealed pull-wires, it will glide away. When the lights go up, there will be no sign of the flag. It will look, again, like one of Horden's prophecies—and all his earlier prophecies have come true.

'After that—'

Garcia shrugged.

'Yes?'

Dawlish's voice sounded calm, as if he were interested in the problem from a completely detached point of view.

'After that, word will go out to our agents to act. The atomic piles will be taken over. Our agents in the Government

Departments will take over from the normal leaders. Our agents in the gas, electricity and other essential services will take over. They will be able to disrupt the whole industrial and economic life of the nation for a day or two—until we have completed the coup.'

'We?' asked Dawlish, mildly.

'Those of us who have been in it from the beginning,' said Garcia. He looked at the luminous dial of his watch. 'It is nearly twelve o'clock; we are ready to start. You will be with us as a spectator, Dawlish. And you remember that if there is any attempt on your part or on Marrick's to disrupt proceedings—there are the hostages.'

Was there a way out? Was there hope? Garcia had spoken with overwhelming confidence—he had the agents, ready to act.

If it were possible to break out—

Dawlish felt the sudden movement behind him, but moved too late to evade the blow which knocked him out.

Dawlish, his head aching but otherwise unhurt, looked at the forty men who had filed into their places. He knew most of them from their photographs. All were either wealthy or highly placed in positions of trust. They sat with pencils and paper in front of them, like any group at an important business or political conference.

Hard-headed business men, they had profited by believing Charles; they had played with corruptible material, and themselves become corrupted. They were utterly controlled by Garcia now.

Dawlish sat in the room opposite the empty platform, bound to a chair at wrists and ankles. A guard sat on either side of him. Others lined a gallery round the walls, high above the main body.

Marrick sat below, near the rostrum; even from here, his face showed deathly pale.

Then Charles came in.

He smiled serenely as he took his position on the rostrum; still smiled, as his hands were manacled to his chair. Above him there was the plain wall; no draperies, nothing to suggest that a red flag, hammer and sickle had been there. He sat down, and no one was near him—no one was within ten feet of him.

Garcia sat by Marrick's side.

Dawlish felt the perspiration gathering on his forehead as he waited. There was a hush over all of them—until, suddenly, the lights began to dim. They didn't go out all at once. It must have been fully a minute from the first dimming until pitch darkness descended upon the room. Dawlish remembered the seance at *Four Ways*; the rustling sound of breathing; and he heard it now, like distant sighing. Tension, like an electric current, ran from body to body.

Outside—

What had *Trivett* done?

Then a new sound crept through the chamber; a gasping, groaning sound; and it came from Charles. Dawlish stared towards the centre of the rostrum; heard that agonized breathing, heard manacles rattle as Charles strained and struggled, caught his own breath and felt the sweat icy cold on his forehead. It seemed to go on for an age—but, gradually, light came.

It was just a mist—a faint mist, showing only Charles's face. The face was distorted, as if his limbs were tugging at their bonds.

And then the voice began, hollow and whispering, yet every syllable clear. The misty light grew brighter, showing Charles's head and shoulders, but nothing beyond or on either side.

'*The world*—'

The voice stopped, the writhing grew worse.

'*. . . is in grave . . .*'

'*. . . danger. Save it, save it.*'

There was a sigh from the assembled men; a greater tension; and then the hollow voice came again, every word isolated, a pause between each.

'*The—world—is—in—grave—danger. Save it—save—it.*'

'*The world—*'

Charles sank back in his chair. Then the voice came again. Dawlish, waiting for it, prepared for it, knew that this was the fake voice Garcia had so cleverly prepared, knew how easy it would be for the others to be taken in.

'*There is only one way to save the world. By the domination of true democracy—the only true democracy, by the rule of the hammer and the sickle.*'

Then the misty light grew brighter; and fifty pairs of staring eyes saw the gradual manifestation of the flag and its symbols; saw it high above Charles's head. A man and a woman sat there, beneath it, as if enthroned. The man was Garcia. The woman—was she a vision? Or was she real?

Dawlish knew.

Estelle Marrick sat on that throne swathed in a red gown, a sickle in one hand and a hammer in the other. The likeness between her and Garcia was unmistakable; they were father and daughter.

Silence.

Silence, except for the hushed breathing of the gathered men—and then a sudden stifled cry. That came from Marrick. The voice did not come again, and the vision began to fade as the mist dimmed. But before it went out, while the man and woman still sat there, Charles moved. He stood up, quietly and slowly, vaguely discernible in the hazy darkness, and he spoke clearly and in his own voice, without beauty, but stern with courage.

'The vision is a fake.' He stretched up his hand, and the chain fastening him to the chair was taut. He pulled at the flag and tore it from its fastenings. 'The woman is as false to you as she is to her husband. As false as Garcia's doctrine and as false as all of you who are here by your own free will.'

The woman hadn't moved—but Garcia and the guards were moving. Bright light shone for a scintillating second, showing guns pointed at Charles. *Then the lights went out again.*

'*Light!*' screamed Garcia. 'Put on the lights!'

But there was darkness, and scrambling, struggling men— and then suddenly a powerful voice, coming through a megaphone, with a ring of authority which Dawlish knew well.

'You're surrounded by the police. Take it easy.'

The scuffling stopped for a second, only to begin again with greater violence.

Then the lights came on, and Dawlish looked searchingly about him.

Police were streaming into the chamber, Trivett, Wilson and several whom Dawlish knew were leaping across the tables towards Garcia. Garcia was standing upright, with a gun pointing towards Charles. Trivett had an automatic, and two shots rang out.

Garcia fell.

Charles smiled at Trivett; not a serene smile as if he were out of this world; but an amiable grin.

Amid the tumult, Dawlish saw Marrick standing a few yards from his wife. Dawlish couldn't see his expression, but saw the smile on Estelle's face as she raised the sickle and drew it across her throat.

*　　*　　*

So Trivett had taken the warning seriously, but—*Charles*. Explain *Charles*.

Marrick buried his face in his hands. Charles and Trivett went up to him, while detectives came hurrying to free Dawlish. Flexing his stiffened wrists, Dawlish went down to the main chamber. Trivett looked round at him with a drawn smile. The crowd was being driven towards the doors, and just here the room was clear.

'Hullo, Pat.'

'What's this?'

Dawlish's voice was cracked.

'Take them one at a time. You now see why Marrick didn't tell you all he knew. He was aware that his wife was involved, but not how deeply. The whole pretty business had turned on her. We've always known there was a mysterious leader, but couldn't find out who it was. Garcia mixed the trails well, always keeping her in the background or making her pose as one of Horden's victims. And until we really knew the leader's identity, we didn't want to swoop. Now we know she was Garcia's daughter: married Marrick, to get him into the business, no doubt. But we swooped—'

'You left it pretty late.'

Dawlish hardly recognized the sound of his own voice.

'But not too late. We've already been through the rest of the house, and have all the records. Word's gone out up and down the country. You'll find your newspapers full of it in the morning. Top of the list will be the mob we caught here. But we had to wait until the last moment, because we didn't know that leader, and we had to find out. If she'd remained free, it could have started again. Not a bad job, was it?'

'I haven't got it yet.'

But Dawlish saw the truth of some things. Why Garcia

had needed Charles, why Estelle Marrick had behaved so oddly, just to get near Charles, to get him away from Dawlish, and back in the Circle. She had caused anguish for Marrick with a cold cruelty of purpose frightening in itself. But there were other things to learn.

Trivett laughed shortly.

'Sorry, Pat. From first to last we used you as a decoy. Even when Horden asked Felicity for help, we were behind it. That's why we were able to leave Horden with you. I knew you well enough to be sure you'd get the right scent, and you soon made it obvious that you had. I kept you uninformed because I was under sealed orders. Then I began to get worried. Horden seemed to change people from good to bad. I forced that row with you at Garcia's flat because I wanted to see how you'd react. I had a pretty shrewd idea of what you'd do in order to get into the Circle, but—I wasn't sure you were really yourself. Then, being confident that he had Marrick so tight the man would never get free, Garcia went beyond himself. And I learned the truth about Horden in time to have no more worries. You've done exactly the job we'd hoped and expected you'd do, Pat, keeping Garcia's eyes off his main danger—the enemy within.'

Dawlish echoed slowly: 'The enemy *within*?'

Trivett chuckled, and turned to Horden.

'Meet Charles Horden, of the Secret Intelligence Department,' he said. 'I didn't know that myself until a few hours ago.'

Felicity was by Dawlish's side, the other women were in the big room, several of them with their husbands. Police stood about, watchful, but there was little left to watch. The two houses had been cleared of Garcia's men and the two bodies taken away.

Dawlish had just told Felicity what Trivett had told him, and added:

'If they're going to tell me blithely that Charles was a fake from beginning to end, I'm going to throw myself under a bus.'

'You say the *police* made Horden get in touch with me?'

'That's it. Trivett says that they discovered a plot of some kind, more or less in its infancy, some time ago. They didn't know much about it, but didn't like the way it was going. There was a spiritualist angle. Horden wasn't in Intelligence then; he'd dabbled in the occult, was extraordinarily good at it. He discovered some Red plot. He reported, was given a job, and foisted on to Garcia. Charles played his double game perfectly. It was Charles, though, who warned the authorities when tonight's show was to start. Charles managed to keep informed all the time, while hanging on until he found the leader. Wonderful Charles! But—'

Trivett and Charles came across to them.

Felicity said clearly: 'I do *not* believe that you fooled us at *Four Ways*, Charles.'

Charles gave an engaging grin.

'I didn't, Mrs. Dawlish. I *am* clairvoyant; I'm told I do get some remarkable results. I used to find it embarrassing because so many impressionable women fell for me—oh, well. That made me feel a heel. So did my attitude over my uncle's death, but—'

'Forget it,' said Dawlish.

Charles said: 'It's hard to do that. Well, to get on. I've always been a dabbler in literature, too—and I've a brother who is quite a man in the C.I.D. He persuaded me to offer to help. One difficulty was that in the trances I don't know everything that's going on about me, but after a lot of practice I was able to keep partly conscious, and tell the police enough for them to work on. Between spells, I'm an ordinary human being. Keeping up the Wonder Man act for so long has been a bit of a strain—that crack-up of mine was genuine, you know.

'Keeping up with Lady Marrick was one of the worst parts of the job. I wasn't sure whether she or her husband were behind it. Another nasty patch was stalling Fay,' he added, and frowned slightly. 'It wasn't easy to pretend that I didn't care a cuss about Fay. I think she's—'

Fay came in.

No one remained in any doubt as to what Charles thought of her.

They found John Downing later that night, near *Four Ways*. He had been injured, when escaping, and hidden by friends until able to move about. He had believed Dawlish was working with Horden; had suspected the political significance of the business, used the other reasons for his prying and probing. He looked tired and ill—but delighted at finding Fay safe. He had released Long Nose simply because he thought Dawlish a crook, and wanted to hamper him.

Tim, patched up with plaster, and Ted, with hardly anything to show for the smash, joined the others at Tim's flat next morning. None of them had much to say; all were buried deep in newspapers. The cleverness with which the Press referred to a 'gigantic plot' and a *'coup d'etat'*, without mentioning the hammer and sickle or the red flag or any Party, was astonishing. Not one organ of the Press betrayed it, yet the secret leaked out, the world knew what had happened, and Garcia's agents by the thousand were rounded up.

Dawlish didn't know, and didn't care.

In the afternoon he went out; and on his return placed a book in Felicity's hands.

'What's this?' she asked.

'A present for you.'

'Thank you, darling. What is it?'

'A book.'

'Yes, idiot, I know; but what kind of book?'

'*Mrs. Beeton's Cookery Book*,' said Dawlish. 'That's the literature I recommend for you in future, sweetheart!'

ABOUT THE AUTHOR

John Creasey, born in 1908, was a paramount English crime and science fiction writer who used myriad pseudonyms for more than six hundred novels. He founded the UK Crime Writers' Association in 1953. In 1962, his book *Gideon's Fire* received the Edgar Award for Best Novel from the Mystery Writers of America. Many of the characters featured in Creasey's titles became popular, including George Gideon of Scotland Yard, who was the basis for a subsequent television series and film. Creasey died in Salisbury, UK, in 1973.

THE PATRICK DAWLISH MYSTERIES

FROM OPEN ROAD MEDIA

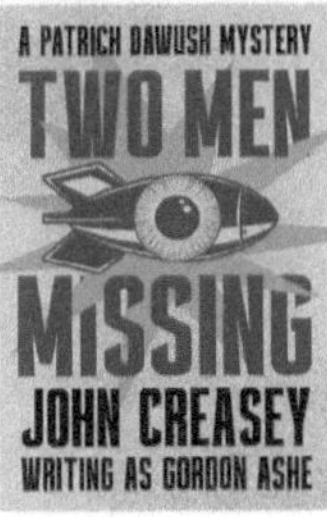

OPEN ROAD
INTEGRATED MEDIA